STRAY WOLF

Warning: Author is dyslexic as hell.

Beta reading team: Mary Alegre, Gary Anderson, Lesa Chang, Martha Collins, Mindy Kane, Lauren Maghoo, and Kirstin Potter

Professional Editing: Amanda Brown, LLC
Cover Art: Ryn Katryn Book Covers

Content Warnings

There is talk about past sexual asult.
Reference to physical and sexual abuse.
Violence and fighting on page.
Conversations and evidence of abuse of power.
Characters experience pain and die on page.
There are several scenes containing explicit, consenteual sex.

DEDICATION

To Lesa C-H: Your friendship is invaluable to me. Between our mutual love of dogs, motorcycles, and food, we've had some damn good times, and hopefully we'll have many more in the future.

To Scott H-C: Love you, man.

CHAPTER 1

The only reason Steph sees the man sitting on the park bench is because she's looking for him; otherwise, she might not have noticed him at all. No one else seems to notice him. Neither the runner nor the mom with the double stroller spare him a glance, even though they're actively scanning their environment. Not even old Mrs. Leland sees him, and she prides herself on being the most active member of the Neighborhood Watch. Steph watches Mrs. Leland make slow progress past the man without even giving him a squinty, suspicious glance.

Mrs. Leland still gives Steph squinty, suspicious glances, and she's lived in this neighborhood for three years. Of course, that might have more to do with the fact Mrs. Leland doesn't like dogs and Steph has three of them. But still, Mrs. Leland is an advocate of "guilty until proven innocent" with all the new faces in the area, and this man is most definitely a new face.

Judging by his face alone, Steph feels like this man deserves a first, second, and third glance. He's not classically handsome. His face is too harsh for that. With a prominent brow ridge, high cheekbones, and a wide flared nose, he makes her think of the old-style mockup of Neanderthals. The word primitive surfaces in her mind.

His dark brown hair, mussed and falling to his shoulders, and his beautiful dark-tanned skin softens his appearance slightly but not enough for her to think her friends would say he's gorgeous. Despite the ill-fitting clothes, she can see he's well-muscled.

If his looks didn't catch Steph's attention, the way he acts would have. He's sitting there, perfectly still, while the world moves around him. It makes her think of a Buddhist monk meditating.

No, that's not right. His stillness isn't peaceful like someone searching for inner calm. His stillness is more like that of a predator—a motionless hunter waiting for prey to wander close.

Despite all that, he doesn't feel dangerous to her. He feels entrancing.

Or maybe it's because he looks lonely, and she's always been drawn to engage with lonely people.

By her reckoning, he's been sitting on that same bench for half the day. She saw him when she ran home on her lunch break to give one of her dogs' medication. Now, returning home from work hours later, she drives past the park to see him sitting in the same spot on a wooden bench under the shade of an oak tree.

He's wearing old worn jeans that are a couple of sizes too big for him, no shoes, and a t-shirt covered in oil stains with lettering so faded it's illegible. He's sporting at least a day's worth of stubble on his face, adding to his disheveled appearance. But his hair doesn't look dirty or greasy. His clothes scream homeless, but the clean state of his hair and healthy physique tells a different story. In her experience, homeless people don't tend to have clean hair, healthy skin, or toned muscles.

No, he's not homeless, but something is wrong with him. He has the same expression on his face now as he did when she passed by him at lunch—blank and unfocused with his eyes staring off into space. He doesn't react to any of the activities happening around him: screaming kids on the jungle gym behind him, the barking dogs running after toys to his right, or the game of tag football to his left. None of the noises or movements seem to affect him. He doesn't look around, doesn't move his eyes, and doesn't even tilt his head as people and things bounce in and out of his peripheral vision. But for some reason Steph gets the feeling he's aware of everything despite his lack of response.

The other strange thing about this individual is how everyone avoids him without appearing to see him. Even though it isn't even the weekend yet, all the park benches and tables are full. It's a popular place, especially during the long days of summer. The park draws people to play on the thick green grass, picnic under the large trees, or barbeque at one of the many pits.

Yet, despite how crowded the park is, no one sits or plays anywhere near this man. A bench just next to his, a prime spot in the shade, sits empty while every other place is full. No one looks at him, but everyone hurries by as if an invisible force pushes them along.

But not her. She sees him just fine, and more than that, she can feel him. She's never told anyone about her "gift." But that gift allows her to just know things, and she's sure about two facts regarding this stranger.

One, he needs her. She doesn't know how or why, but a part of her screams that he needs help and she can provide it.

Two, he's not a danger to her. Her gift is ready and willing to warn her of danger, and she almost always listens. If her gift tells her this guy isn't a threat to her, she has no reason to fear.

Besides, she's used her gift to defend herself in the past. There's no reason to think it won't rise up to defend her in the future. It makes her fearless in a way that appalls many of her female friends.

The light in front of her turns green and she presses on her gas pedal. Her house is just around the corner, and she thinks about what to do as she finishes her drive home. Parking in her driveway, she grabs the lunch she didn't eat and turns to walk back to the park. She can hear her three dogs inside the house barking loudly in protest.

"I'll be back," she calls to them as she walks away. "And I promise treats."

It only takes a few minutes to walk back to the stranger. An odd, unfamiliar anxiety builds in her chest as she gets closer to him. It presses against her like a winter day when you open the front door and leave a nice warm house to face the cold outdoors. She concentrates for a moment and pictures a ball of warmth surrounding her, causing the feelings of anxiety and fear to dissipate. She can breathe again, which makes her smile in relief. That's when the man moves.

She shouldn't be startled. She knows he's alive and not a statue. But he's been so still for so long that when he moves his head to focus his intense gaze on her, her breath hitches.

"Hello," she greets as she steps up to the empty side of his bench and takes a seat. Canting her body toward him, she keeps her face pleasant, even if she feels a little nervous. He moves his eyes slightly to follow her motions but otherwise remains completely still, which Steph finds mildly unnerving.

"I saw you here earlier today," she explains. "And you're still here." He says nothing and doesn't even blink as he just watches her with bright green eyes. She's not sure she's ever seen anyone with eyes that color. They even appear to glow with their own light.

"You seem a little down on your luck at the moment, and I thought you might be hungry," she continues, undaunted. She opens the colorful cooler she uses as a lunch tote and pulls out a cellophane-wrapped sandwich to offer to him. "It's egg salad. It's probably a little soggy now, but it'll still taste good. I make a mean egg salad sandwich."

He shifts his gaze to the sandwich and then back to her. He doesn't move to take the food but just stares at her. "I promise it isn't poisoned or roofied," she assures him. No movement, no response. "Right," she murmurs and sets the sandwich down on the bench between them. "I'll just put that there in case you change your mind."

She feels the anxiety and fear push at her again, harder this time. It's coming from the stranger sitting next to her. She's not sure how she knows that, but in some strange way the power "feels" like him. He's trying to make her get up and leave, but she resists it easily.

She lifts an eyebrow at him and puts more effort into feeding the warm ball of light she pictures. It works again, and the stranger's expression changes from blank to mild surprise and then to a scowl. He pushes more power at her. She counters it and builds more power on her side until she can push back against him instead. She doesn't push hard but uses enough force to let him know that this show of strength isn't going to get him anywhere with her.

"Don't do that," she admonishes him softly. "Don't drive me away. You can ask me to leave, and I'll go. But don't be unkind like that."

His unwavering gaze shifts a little, and his eyes seem to flash a brighter green. "I haven't done anything." His voice is low and gravelly.

No, that's not correct, she thinks. *It's not gravelly. It's rusty from lack of use.*

"Well, don't do what you haven't been doing," she quips with a little smile. She takes it as a positive sign that he didn't ask her to leave. "I have some cookies in here too, if you want to start with dessert."

"I'm not hungry."

"That's fair." She digs out the cookies and puts them on the bench next to the sandwich. "I'll just leave them here in case you get hungry later."

He regards her thoughtfully for a moment. "This charity… are you trying to get in good with your god?" he asks with derision. "You think I might be one more soul to save? A good deed for the day? Trust me. Saving me won't win you any points with your deity."

She's much too fascinated by the way he talks to take offense at his words. Besides, working as an office manager for a trucking company forced her to grow a thick skin. Those attempted insults don't even register across her bow.

"You speak very eloquently," she tells him, and this time the surprised expression sticks.

"Lady, you're a strange one," he mutters, making her laugh.

"And here I've been calling you 'the stranger' in my head since I saw you earlier today," she confesses. "I guess we both get to be strange today."

She watches a reluctant smile form, transforming his face from interesting to handsome. "You saw me earlier?" he asks.

"Yup," she confirms. "Drove by in my car around 12:30. I live just around the corner." She points back toward her little house. He doesn't look to where she points, and his entire focus remains on her.

As she drops her hand back into her lap, they lapse into silence—him staring and Steph trying not to fidget. The man sure has an intense set of eyes.

"Are you homeless?" she finally blurts out and then cringes. She meant to broach the subject more delicately, but instead she just burst right out with it. *Smooth, Steph*, she berates herself. *Really smooth. Can't imagine why you never seem to get a second date these days.*

The man goes back to being expressionless, and Steph hurries to do damage control. "Being homeless isn't something to be ashamed of," she says quickly. "Lots of people end up homeless for a lot of reasons. Heck, dogs end up homeless too, and they don't even have opposable thumbs." She holds up her hands and wiggles her thumbs at him. When he doesn't even smile, she drops her hands back in her lap with a little sigh. It sounded funny in her head.

"I guess what I'm trying to say is if you're homeless it's not a reflection of your character or self-worth. No more than being rich or poor is either. I was homeless for a week. I slept in my car and got the worst stiff neck. It took months before my neck stopped hurting. Turns out I like being able to stretch out, so if I'm ever homeless again I know better than to try and sleep in my car."

Now his expression is downright amused, which only encourages her.

"I have a friend who runs a shelter. It's not far from here. The beds are dormitory-style, but they're comfortable. She'll feed you dinner tonight and breakfast in the morning. There are showers and a TV room and everything," she enthuses, but before she can finish extolling the virtues of the shelter, he holds up his hand. It's the first time he's moved anything but his head, and she finds herself staring at his callused palm, oddly fascinated.

"I can't go indoors right now," he tells her.

"Oh, right, okay then," she nods, reassessing her strategy. He might be a veteran suffering from PTSD. Being indoors could be a trigger for him or he might have claustrophobia. Best not to push. Let him tell her in his own time. She knows a few people who counsel veterans for free. She can get him to see one of them when he's ready.

"How about this? I have a patio with one really comfortable lounge chair. I fall asleep in it all the time. I've got a spare pillow and blankets, so you can still sleep outside but in comfort. Like camping, except you don't have to worry about bears. Or raccoons. The last time I went camping raccoons stole a bunch of my food. But I have a bear and raccoon-free backyard, so you're safe."

He lowers his hand and tilts his head to the side as if considering her words. "You're genuine. Aren't you?"

She's not sure what he means by that statement, but she smiles and nods, "The offer is real with no strings attached. You can sleep on my patio and use my bathroom for however long you need."

He blinks a few times as if he's shocked by her words. "I could be a rapist or a murderer."

"Nope," she says simply. "You're good." Again, he blinks at her, and the silence between them stretches. She's tempted to start chattering again but feels like it's important that he has a moment of silence to think and assess her offer.

"You make no sense," he finally states.

"I hear that a lot," she confesses with a grin. "Mostly from guys on the first date. That's probably why I don't get asked on second dates. Their loss really because I make an awesome girlfriend. I like action movies and baseball. I'm pretty darn mellow. I don't expect flowers or chocolates, and I don't really wear jewelry, so no need for expensive gifts. A quiet night on the couch with pizza and beer is my idea of a great time. Throw in some mozzarella sticks, and I'm your sex slave." She colors a bit at those last words. She didn't mean to turn her little speech sexual, but it just slipped out. But to her relief, the guy doesn't leer at her. He just gives a soft smile, and she doesn't care that she overshared any longer.

"What's your name?"

"Stephanie Garmin, but everyone calls me Steph," she holds out her hand to shake. "What's yours?"

"Eli," he says, taking his hand in hers. "Just Eli." She doesn't realize how big his hand is until it engulfs her own. She feels a little fission of power as their palms meet. He must have a gift like her.

Maybe he sees ghosts and is haunted by those who were unable to complete some kind of task during their lives.

Or he can see future events, but he can't fix anything and it's driving him to a lonely, homeless existence.

Or he can read people's thoughts, and his mind is full of everyone else's emotions, overwhelming him.

Or she could just be letting her imagination run wild again.

Get it together, Steph. It's probably just static electricity. He releases her hand and seems to draw back a bit, his face returning to that blank mask.

"So, is that a yay or nay on the patio bedroom?" she asks. "Because I can sweeten the pot a little. There's homemade lasagna at my place too." He's silent for so long she thinks he's going to refuse when he abruptly stands up, towering over her. She scrambles to her feet as he scoops up her lunch tote, puts the cookies and sandwich back in it, and then slings it over his shoulder.

"I would be honored to accept a meal and lounge chair bed for the night."

She freezes for a moment, intimidated by his quick movements and imposing size. Now that he's standing, she can see he's much larger than she first thought, and for just a moment she questions her offer.

But only for a moment.

"Right this way, good sir," she says in her best butler voice and starts walking them toward her house. "A scrumptious meal and grand bed with a view of the stars awaits you."

CHAPTER

2

Eli can't believe he's following this little, defenseless human home. More than that, what is she thinking? Why is she offering a stranger access to her personal space? Doesn't she have any common sense at all? He's not just a stranger but a large and powerful male. Even if he didn't have an animal waiting to burst out of his skin, his human form could do plenty of damage. This woman needs protection from herself.

She chatters as they walk, and that's another thing. Normally he doesn't like talkative people. He likes quiet. That's the reason he built his home in the middle of the forest at the end of a ten-mile long rutted, gravel road. That's also why he was putting a lot of energy into his shields, keeping people from noticing him or getting too close. But Steph noticed him, walked right up to him, and started talking.

And talking.

But for some odd reason, he doesn't mind her talking. She amuses him. Makes the oppressive weight of his current dilemma lighten. While she chatters along, he listens with half an ear, enjoying the way she flitters from topic to topic with the most tenuous connections. He doesn't need to pay attention because she doesn't expect him to respond, so he's free to let his mind wander as her tone soothes him.

She leads him to a small house painted a soft yellow. The quaint home fits her, not just because it's painted such a cheerful color but because it practically glows with warmth. When she opens the door, he feels drawn inside.

Normally he hates being in other people's homes and surrounded by their things, their memories, their smells. He feels clumsy and awkward, trying to negotiate someone else's space. But Steph's small house is different. The front door opens into the living room where a big comfy couch faces a TV. It amuses him to notice the TV is supported by planks of wood and cinderblocks.

He could make her a nice wooden stand, using a dark wood to go with the hardwood floors. And he could make it a little taller than what the TV's currently sitting on. That would make it better for viewing and allow him to add a few shelves below for storage space. He could…

What's he doing? Thinking about making her furniture? He's only here for the night. Hell, his wolf probably won't even last the night. He'll end up shifting and running to the closest woods. His wolf might even try and take him back to his woods. The wolf keeps trying to drag him home, but he's been fighting it. He hasn't been home in days. If he loses control of his wolf and ends up back in Hunger Valley territory, people will end up dead, or he'll end up dead. It could go either way.

"Hey, there." Her voice is soft and worried, making him realize he's been standing stock still in her living room, staring at her blank TV for a while. "It's okay. You don't need to stay in the house if you're uncomfortable. Let me put the dogs in the kitchen and I can take you out to the backyard."

When she mentions dogs he notices the smell of her pets. Three distinct canine voices are crying out for her attention. She disappears through a door, and he hears the click of a lock followed by another door opening and the ecstatic whines of excited canines entering. She talks to them, praises them, tells them how much she missed them, and encourages them to be patient a little longer. When the cacophony dies down, she emerges from the kitchen, wiggling her way through the half-closed door while trying to keep the excited pets from following her.

"I locked them all in the kitchen. I can introduce you to them later, if you want," she offers. "They're all friendly once they meet someone. Or I can keep them in the house for the night. It's up to you."

"They won't like me," he warns her. Dogs don't like his wolf.

"Other dogs might not like you, but my dogs will. I have the best dogs," she informs him with a wave toward the kitchen. He just nods and hopes he doesn't end up hurting one of her pets because it attacks him.

"Let me grab some stuff," she says as she opens a hallway door and fills her arms with bedding. He steps forward to help. When he reaches over her head, his nose fills with her scent.

He almost stumbles. Nothing has ever smelled so good. He leans a little closer to fill his lungs and savors her scent, letting himself get caught up in what it's doing to calm his mind. That's why when she steps back, he isn't ready. Because he's leaned over, she slams the back of her head into his face.

The impact sends her to her knees and drives him back several steps. He cups his hand over his throbbing nose and breathes through the pain.

"Oh my god!" she cries out, scrambling back to her feet and rubbing the back of her head with a hand. "I'm so sorry! I didn't know you were right behind me. Are you okay? Let me see your face. Oh, please tell me I didn't break your nose! Of course, if I broke your nose, I'm totally going to brag about it at work, but I'm going to make it sound like you were a mugger in a dark alley and I punched you instead of just accidentally running into you with the back of my head." She smacks herself in the forehead with the heel of her hand. "What am I thinking? Did I just say that? You must think I'm insane. Before you run off and call the cops on me for abuse, let me get you some ice." She hurries past him and wiggles her way back into the kitchen.

While she's gone, he gingerly runs his fingers over his nose. Yup, it's broken. Bracing himself he cracks it back into place, gritting his teeth through the pain as he waits for his shifter healing to take effect. He's not known for his sophistication, but even for him, this is a new low—receiving a broken nose from a good Samaritan as she tries to get him blankets.

This is a good example of why he rarely leaves his cabin, let alone his clan's territory.

"Here you go!" she calls out cheerily as she wiggles back through the door, forcing it closed behind her despite the weight of the dogs pushing against it. Triumphantly she holds up a bag of ice as she jogs to him and thrusts it into his hands. He reaches out to take it. At the same time, she leans in to get a better look at his face and he almost slaps her across the cheek with his hand.

This woman is a menace!

"It doesn't look too bad, actually," she comments, not even realizing how close she came to getting backhanded by accident. "That's good because I felt guilty. I hate feeling guilty. I hate it even more than lutefisk and that's saying a lot."

Finally able to pluck the icepack out of her hand, he dutifully holds it over his throbbing nose. In a few minutes he'll be fine, but for now, it's better to feign human weakness. The icepack will help cover the rapid healing of his nose. "What's lutefisk?"

"It's a traditional Norwegian dish. Basically, it's cod treated with lye. It ends up translucent and gelatinous. Smells bad too." Her description sounds revolting, even to his wolf who isn't a picky eater. His disgust must show on his face because she laughs and pats his arm reassuringly. "Don't worry. This house is a no lutefisk zone. It's not allowed, even during the holidays, no matter how much my friend Sara tries to talk me into it."

She turns back to the pile of bedding now on the floor and scoops it up. "Let me show you to your room, good sir. You can rest and recover from my natural clumsiness." He wants to tell her it's not her fault, that he got too close and wasn't paying attention. With his shifter speed, he should've been able to move out of the way long before the impact. But she brushes past him and her scent hits him again, making him lose the power of speech.

She's out the front door before he can think again. Hurrying after, he follows her around the house and through a gate to the backyard. Then he stops dead, shocked at the state of the place. Except for the small stone patio, the entire backyard is nothing but bare earth, weeds, and piles of rubbish. He hasn't known her for long, but this doesn't seem like her style at all. He looks over to her and raises an eyebrow.

"I know. It's a mess," she admits as she dumps the contents of her arms onto the lounge chair. "I bought the house as a fixer-upper. I focused on the inside first and then the front yard. Now I need to do the backyard, but I've lost my enthusiasm. There was nothing but trash back here when I bought it, so I'm proud I got most of that cleared away. But I just don't know what to do with the space. I want flowers, a little veggie garden, and a couple of trees, I guess. But I can't decide what I want exactly and where to put it."

She's about to say something else when her stomach rumbles, making him frown. Why was she trying to feed him her lunch when she's hungry?

"And that's my cue to get the lasagna in the oven," she declares. "I'll be right back." She turns and hurries away, leaving him standing in the wreckage of her backyard.

To give himself something to do, he unfolds the bedding. He's been sleeping in the woods in his wolf form the last few nights, but stretching out on a bed, even if it's a lounge chair, sounds like a nice change. Then he gets a look at his bare feet. He stole clothes after he shifted to his human form that morning. He doesn't feel guilty about stealing an old pair of jeans and a battered shirt, but shoes have real value and he couldn't bring himself to take a pair. Consequently, his feet are filthy. That leads him to the realization that the rest of him is probably almost as dirty.

He winces. No wonder she thought he was homeless. His clan would shake their heads if they saw him now, and they even know about his issues. That makes him want to explain things to her.

But explain what, exactly? Rarely do humans knows about the magical world. If he can't tell her about his wolf side, what good would any attempt at an explanation be?

He could at least say something appreciative.

Without thinking he walks through the door she disappeared through, which leads to a small bright kitchen. She's crouched next to a stove, with three mutts watching her with rapt attention. He forgot about the dogs. Hoping to sneak out before they notice him, he eases himself backward, but it's too late. The smallest of the mutts sniffs, turns, and bounds toward him with a fierce growl. The other two are only a millisecond behind the first, and those two are substantially larger.

He doesn't want to hurt Steph's dogs so he braces to take the bites, hoping to minimize the damage to just one arm and maybe a leg. But when she turns to see why her dogs are moving across the kitchen, she acts decisively.

"Sit!" she bellows in a voice that would do any drill instructor proud. All three of them sit so quickly they slide a little. Eli feels power brush past him, making the hair on his arms stand up and his wolf whine. He has to fight the urge to plop himself down on the floor right next to the panting dogs. This woman might smell human, but something more is going on here. Something powerful.

Her voice goes back to its normal cheerful tone. "Eli, I'd like to introduce you to my motley crew." She takes a few steps forward to place herself in the middle of the three dogs. She points to the littlest one. The dog looks to be about fifteen pounds and mostly white with a few large brown spots on his short fur. "This one is Terror. Terror, go greet our guest." The dog stands and trots over to him, stubby tail tucked submissively.

"What do I do?' Eli asks her as the dog stands at his feet, looking at him expectantly.

"Hold your hand out so he can sniff it." Eli does as she instructs. Terror gives him a sniff and a lick before trotting back to her.

He looks back to Steph, and she points to a long-haired beast. The dog is the largest of the three and mostly dark brown with black legs and a big bushy tail. The beast's mouth opens to pant, showcasing a set of teeth that would make any predator proud. Terror might be the vigilant one of the group, but this one is the enforcer.

"This is Mesa. She's a great cuddler. Like a living blanket in the winter," she says. "Go say hi," she orders Mesa, and they go through the same sniff-and-lick routine.

She points to the last dog, and even Eli with his lack of dog experience knows this one is a pit bull. His short gray coat does nothing to hide the dozens of scars crisscrossing his body. Both ears are almost entirely missing and a chunk of muscle in his right shoulder is gone, making it dip in the wrong way. Despite the damage, his body is muscled and strong. As Eli examines him, the dog yawns, his giant square maw opening wide. No wonder they use this breed for fighting. The thing's mouth would do any shark proud.

Out of all the dogs, the pit bull's body is the most relaxed and laid back. Mesa might be watching him distrustfully, but this second dog, just like his owner, isn't concerned with Eli's presence at all. Aren't pit bulls supposed to be aggressive and dangerous? This one, now with his tongue lolling out sideways, looks more stoned than threatening.

"This is Grey, spelled with an 'e' instead of an 'a.' I know. It's not a very original name, but I didn't pick it so we're all kind of stuck. Anyway, Grey was rescued when a dog fighting ring was broken up. Don't let his looks fool you. He's a sweet guy. His feelings are easily hurt, so don't mention the s-c-a-r-s."

Eli ignores the fact that Steph thinks her dogs can understand human speech to the point that she needs to spell out words instead of saying them. He holds out his hand for the pit bull to give him a sniff. Unlike the other two, Grey stays close to him after doing the sniff-and-lick routine. He pushes his big body up against Eli's leg and makes a snuffling sound.

"Oh, he likes you!" Steph exclaims. "It can take him a while to warm up to men, so you should feel special." Going on instinct, Eli reaches down and gives Grey a scratch behind his ears. The dog relaxes under his touch, leaning even more of his body weight against Eli. He regards the scarred dog thoughtfully.

I know how you feel, he thinks. *I've been forced to fight for the gain of others too.*

"It's going to be a while before dinner's ready," she informs him. "Would you like a shower?" Eli nods, and when he moves to follow Steph out of the kitchen, Grey stays with him, even settling down on the bathroom floor when Steph hands him some towels and a robe.

"This should fit you. If you give me your clothes, I can run them through the wash while you shower," she offers. He shrugs and starts stripping. She squeaks and turns her back. "I guess you're not shy," she mutters, and he grins.

Shifters end up naked around each other so often that nudity is just a fact of life. It's been a long time since he interacted in the human world, so he's forgotten how prudish they can be. He tosses his clothes at her feet, and without turning around, she leans over and picks them up.

"I'll just go take care of these. I'll meet you in the backyard when you're all done," she says and rushes out of the room. He looks down at Grey who grunts as he lets his big head flop to the tile floor. Eli just raises an eyebrow at the pit bull and then focuses on getting himself clean.

The shower feels luxurious. Hot showers are rare for him because he never bothered installing plumbing in his cabin. Usually, he just bathes in a nearby stream or heats a little water on the wood stove and makes do with sponge baths.

The robe she gave him doesn't fit at all, so he wraps one of the towels around his waist and hopes that's enough for her human sensibilities.

Padding through the house, it doesn't take long for him to find her in the backyard. She's curled up in an Adirondack chair and tapping furiously on her phone. While he was showering, she unfolded the lounge chair and made it into a bed with a massive pile of blankets and a few pillows. He wants to tell her not to worry. He won't get cold, but that might open up a line of questions he can't answer.

She looks up when he steps out the back door, giving him a little smile when she sees him clad in only a towel. "I guess the robe was too small. Sorry about that. You should take that as a compliment. You're too muscled and manly to fit in my little feminine robe." He looks down at himself and back at her, noticing that she's blushing and trying to look at everything but him.

Trying to puzzle out why she appears embarrassed, he makes his way over to her and lowers himself down on the lounger, being careful to keep from accidentally flashing her. Once he's sure the towel will stay put, he points at the beer sitting on the edge of the firepit.

"Mine?"

"Yup, that's for you," she tells him, setting her phone down. "You strike me as the beer type. I hope the brand works because it's all I have." He points to the glass of wine and cocks an eyebrow, remembering one of her little spiels earlier when she mentioned liking pizza and beer. She smiles at him, not missing a beat.

"I switch back and forth," she explains. "Depends on my mood. Tonight feels like a wine night." He nods and takes a long pull of the beer. It tastes good and feels satisfying sliding down his throat. Grey settles down at his feet, one paw resting over his right foot. Mesa is curled up at Steph's feet, eying him with mild distrust. Terror is nowhere to be seen, but the sound of little feet running tells Eli the small dog is at the far corner of the yard chasing something.

He points to Mesa and then Grey. "Are these the reasons?"

She tilts her head in confusion. "Reasons for what?"

"The reason you're not afraid to invite a stranger into your home?"

Steph looks down at the dogs with deep affection. "I'm sure they could be dangerous if pressed, but no. I don't rely on the dogs for protection. I don't need to. They're here because they picked me, not for any other reason."

"Picked you?"

"Mesa was first. I came out of my work one night, and she was sitting next to my car. No collar, no chip, and she was filthy and underweight. There were dozens of cars, but she picked mine. She picked me." Reaching down, she scratches Mesa's shaggy neck. For a moment the dog's eyes squint with pleasure. "I thought for a brief second about taking her to the shelter, just in case some family was looking for her but decided not to. I know Mesa didn't run away from her people. She's had tons of opportunities to escape and never took a single one. That tells me she wants to be here. That she's decided I'm her person."

She stops petting the dog and sits back up. "Terror showed up a few months later. He dragged himself to my front porch. He probably got hit by a car. He had a broken leg and cracked pelvis. The poor little guy hated being in a cast." She chuckles at the memory and then sobers. "If I'd taken him to the shelter, they probably would've put him down. He's like Mesa, no collar and no chip, and his vet bills ended up being pretty darn expensive." She smiles fondly. "We had to eat a lot of generic brand food for a while, but I don't mind. He's a great dog. I haven't had a rat problem since he came into my life, and he always warns me that someone's at the front door. He's my furry doorbell."

Grey picks that moment to yawn and roll to his side, his paw still on Eli's foot.

"And then there's Grey," she says with a sad little smile. "He's pretty new to our little family, and I'm sure you can tell he's had a rough time before he got here. A friend of mine works with a pit bull rescue and they needed foster homes, so I offered. When I showed up to pick up a young female, Grey got loose and got in my car. He wouldn't get out. My friend tried to drag him out, but he bit into my seat and wouldn't let go, so I brought him home. Technically he's still a foster, but no one has ever even asked to meet him, so I think he's staying too. I don't mind. I adore him, and he fits right in. I guess they call it a foster failure when the people fostering the dogs end up adopting them."

She gives Eli a big grin. "It's one aspect of my life where I don't mind being called a failure!"

If she's the type to collect strays, is he the latest one? He doesn't like that. He doesn't want to be another lost soul to her. She needs to know he's strong and capable, not just a stray wolf in need of a home.

"I have a cabin," he says.

There's no confusion from her at his seemingly random comment. She just smiles and nods encouragingly. "Is it close by?"

He shrugs. "It's in the woods outside of Hunger Valley."

"That's not too far. I can drive you home tomorrow." Her offer makes him scowl. That wasn't what he intended at all when he mentioned his cabin. Not only does he want to stay away, but the last thing he wants to do is bring this innocent woman anywhere near his clan.

"Or not," she amends when she catches his expression. "The offer's still open to sleep here for as long as you need. If you're up for it, you can even move into my guest room."

He nods and takes another pull on his beer. The silence stretches between them, and he's disappointed she doesn't fill it with her chatter.

He's not sure why, but he wants to confide in her. He wants to tell her about his troubles, the horrible decision he needs to make, and the obligations tearing at him. Instead, he finishes his beer and sets the bottle down. When he looks up to meet her gaze, he finds himself transfixed. The expression on her face isn't one of pity or sympathy. It's one of profound sadness.

"Something bad is going on. Something that's tearing you apart inside," she says softly. "When you're ready, I'll listen, and I'll help as best I can."

His mouth drops open in shock. What does she know? She's human. What can she possibly know? Maybe she's part druid or witch. If either of those blood lines run through her, she could have power but smell human. Of course, neither of those groups tend to like shifters, so he hopes she doesn't know what she is or he'll be forced to leave long before he's ready to.

"Are you a mind reader?" he demands, and she laughs, the light sound easing the pain in his soul.

"Not really. Your secrets are safe," she promises him. "I can just feel things sometimes."

Unsure how to respond to that, he takes another drink of his beer. She doesn't chatter on like she normally does, and the silence stretches between them. A buzzer goes off in the kitchen.

"Saved by the bell," she murmurs as she stands. "You stay here. I'll bring dinner out. We can dine al fresco tonight."

He watches her walk back into the house and takes that moment to check in with his wolf. Is she a danger to them? Should they walk out the gate and disappear into the coming night?

The wolf, normally ripping at his insides and demanding release, rolls over and closes his eyes. *Here*, the wolf tells him cryptically. *It's here.*

As if he didn't have enough troubles to deal with already, suddenly his wolf is turning vague and mysterious.

Just great. Why couldn't he have been born a coyote instead of a maned wolf? Or, even better, he could've been a badger—the only shifter that can live outside a clan with no consequences. No one fucks with badgers.

He would have made a damn fine badger.

CHAPTER

3

Steph comes out of the store and hands him a bag and a shoe box. He takes the items, and thinking she wants him to carry them for her, he tucks them under his arm and waits for her to lead him to the next spot on her morning to-do list. Instead of walking, she points to a nearby alley.

"If you're not comfortable going into the store, you could just duck in there and change," she tells him, and that's when he realizes the bag of clothes and the box of shoes are for him.

"I don't need these," he says and tries to give them back to her but she links her hands behind her back and steps away with a big grin on her face.

"You're holding them, and possession is nine-tenths of the law, so they're yours now."

"That's if I was trying to steal them," he huffs out.

"Refusing gifts is bad luck," she informs him.

He eyes her. "You just made that up."

"Maybe," she says unrepentantly, her grin never wavering. "And I'll need you to come into the nursery with me to buy plants so you better put those shoes on at least. I had to guess the size since you wouldn't tell me. I hope they fit."

He stares at her, holding out the purchases to her. She doesn't move to take them. He pushes a little power at her to see if he can bully her into taking back the items. Her reaction isn't anything he expects. Instead of intimidating or frightening her, she just gives him an even wider smile. Then he feels it. Warmth runs along his skin, raising the hair on his forearm and teasing his shields.

She's not a shifter, or druid, or any other creature he knows. Her magic is unique, both in feel and ability. He doesn't know anyone in the clan who can make someone feel good like she does. Coyote magic is as close as he's ever experienced to what she can do. Coyote magic is joyful and can make you feel drunk on happiness. But her power is different. Warmth and caring radiates off her, pushing against his shields and pressing to get inside him.

Maybe if a clan leader is powerful enough, they could transmit feelings through the clan tie. But he's never heard of any clan leader ever being that powerful. And this woman isn't even a shifter or a member of a magical group he knows about. She's a mystery, and he's both intrigued and wary.

"What are you?" he asks, rubbing his arms where her power made his skin feel warm.

"What are you?" she counters, and he nods his head in acknowledgment of all the secrets they aren't going to share.

Without another word, he ducks into the alley to change clothes. She tried to get him to enter the store with her, but his wolf protested so strongly he almost ended up on his knees because of the amount of effort he had to use to keep from shifting. Now, as he pulls on a brand-new pair of jeans, work boots, and a shirt, he wonders why he's still with Steph.

He should have left last night. He expected his wolf to rip out of him in the wee hours of the morning and send him loping into the woods and back to Hunger Valley territory. Instead, he woke up to the smell of pancakes and the weight of Grey curled up on his chest.

He's not sure what's more shocking—the fact that his wolf wanted to stay, or that he managed to sleep through an eighty-pound pit bull climbing onto him.

Of course, waking up with Grey snoring and drooling all over him was nothing to the realization that his wolf was content and quiet the entire night. Then, just as he thought he'd turned a new page with the troublesome animal half of himself, the wolf went crazy when he tried to walk into a store with Steph. Fighting his wolf made him start sweating, even after Steph left him on the sidewalk while she ran inside.

Tucking his stolen clothing into the bag, he catches a faint smell. Going still, he takes a deep breath in through his nose, trying to tease out the aroma. Then he figures it out. A bear shifter is close. Scenting the alley a few more times, he realizes the smell of bear is coming from a back door leading into the store where Steph bought his clothes.

That's why his wolf raised such a fuss when he tried to walk in. His wolf scented the bear and didn't want him going near it.

Good wolf, he thinks. *We don't need the local clan to know we're here. We've got enough fights waiting at home. No need to add to the list.*

His wolf sends him an amused feeling and goes back to sleep. It's a strange thing to have his wolf be agreeable. Most days, he and his wolf argue, and sometimes it feels like a full-on battle.

Most shifters blend seamlessly with their animal but not him. He and his wolf argue, fight, and occasionally ignore each other. Come to think of it, this is the calmest his wolf has been in a long time. He risks poking the beast, taunting him with images of their cabin and the Hunger Valley wilderness. The wolf doesn't rise to the bait and instead just gives a snort and sends him back an image of Steph's face.

Well, that's new. Generally, his wolf doesn't like anyone, even other shifters. But apparently, he likes Steph. *It makes sense you'd like her so much. She's fond of dogs,* he tells the wolf.

The beast inside of him growls, and with a silent laugh at his irked wolf, he makes his way out of the alley.

"Looks like I got the sizes mostly right," she says as he comes into view. For some reason he suddenly feels mildly shy as she examines him from head to toe. Annoyed with himself, he stands up tall and scowls. To his bewilderment, she laughs.

"Arrogant looks good on you," she comments gaily. "That scowl brings out your cheekbones. If you decide to go into modeling, you should practice that look." He finds himself unwillingly smiling at her unrelenting good humor.

"Are you ready to hit the nursery?" she asks. "Because I'm ready to put you to work in exchange for those clothes." He nods and follows her back to the truck she borrowed from one of her neighbors. *Does anyone ever say no to this woman?* Actually, the more salient question is whether she would ever bother to pay attention to the word *no* if someone attempted to use it.

CHAPTER 4

Her intentions might have started out altruistic, but having shirtless Eli laboring in her backyard makes her admit there might be more driving her than just a wish to help someone down on his luck. In a word, the man is perfect. His upper body is nothing but muscle covered in tanned skin. She bets if he took off his pants, his lower half would be just as perfect.

A few substantial scars mar the skin on his back. As curious as she is, she manages to keep herself from asking about them. If he wants to talk, she'll listen, but she knows he's not one to appreciate prying.

It's also becoming obvious that he's the kind of guy who likes to be left alone to work. So far, he's refused to let her help once they brought the plants and bags of soil back to her place. He unloaded the truck she borrowed, growling at her every time she tried to pick up anything. When she brought out a shovel, he snatched it from her. Hauling the garden hose from the front yard got her a glower, and attempting to unpot even one of the bushes got her snapped at.

With a shrug she retreated into the house, leaving Eli to his labors. At least the dogs are out there to help him. She chuckles a little as she glances out the kitchen window into the backyard. Grey is lounging in the sun. Mesa's watching Eli with barely concealed suspicion. And Terror is trying to help dig holes in all the wrong places.

Eli doesn't seem to mind his dubious helpers. He just keeps digging and planting, uncaring of the sun beating down on his bare back or the woman admiring his half-naked body from her kitchen window.

Blushing at her thoughts, she busies herself with making a pitcher of iced tea and mixing up a big batch of cookies. She insisted on buying him lunch after loading the truck with plants, soil, and paving stones. She took him to her favorite hole-in-the-wall Mexican restaurant and ordered enough to feed four people because he wouldn't tell her what he wanted. It seemed like a lot of food when it was all delivered to their small outside table, but to her astonishment, he managed to eat his way through most of it.

Thinking about the amount of food Eli ate makes her realize she needs to stock her kitchen if he's going to be staying much longer. She's got a casserole to heat up for dinner, but after that all she's got in the cupboards is pancake mix and bread. She doesn't even have enough cheese or deli meat to make a few sandwiches.

She slides open the kitchen window. "How do you feel about pancakes for breakfast again tomorrow?" she calls out. Eli doesn't look up and just gives a grunt and nod. "Great," she yells to him and then leaves the kitchen window open in case she thinks of any other questions to ask him.

The timer goes off, and she swaps one baking sheet for another. The kitchen is starting to fill with the vanilla smell of fresh sugar cookies. She catches Eli pause in his planting and sniff the air; then he looks over to her. She knows the hungry look is because he smells the cookies but wonders what it would feel like if that look was for her.

Get those thoughts out of your head, she admonishes herself. *The guy needs help, not you ogling him and wondering what those callused hands would feel like on your skin.*

But what would those hands feel like?

Ugh! Annoyed with herself she decides to keep herself busy by making another batch of cookies. Peanut butter cookies sound perfect. She turns to the pantry to pull out peanut butter, hoping she has enough for at least one batch.

When she turns, she lets out a startled gasp and stumbles back. Eli is standing right at the kitchen window, staring at her with intense green eyes. She didn't hear him move or even feel his presence. One minute he was digging in the far corner of the yard and the next he's standing right in front of her.

"D-do you want some cookies?" she asks, stuttering over her words. He nods, not taking his eyes off of her as she puts a few on a plate. "The iced tea isn't cold yet, but how about a beer?" He nods again so she pulls a beer out of the fridge.

By the time she's opened the beer Eli has come into the kitchen and is holding out his hand to take the bottle. He doesn't drink it but just keeps staring at her. Feeling disconcerted she reaches to grab the plate and manages to knock it off the counter. Before she can even cry out, Eli has caught the plate without losing a single cookie.

Grey gives a little moan of disappointment from the floor behind him.

Eli's eyes never leave hers, even as he plucks the plate from imminent doom.

Finding his gaze much too intense, she drops her eyes to look at the plate.

"Wow, you're fast. Of course, even if the dish broke it's not a big deal. It's not real china. I could never afford the real stuff. That's just some imitation of an expensive china pattern, but I like it. I broke a bunch of plates in my last move, so I ended up buying a whole new set. But I still have a lot from the original set, so now I have more dishes than I know what to do with. You could probably break a few a week and I wouldn't even notice for a year. Oh, gosh, you're sweating buckets. You should probably drink some water along with that beer. You could get dehydrated. Let me get you some water."

Throughout her nervous monologue, Eli remains silent, but his face softens slightly, and a small smile curls the corners of his lips. She knows she's talking too much. It's a habit she's tried to break most of her life. But at the moment the power to stop the words pouring out of her mouth absolutely eludes her.

He stands much too close as she pulls a glass out of a cupboard and fills it with water. "I'm sorry I don't have any ice. The ice maker on the fridge broke, so normally I just keep a bag of ice in here. But last week I had friends over for dinner and drinks and we used up the last of the ice making ice cream. And a few margaritas."

Stopping babbling, she commands herself as she exchanges the glass of water for the bottle of beer. He's so close she can feel his body heat, so she takes a few steps back to give herself some breathing room. Moving doesn't help because Eli moves with her, keeping the distance between them at about a foot. His proximity sets her off again.

"So, I was thinking I'd heat a casserole for dinner. Mrs. Martelli at the end of the cul-de-sac made it. I know it's good because she's a great cook. Well, not her cakes so much, but everything else she makes is really tasty. Her cakes are always dry, which is weird because I know she uses mixes. How can you mess up when you use a mix? We don't tell her though. No one wants to hurt her feelings. Anyway, last time I helped her with her son she made me a casserole and told me to freeze it until I felt like eating it. I probably should have heated it up sooner because I've had her casserole pan for, like, ever! But I just keep forgetting it's there. Well, until you showed up. And you eat a lot of food so the casserole should be perfect."

She pauses to breathe, and that's when she realizes he's staring at her lips. Probably because she's talking a mile a minute so he could very well be trying to figure out how to get her to shut up. She can't blame him. Even her parents couldn't stand her like this, and they were supposed to love her.

Wincing, she drops her gaze to the floor and lets her shoulders droop. "I'm sorry. I'd love to say I don't normally chatter like an idiot, but that'd be a lie." She hears him set the water glass down but can't bring herself to meet his eyes. "I've always talked too much, and I know it's annoying and I should be able to control it by now—"

Broad fingers under her chin urge her to look up and cut her word off mid-sentence. Eli is smiling now, widely enough to show off a nice set of even, white teeth. And rather pointy canines. Has she ever met anyone with such prominent canines before? They're fascinating, and she curls her hands into fists to keep herself from putting her fingers in his mouth to feel how sharp they are.

Inappropriate impulse much?

"It's fine," he tells her, and she's not sure if he's referring to the casserole she's prattling on about or her inability to shut the hell up. Or maybe he figured out she was having weird thoughts about putting her fingers in his mouth?

Her face must have shown her apprehension, but his smile only gets wider. "I like just about any food. And I like your voice," he explains simply. Then he leans closer to her. "And I like your smell."

She wants to tell him she likes his smell too, but then his mouth is on hers and her entire body flashes hot. She leans into the kiss, opening her mouth and grabbing his biceps with her hands to steady herself.

Although she might not be as worldly or experienced as many of her friends, she's not some blushing virgin. She's dated, kissed, and had sex with a handful of men. From what she's experienced so far, Eli's kisses are better than anything she's known. Electricity zigs between them, warming her lips and sinking down, making heat pool in her belly.

With a little moan, she pushes her body against his. She hears the clink of a plate set on the counter, and then Eli's hands wrap around her. One hand goes to her ass and the other rests on her back between her shoulder blades. The hand on her ass squeezes and lust rockets through her system.

Her own hands come to rest on the sides of his torso. She wants to grab him back. Run her hands over all his delicious sweaty skin, but between his kiss and his hands, she's forgotten how her own body works. Before she can figure out how to get her hands to move, a warm furry body is forcing itself between the two of them with a low threatening growl.

Eli releases her and steps back. She's not sure, but he seems to growl right back at Mesa, who's now showing teeth and snapping her jaws threateningly.

"Mesa!" Steph gasps. The dog has always been possessive and protective of her, but this is the first time Mesa has threatened anyone she's been introduced to. Introductions are Steph's way of telling Mesa and the other dogs that the new person in their lives isn't a threat, and it's never failed. Until now.

Lifting a lip to show off one of those long canines, Eli growls back at the dog.

Wait, did that canine get longer when she wasn't looking? Dog and man growling at each other pulls her out of her wild thoughts.

"Eli!" Steph gapes, and he looks up, the growl dying in his throat. A worried expression replaces the aggression on his face.

"Mesa, out!" she orders the dog and points toward the living room. The dog tries to ignore her, but when she repeats the order along with a push from her gift, Mesa gives a little whine and slinks out of the kitchen.

When she turns back around, Eli is gone. A glance out the window shows him back out working on the planting as if he hadn't been standing right next to her seconds ago. The plate of cookies, glass of water, and beer are sitting untouched on the counter. It's almost as if he was never in the kitchen in the first place. Except for a few muddy boot prints on her floor.

"At least I'm not crazy," she mutters to herself as she gets out a rag to clean up the floor. "Or more accurately, at least I'm not hallucinating. The jury might still be out on the crazy part."

What was I thinking? Eli berates himself as he sinks the pickaxe into the hard ground. He's finished planting what they brought home from the nursery, but unwilling to stop working, he starts breaking up the hard ground where she told him she plans to start an herb garden.

The smell of the cookies drew him to the window. But the sight of Steph, humming to herself as she went about the kitchen, mesmerized him. He knows his unrelenting gaze can unnerve even other shifters, so he's impressed Steph didn't run away from him, especially after he used shifter speed to get into the kitchen. He didn't even realize what he'd done until she was handing him a beer and talking nonstop.

Even though he doesn't remember anything she said, he's still feeling the unique calm the sound of her voice creates inside him, which affects both him and his wolf. The sound of her chattering made the wolf wake up inside him. His wolf whined with pleasure at her voice, radiating a contentment Eli doesn't think he's ever felt before. The wolf loves her voice. Her magic. Her smell. Her taste.

Goddess, her taste.

The wolf had pushed him to kiss her.

She liked it, his wolf grumbles. *She likes us. Why did you stop? We're going to keep her. She's perfect.*

She's human, he reminds the wolf and only gets a harrumph back. His wolf isn't interested in the fact that she's human and doesn't even know shifters exist. If she knew about shifters, she wouldn't have been so surprised at his speed. Her shock was genuine, and remembering his carelessness makes him wince. He growled at her dog. Did she realize human throats can't make the sound he made? Did she notice his teeth? He's pretty sure his canines dropped.

I need to leave, he tells himself, but instead of doing that, he sinks the axe into the ground again. He can feel his wolf ready to fight him if he tries to leave. The wolf is determined to stay.

You hate humans. You barely tolerate other shifters, and you don't like being in town, he reminds the wolf.

Not this human, not this town, wolf responds mysteriously.

His wolf is the reason he lives in a cabin far in the woods and rarely visits town. Now, all of a sudden, his wolf wants to settle down and play house?

Agitated by both the ideas of leaving and staying, Eli uses too much force on the pickaxe and the handle breaks right at the metal top.

"You're an asshole," he mutters and drops the pickaxe handle to the ground. He's been working steadily for hours, and he can feel the fatigue in just about every muscle in his body. Steph came out once to bring him iced tea and cookies, but he didn't look at her. He just grunted and waited until she left before he ate and drank. That was a while ago, and now he's hungry and thirsty again. But he's afraid to go inside and let his wolf get too close to Steph. And he can feel that his wolf won't let him leave.

"Such an asshole," he grumbles as he straightens up his body and stretches his back. Grey looks up at him, his tongue lolling out and body relaxed where he's sprawled out in the last bit of sun still shining in the backyard.

"Not you," he assures the pit bull. "I like you. You're not an asshole at all." As if he understands Eli's little speech, Grey gives a happy little huff and thumps his head back down to continue with his lazing about.

Great, now he's talking to dogs.

Stretching his arms over his head, he sniffs the air. By the smell of it, whatever's in the oven is probably done. She'll come out soon to tell him dinner is ready. He needs to be nicer to her. It's not her fault he's warring with his wolf side, and it's certainly not her fault his wolf's a pain in the ass.

But it's entirely her fault she's so delectable that he can't resist taking liberties.

Maybe his wolf isn't the only asshole.

As if drawn out by his thoughts, Steph appears in the doorway to the backyard. "Dinner's just about ready," she calls out, looking around the garden with wide eyes. "Wow, you've done amazing. Look at all this. You got everything planted and even put the paving stones down. How did you get them so even? You didn't even have sand to put down under them. You should do this professionally. You're really good."

Walking around the backyard she points out every little thing he did, and he feels himself preening under her praise and enthusiasm. The sweet smell of the cookies she made clings to her, adding to the delicious scent that seems to taunt him every time he gets near her.

Touch her, his wolf demands.

Shut up.

Touch her, his wolf pushes. *She likes us. She wants us. You can smell it.*

The wolf pushes his superior sense of smell to the forefront of Eli's consciousness. Now the slight scent of Steph's arousal hits him. He noticed it earlier when they kissed but ignored it in favor of lambasting himself for his lack of control. Now he feels his dick get uncomfortably hard in his jeans.

He's not completely inexperienced. But he's also very careful about who he sleeps with. Usually, he seeks out one of the big cats. Those shifters are powerful enough to keep his wolf in check if his inner animal decides to rear up and act out. It's never happened, but he lives in fear anyway.

And he's never had a real relationship with any of them. All his dalliances were emotionless fucking, fulfilling a base need for both parties.

What he wants to do to Steph feels different. Yes, he wants to bend her over and take her hard, but he also wants to hold her, nuzzle her, and fall asleep with her in his arms. He's never had these impulses before. Between that and his wolf's interest in her, he should be freaking out. He should be trying to understand why she's different and why his wolf is acting out of character.

But he doesn't do any of those things. Instead, he just follows Steph around the backyard as she "oohs" and "ahs" over every little thing he did.

"I can't believe you did all this," she chatters as they come to the section of hard-packed earth that would eventually be the herb garden. She spies the broken pickaxe and leans over to pick up the iron axe head. He fists his hands and breaks into a sweat from the effort to keep from reaching out to touch her ass.

Touch it. Touch her.

No! Shut up! Do you want us to get kicked out? The wolf doesn't like that idea but doesn't stop pushing him.

We can just get back in. She can't keep us out. Touch her. Strip her. Claim her. Heartmate with her.

Those words send a shaft of fear through him. He's not even sure a human and shifter can Heartmate each other. The process might kill her. Ruthlessly he fights the wolf into submission. Steph doesn't notice his internal struggle as she exclaims over the broken tool.

"It was old anyway. I found it in the garage when I moved in," she states with a bright smile as she turns, holding up the pickaxe head.

"Sorry," he mumbles and drops his gaze to the ground. He knows his eyes are probably shining as he fights his wolf for control. Worried that he'll frighten her if she sees his glowing eyes, he shoves his fisted hands into his pants pockets and focuses on her feet.

"Don't worry about it," she says. "I don't mind getting a new one. Besides, it died for a good cause." Her tone is teasing, but her voice is softer now. She takes a step forward and places a hand on his forearm. He should move back before he loses his fight and grabs her. He should run deep into the woods before the wolf forces its way out and makes him do something irreparable.

But he can't do those things. He can only stand there, shaking with the effort to keep his wolf in check.

What you want to do is rape, he screams at his wolf.

Not rape, the wolf insists, pushing Steph's smell at him again. It almost sends Eli to his knees with lust.

"Easy," she whispers. "It's okay. If you need to leave for a while, you can. If you don't come back that's okay too. If you want to leave and come back, you're always welcome. Take some deep breaths for me. Whatever's going on I promise you're safe here. No one's going to hurt you. Just keep breathing for me."

At her soft words and gentle touch, the wolf stops fighting him. His inner beast calms. If he was in his wolf form the animal would be rubbing up against her and nosing her hand to pet him. The wolf recedes with a soft huff, content to let Eli be in control now that she's touching him, even if it's only her hand on his arm.

Able to breathe now that he no longer needs to wrestle with the wolf for control of his body, he takes a few jagged breaths. Steph keeps talking to him the entire time. Her voice urges him to keep breathing, to concentrate on the pull of air into his lungs. Her voice soothes something deep inside of him. Her power brushes against him with gentle, warm insistence.

"Sorry," he mumbles again, exhausted from his internal struggle. He sways a little and Steph steps up and puts her arm around his waist to steady him.

"Hey now, none of that," she soothes. "We all struggle. We all have demons. Let's go sit down." He lets her lead him to the lounge chair. His legs give out at the last minute, and his bulk crashes down. Thankfully the lounge chair is sturdy and holds up under his weight. She sits down next to him, her hand rubbing circles on his naked sweaty back. Grey soundlessly climbs onto the lounger to curl up on his other side, resting his big square head on one of his thighs.

Steph doesn't press him for an explanation. She just sits and quietly tells him about how thankful she is that he's there. When his eyes close and he slumps forward to rest his head in his hands, she brings her hand up to start running her fingers through his damp, dirty hair. He's filthy, but she never balks as she touches him.

Being a shifter means he recovers quickly, and by the time a buzzer sounds in the kitchen he feels strength returning to his body. He doesn't want to move. He doesn't want her to stop touching him but knows she needs to check on the food in the oven and he needs to take a shower. If she's willing to touch him while he's filthy, perhaps she'd do more than just pet his head and back when he's clean.

The wolf perks up at that thought, and he ruthlessly shoves the beast down. *Don't ruin this*, he begs the beast.

Don't you ruin this either, the wolf snaps back and then rolls over and goes quiet in his mind.

I'm trying, he thinks. *I'm trying damn hard.*

CHAPTER 5

Steph can't sleep. Picking up her phone to check the time, she sighs when she sees it's nearly one in the morning. She's been in bed for several hours, tossing and turning with images of Eli floating through her mind. Mesa grew so annoyed with her restlessness that the dog got off the bed with a disgruntled huff and settled on the dog bed in the corner.

Grey is outside. He decided to stay with Eli rather than join her and the other two dogs in the house. The pit bull has bonded to her guest. It's a good thing. Dogs are like Prozac. When she first moved into this house, she felt horribly lonely, despite having friends over all the time. When Mesa pushed her way into Steph's life, everything got better. That feeling only increased with the additions of Terror and Grey.

Surprisingly, Eli's reacting to Grey's attachment with bemused acceptance. When he first commented that dogs don't like him, she thought he might have had a few bad experiences. Now she thinks differently. The way her dogs reacted when he first came into the kitchen was stronger than normal. Mesa forcing them apart and threatening Eli shocked her.

Him growling right back at her dog was eye opening as well.

That's probably why dogs generally don't like him. That and the way he can make his aura menacing. Half the time he probably isn't even aware he's doing it, like people who scowl when they're thinking. They look mean and unhappy, but they aren't. It's just the way their face is. Maybe that's just the way Eli's aura is. Dark and threatening. His dark aura isn't a reflection of cruelty. She thinks it's an unintended consequence of internal suffering. There's no question in her mind. Eli is suffering from some pretty deep emotional wounds.

If she can get him to stay for a while, maybe she can try talking him into seeing her therapist friend. Lieta always keeps spots open that are paid for by a local charity. Usually, those spots are reserved for retired soldiers suffering from PTSD, but if she can't get Eli in one of those spots, she'll just pay Lieta out of pocket. She'll just need to make sure he never finds out. Maybe she can convince him that she needs him to stay to help her. He strikes her as the helping type, willing to give in if he thinks she could be in any type of distress. They could work out a trade—his labor for room and board. Of course, if he keeps up his current pace of work, she's going to run out of projects fast.

Despite his willingness to help, she knows Eli's a flight risk, ready to run at any moment. Leaving both the back door and her bedroom door open so Grey can come inside to tell her if Eli decided to leave, she takes comfort in the fact that the big, laidback pit bull has yet to make an appearance.

For now, Eli seems content to stay. She just needs to work on making this arrangement permanent. Get him used to the idea of settling in.

Earlier that evening she started a little fire in the backyard firepit and brought their dinner out. She sat with the silent man, babbling about anything and everything. She talked so much that she barely touched her food while he ate several helpings of the casserole.

His silence led her to talk and talk and talk. Even now she wants to groan a little in embarrassment. Did she really tell him about the time she climbed a wrought-iron fence and got the back of her pants caught on one of the spikes? She spent several minutes dangling, her butt hanging out while her friends laughed too hard to help her untangle herself. And that wasn't the only embarrassing story she told. Mortification fills her as she thinks of all the random stories she told in an effort to fill the silence.

For his part, Eli didn't seem to mind her verbal diarrhea. After eating, he focused his intense gaze on the fire for the rest of the evening. Very occasionally he asked a question, telling her he heard every word she said. And that only encouraged her.

Only when her throat started feeling a little raw from all the talking did she realize hours had passed. Feeling like he might need time alone with his thoughts, Steph finally called it a night and retreated into the house.

Part of the reason she babbled so badly was because of the struggle she witnessed earlier that day. Waves of distress were coming off him and crashing against her. Even without her gift, his tense body and unwillingness to meet her gaze would've clued her in to his internal battle. He was visibly shaking with the effort to hold himself together.

Why do people always assume all wounds and scars are on the outside? The ones that leave marks on souls can take much longer to heal and even fester for a lifetime. Without a doubt, Eli's dealing with such a wound.

Working on instinct, she just waited him out and kept up a soothing presence, both with her gift and her physical body. Normally she wouldn't touch someone in such a state, but her gift pushed her to approach him. It encouraged her to touch him and keep talking to him. It seemed to work, and she'd felt reluctant to pull her hands away from him when he came back to himself.

Now, thinking back, she wonders if she doesn't feel more than compassion for Eli. He's got some kind of gift, like her, and maybe that's why she's determined to help. Like recognizes like. It would be nice to have someone to talk to about it. Someone to confide in. Perhaps that's the next step, admitting to him that she isn't normal. She should make herself vulnerable to him so he can feel safe to divulge his secrets.

Her stomach clenches at the idea of telling anyone about her gift. Is she ready to be that exposed?

The chirp of her cell phone brings her out of those deep thoughts.

Grabbing it, she wonders who might be contacting her so late. Most of her friends know she tends to go to bed by ten, even on the weekends. When she sees the name on the screen she sighs and sits up.

Ashley "Ash" Bridge is a gorgeous and vivacious woman. Steph loves her but isn't blind to her tendency to party too hard and end up in unsavory places—where Ubers, Lyfts, and taxis tend to avoid—without a ride home. This isn't the first late-night request for a pickup she's received over the years. Steph never refuses or rebukes Ash for fear her friend might not reach out when in need.

Especially considering the woman doesn't seem to have many real friends and no family close by. One time, when Ash was particularly distressed, she told Steph she was trapped and she hated her life. Then she looked scared and refused to talk about it anymore.

Something is deeply wrong in Ash's world, but until she's willing to confide in Steph, there's nothing she can do to fix it. She can only be there for Ash as best she can. Like now.

The text from Ash is a common one: *Can you pick me up?*

Her response is just as predictable: *Of course, where are you?*

Falls Tavern. Please hurry! That gets Steph's attention. Ash isn't one to be demanding when she's asking for a pickup. There must be trouble.

I'll be there ASAP! Call 911 if things get bad. You need to keep yourself safe. I'm coming no matter what.

I'm fine. I'm just going to hang out in the parking lot until you get here.

Steph knows Ash well enough to know that "hang out" really means hiding and waiting for rescue. The fact that Ash never calls 911, even at Steph's urging, makes her hurry to pull on whatever clothes she can find and rush to the front door.

A hand slaps over the door just before she can open it, making her yelp and twist around ungracefully.

Standing there with eyes glowing in the darkness and his face unreadable, Eli keeps his hand on the door, his muscled arm just above her shoulder. His face is so close it would only take a small movement for her to touch her lips to his. If she kissed him, would he jump away from her or return the kiss?

"Where're you going?" he growls out. His words break through the lust muddling her brain. Giving herself a mental shake, she focuses on the task at hand.

"I need to go get a friend," she explains. "She just texted me and I need to pick her up."

With a nod, Eli removes his hand and takes a small step back so she can open the door. "I'll go with you."

"You don't need to," Steph answers even as relief courses through her that she won't need to face Falls Tavern by herself.

Although the name might lead one to believe the place is a quaint bar, the reality is far grittier. Calling it a dive bar might be an insult to dive bars. She doesn't know why Ash would decide to party at a place notorious for violent altercations, but the bar's reputation only means Steph wants to get to her as fast as she can. Having the large Eli accompany her will probably go a long way in dissuading anyone from trying to stop Ash from leaving.

Without responding to her initial refusal, he opens the front door. Following her out to the car, he silently slides into the passenger seat. He showered and changed earlier in the evening, but that doesn't stop his clean masculine scent from filling the car as she drives down the mostly empty street toward the outskirts of town.

She can feel him getting tenser as they approach the bar and even hears a little growl come out of him.

"This isn't good," he mumbles.

She can't argue with that statement. Pulling into the parking lot, she's disheartened to see that despite the late hour, the place is still full of vehicles. Hopefully, they can just grab Ash and go without anyone being the wiser.

That hope is dashed when she pulls to a stop and sees Ash running toward her. She can't make out the expression on her friend's face, but the high-speed sprint tells the whole story. Ash can't get away from Falls Tavern fast enough. What is she even doing here? She lives and works across town and told Steph she doesn't like this area of Lowell.

The woman's momentum is suddenly checked when a large body slams into her, putting both of them on the ground and out of sight behind a line of parked cars. Stunned by the speed and violence of the attack, Steph doesn't move until she hears a pitiful cry of pain and fear.

"Fuck," Eli grounds out, and he's out of the car and sprinting toward Ash so fast Steph can't even track his movements. Stumbling out of the car, she snatches up her weapons and hurries to follow.

By the time she gets to the three of them, Eli has Ash's assailant by the throat and, in a show of superb strength, holds him off the ground with just one arm. Even as the man flails against the grip, Eli doesn't even seem to be struggling to hold the massive man aloft.

More concerned with the sobbing woman on the ground, Steph ignores Eli and drops to her knees to gather Ash in her arms. "Are you hurt? Can you walk?" she asks.

Unable to talk through her tears, Ash simply nods her head and struggles to stand up. Keeping her arms around the crying woman, Steph helps her to her feet and then starts leading her to the car, only to be brought up short when she finds their path blocked by several men, just as big as the guy who tackled Ash.

Where are all the smaller guys? This can't possibly be an accurate cross-section of men living in Lowell. Couldn't some smaller men decide to attack them?

"Where do you think you're going?" one of the men asks.

"We aren't here to cause any trouble," Steph says, trying to keep the fear out of her voice. "We're just going to leave now."

"I'm not talking to you, cow," the man growls out and then turns his attention back to Ash. "You know better than to bring cattle here. What were you thinking, girl?"

Ash cringes against her. "Please," she whispers. "I don't want to be with Glenn. Please don't make me."

"It's done," the man states harshly. "You know how it works, but you teased him and then all of a sudden decided to run. You know I'm going to have to punish you for that. And for her." He thrusts a finger at Steph. "We're allowed to make a few cows disappear from the herd. Maybe she's gonna be one of them."

That's it. She's decided she's had enough. Bringing up the can of pepper spray, she hits the guy full in the face and then turns it on his stunned friends.

The three of them drop to the ground howling, and Ash jolts against her. "Oh god," the woman sobs out. "They're gonna kill you now."

"Fuck them," Steph mutters, feeling justified for her cruelty by the man's threats.

Not to mention he called her a cow. Rude!

"What did you do?" Eli steps up behind her. Steph glances back to find the man he was holding lying in an unconscious heap on the dirty parking lot tarmac. She relaxes slightly, feelingly a modicum safer to know the imminent threats are all neutralized for the moment.

"Pepper spray," she explains. "It's my favorite accessory when visiting dive bars in the wee hours of the morning." She's not sure, but she thinks she hears Eli give a muffled snort of laughter.

"Not helpless," Eli mutters approvingly and then grabs her and Ash and starts dragging them back to the car. Pulling her arm free, she jogs to the car ahead of him and jumps into the driver seat to start the car. Eli focuses on getting the weeping Ash into the backseat. Just as Eli's about to slide into the passenger seat, the tavern door opens and several more men emerge from the crowded, raucous bar. Eli turns his head to look at them, probably gauging them as potential threats. They're too far away to stop the three of them from leaving, but Steph worries about what weapons they might be carrying.

"Don't do this, Eli," one of the men shouts out. His tone is almost friendly and Steph freezes in the process of starting the car. They know each other? Could Eli be friends with these horrible people?

"If you do this there will be repercussions," the man continues, stopping a few feet from the bar's entrance. Just like the other men, this guy is massive and exudes menace. Steph grips her pepper spray in shaking hands and puts her other hand on the gear knob. Now she wishes she'd brought her baton and taser with her. Next time, she's not leaving the house without them.

"Don't care," Eli shouts back.

"I hear you're in line for clan leader," the man comments with deliberate casualness. "Could be I can help with that. But if you take Ashley, there won't be any understanding between us." Eli and the man stare at each other for several long moments. It turns out Eli's stare can make anyone keep talking because the guy gives up on the silence contest and starts talking again.

"Let me sweeten it even more," and his tone doesn't sound as confident as before. He sounds almost nervous. "I hear your clan doesn't make sure the males are taken care of. It's different here. Give me back Ashley, and I'll give you a beautiful girl of your very own. I hear your kind can be pretty rough. Wouldn't it be nice to have someone who won't say no or complain? I can make that happen."

Stomach twisting with nausea at the man's words, Steph glances over at Eli. His face is hard and his eyes seem to be glowing. The next words out of his mouth make her smile.

"Go fuck yourself!" Eli shouts out and then ducks into the car. Vibrating with anger, he turns those bright green eyes on her. "Go."

Throwing the vehicle into drive, she doesn't even try to maneuver out of the parking lot, instead driving over the curb and apologizing to the car's alignment as she pushes down hard on the gas pedal.

No other vehicles pull out to follow her. Even though that's a good thing, apprehension still fills her. Nothing about the man standing on the porch says he's one to just give up and back off. He was too far away for her to feel his aura, but she would bet good money it's black and tar-like. The guys back at the bar might not have chased after them, but that doesn't fill her with relief.

She has no doubt that trouble will follow them at some point. Another confrontation is looming in their future.

Eli centers his attention on getting the inconsolable Ash into the house and forcing her to drink several glasses of water. In the car he thought he'd need to exert power to keep her from shifting, but her coyote is much too scared to come out. The poor animal is cowering and crying deep inside of her. Instead, he found himself trying to soothe her with his power, something he's never done before. His power acts like an ill-used electronic device and fizzles out at his attempt to assuage Ash's distress. Maned wolf shifters are known for their ability to create fear, not comfort.

This is our female's job, his wolf protests. *Have her comfort the coyote. We need to stay alert for danger. Patrol. Guard.*

Be quiet. Let me concentrate. The wolf grunts and sinks deep into him, disgusted at what he's attempting to do with his power instead of preparing to fight off anyone who might get close to Steph's house.

He doesn't care. He keeps trying to soothe Ash anyway. Distraction is good. As long as he keeps his mind on the here and now, he doesn't have to think about the fact that he's fucked.

So very fucked.

Bend over and forget the lube fucked.

He left his territory to keep from being drawn into a battle for power. Now he's managed to piss off the clan leader of the neighboring territory. He's going to have power-hungry shifters coming at him from all sides.

How did this happen? He worked hard to keep himself away from these types of struggles, and now he's just put a giant target on his back just to rescue some weak coyote shifter. What was he thinking?

She needed us, his wolf comments, making Eli's eyes slide over to Ash.

No, not her, his wolf says derisively. *She's too weak for us. Our human needed us. Will need us. Only us.*

Glancing up to where Steph is wrapping Ash in a blanket, Eli grins. His sweet little human surprised the hell out of him tonight. She was merciless with that pepper spray, and the moment she got into the house, she gathered several other weapons and stowed them on her person. He's not sure any force could daunt this human, certainly not a sadistic clan leader or even his enforcers.

"We need to report this to the police," Steph tells them after taking a seat next to Ash. Eli winces at the idea of bringing human law enforcement into shifter politics. It won't go well for anyone involved. Especially considering that most clans are willing to kill humans to keep shifters a secret. Calling the police might end up getting a few humans murdered by clan enforcers.

"No!" Ash responds adamantly, almost shouting in Steph's face. Eli gives the coyote a warning growl and she shifts her attention back to him, baring her throat in a sign of submission. Steph glares at him but keeps her tone soothing.

"We don't need to call them right now, but those men threatened you," she says gently, rubbing a hand in a large circle over Ash's back. Eli finds himself growing jealous of the cowardly coyote. Steph is his human. The only shifter she should be touching and comforting is him. Ash is stealing his human's attention and affection.

"I shouldn't have called you." Ash starts crying again. "They're going to hurt you. Oh god, Steph, I'm so sorry." Ash manages to meet his gaze with her tear-filled eyes. "Can you keep her safe? Her house is in neutral territory between the clans, but Clyde will come after her anyway. It won't matter." Ash slumps down, drawing in on herself. "This is all my fault. I should have just accepted Glenn. I shouldn't have run away. He would've gotten tired of me eventually."

The coyote starts shaking again, and he's pretty sure it's because she's thinking of the things Glenn would do to her. He can't blame her. He's heard stories about her clan and clan leader. He knows his clan is messed up but nothing on the scale of Clyde and his group.

The Hunger Valley clan would never force shifters into matches. And his clan leader would never seek to deliberately hurt the weaker members. Sure, Clan Leader Richard is much too strict and tends toward draconian rules, but he's never forced a pairing or a Heartmate tie on anyone. That shit went out of style a hundred years ago.

"I'll keep her safe," he promises the desolate coyote shifter, and she seems to calm down slightly at his words.

"I've heard of you," she murmurs. "I know what you are. You could challenge Clyde. You could save all of us, not just Steph."

Shaking his head, he pushes his eager wolf down. "I'm not issuing a challenge to anyone."

"No one needs to challenge anyone," Steph interjects aggressively, and Eli's shocked to realize they just had that entire revealing conversation right in front of his human. "At some point we're going to call the authorities. This isn't something either of your needs to 'handle.'"

Pinning him with determined eyes, Steph reaches out and wraps her free hand around his wrist. The moment her skin touches him, he feels a soft wave of warm power flow over his skin. His wolf stops clambering for control, and his mind calms. He looks down at Ash to see her eyes are closed and her face is relaxing, the tears slowing.

He's not sure if Steph understands what she's doing, but the comforting magic she's providing is powerful. His wolf is already half asleep, metaphorically rolling over on his back with a contented grunt. Ash has gone from frantic weeping and wailing to halfway asleep with a smile on her face.

Just like coyote joy magic, Steph's brand of soothing warmth could easily become addicting. Even more dangerous if the human doesn't know she's doing it or doesn't know how to control it.

What a tangled mess.

A shifter with a deranged maned wolf, a traumatized coyote, and an unaware human with some kind of powerful magic trapped between two brutal clans. If Shakespeare was a shifter, this is the kind of shit he might have written about.

CHAPTER

6

Waking up to the smell of cooking bacon makes Steph smile. Before buying her little dream house, she always had roommates, sometimes many of them at the same time. She didn't mind sharing a house or apartment with other people. Some of her roommates became lifelong friends. That's how she met Ash. They shared an apartment for almost a year before she bought the house. She tried to get Ash to move with her, but the woman refused, giving lame excuses and displaying so much anxiety that Steph dropped the subject.

Now she wonders if Ash's unwillingness to move has anything to do with the large aggressive men at the tavern. A lot seems to be going on in her small town that she doesn't know about—a dark undercurrent that she suspected but never encountered face to face.

After the events of last night, she wanted to scream and yell for Eli and Ash to tell her what's going on. She wanted to demand answers, but instead she took care of business, knowing questions and answers would have to wait.

She helped the exhausted, mostly asleep woman to the spare bedroom, checked on Eli, who was stretched out with Grey on the backyard lounger, and then fell into bed. She expected to toss and turn, but the moment Mesa settled her warm comforting weight next to her, Steph plunged into a deep sleep.

Hearing soft voices, Steph stops lingering and forces her tired body out of her soft bed. She dresses in her standard jeans and a fitted t-shirt, this one sporting the logo of one of the many animal rescues she supports, and makes her way barefoot out to the kitchen. Mesa follows on her heels, abandoning her escort duty to sit by the back door and wait to be let out.

Ash is sitting at the small square kitchen table, wearing a pair of Steph's pajamas. Steph notes sourly that they're practically falling off of her thin athletic frame. It's a good thing she adores Ash. Otherwise she'd have to hate the other women on principle. No one should be allowed to consume the amount of food Ash eats and still be that skinny.

"Morning," Ash says with a small smile. Petty jealousy aside, Steph's glad to see Ash looks much better this morning. She still has dark circles under her eyes and a haunted look on her face, but she's sitting up straight, sipping coffee, and meeting Steph's eyes.

"Morning, Ashy." Steph uses the hated nickname, getting a mock scowl and then a laugh from Ash.

"How did you sleep, Stephanie Ann?" Ash's eyes glint with humor as she uses the full name Steph despises, even throwing in her middle name for good measure.

Wincing, Steph holds up her hands in defeat. "It's too early to spar. I'm sorry I started! You win."

Shirtless and shoeless, Eli doesn't look up from where he's cooking at the stove as he stretches out one long leg and toes open the back door for Mesa. Moments later Steph can hear all three dogs running around and playing in the backyard. It's a cheerful and familiar sound.

"There's coffee," Eli grunts, and Steph's transfixed for a moment staring at his chest. Isn't he worried about getting bacon grease on his bare skin? If she says something, he might put a shirt on, and then she'll be deprived of ogling his beautiful chest. Caught up in her internal debate, she finally realizes Ash is talking to her.

"I'm sorry, what?" She moves to the coffee and then to the fridge for the cream. Once she's finished adding cream and sugar to her coffee, she looks up to see both Eli and Ash staring at her, aghast.

"I was telling you about the dog my neighbor adopted." Ash's face fills with disapproval. "I thought you were going to get better about that," she says softly, eyeing the sweet creamy concoction in Steph's mug.

"I have," Steph says defensively. Always healthy and active, Ash spent most of her time as a roommate trying to mend Steph's unhealthy eating habits. Some of it took. Some. "But today is Sunday. I get to have cake coffee on Sundays."

"Cake coffee. Cream and sugar, not much coffee," Eli grunts as he takes a sip from his mug. "Cake coffee," he grumbles under his breath. "Insult to coffee."

"You should have seen what she ate every morning when we lived together," Ash volunteers. "The amount of simple carbs and sugar would be devastating even to our systems." Although she seems like she is going to say more, Ash suddenly gets quiet and drops her gaze to her mug.

"I might not be as fit as you two, but it seems to me that people who are living in a house for free and eating food they didn't pay for shouldn't give the host a hard time," Steph counters with a grin. After the first sip of sweet nirvana in a cup, her mood instantly brightens. Last night might have been horrible, but they are all alive and safe for now. Sometimes that's all you can ask for.

"About that," Ash begins, but Eli makes an aggressive noise, making her shut her mouth as tears gather in her eyes.

"Stop it, Eli," Steph orders and takes Ash's hand in her own. "What do you need, sweetie? Just ask."

"He won't like it," Ash whispers, her eyes still downcast.

"That doesn't matter," Steph insists and then ignores Eli's grunt of annoyance. "Be quiet, big guy," she commands, unintimidated by Eli's dark look. With a shake of his head, he turns his attention back to the sizzling pan and starts forking slices of crisp bacon onto a paper-towel-covered plate, grumbling something under his breath. Turning her attention back to Ash, she finds the young woman looking at her with wide eyes.

"He's angry, but you're not scared," she whispers reverently. Always easily intimidated by large aggressive men, Ash's anxiety seems to have gotten worse over the last few years. When they stopped hanging out as often about six months ago, Steph assumed Ash was just making new friends. But if the men at the bar are anything to go by, her assumption couldn't have been more wrong.

"It's okay, Ash," Steph assures her, pulling her friend into a tight one-armed hug. "I've got you. Go ahead and tell me what's going on."

"I just need a place to stay for a little while," Ash says, her words rushing out of her mouth so quickly the sentence is almost one word. Her body is stiff against Steph, as if waiting for a violent rejection. A strong feeling of guilt swamps her. She should have kept a closer eye on her vulnerable friend.

"Of course," she tells Ash without hesitation. "You can stay as long as you like. You know I wanted you to move in with me the moment I bought the house. I didn't look for a person to rent the spare room because I also hoped you'd change your mind."

"Really?" The look of hope and relief on Ash's face just about breaks Steph's heart.

"Really. We can go get your stuff today and move you right in." Steph isn't prepared for Ash's strong reaction.

"No!" Ash's voice is only half a decibel off screaming as she clutches at Steph with surprisingly strong fingers. "No, I don't want you going anywhere near my place. There isn't much there. I'll go grab stuff later this week. Just promise me you won't go into town. Okay? You need to promise me!"

"I promise," Steph agrees quickly, willing to say anything to calm the terror in Ash's eyes. "If it's that important to you, I won't go into town." Trying to pry Ash's fingers off her arm she gives the woman a big grin. "But we're going to need to pick up groceries soon. You two are going to eat me out of house and home." The attempt at humor doesn't work. If anything Ash's grip only tightens.

Then Eli's there, looming over both of them. "Release her," he orders Ash, and Steph feels a wash of fear go through her. Next to her Ash lets go of Steph's arm like she's been burned and curls into herself, drawing her legs to her chest and rocking. Tears start streaming down her face, and although she shoves a fist in her mouth, Steph can hear little whimpers coming out.

Steph's gift reacts without conscious thought. She feels the warmth she normally has to concentrate to produce pour out of her without effort. The effects are obvious when the power washes over Ash. She quiets and relaxes a bit, dropping her fist away from her mouth and taking a few deep, sniffling breaths.

But she really feels the results when her warmth hits Eli.

A growl issues out of the man, and for a moment she feels her gift flowing back at her like a wave turned back on itself after hitting a seawall. Instinctively she puts more of herself into her gift, and her warmth pushes past whatever blocked it before.

"Oh, fuck," Eli mutters, but his tone isn't angry or harsh. It's more admiration than anything else. He's closed his eyes, and his body seems to relax also. His expression changes from angry to peaceful.

Although she's always known she has the ability to make those around her calmer, she's never seen such a dramatic display. A little unnerved by the last few minutes, Steph does what comes naturally to her and starts talking.

"I guess we're having bacon for breakfast. I didn't even know I had bacon in the fridge. I don't normally buy it, but it's nice to have it every once in a while, you know? Do I have eggs in there? I can't remember. I'm just asking because scrambled eggs go great with bacon. And maybe toast. But I think the last of my bread is moldy. We're going to need to go to the store. We could hit the little one just down the street. They have a horrible selection, but at least they're convenient. Right? Get it? Because they're a convenience store? Yeah, okay, not my best joke, but in my defense I haven't eaten yet. Speaking of eating, that pan looks like it might be smoking."

At her last words Eli stops standing there staring at her with a strange expression and hurries back to the stove, cursing under his breath as he pulls half-blackened bacon strips from the pan. She looks over at Ash who's now grinning, a vast improvement over the whimpering and crying.

"If I was a lesbian, I'd marry you and have all your babies," she states. At Eli's growl, Ash just huffs out a laugh. "I said *if*."

"If I wanted a wife, I'd totally pick you too!" Steph answers with a matching grin, falling into their familiar banter.

"I know you would, honey. I'm perfect wife material."

Setting down a plate full of crispy bacon between the two chuckling women, Eli gives Ash a hard look. "Mine," he states, and Ash draws back a little. To Steph's relief, Ash's expression is intrigued instead of scared.

"You know what that means. Right?" Ash asks softly and Steph watches Eli give one firm nod and turn back to the stove.

"You guys want to clue me in on the super-secret squirrel club?" Steph asks sardonically as she grabs a slice of bacon. "I'd like to know what we're talking about too."

"Later," Eli grunts and pulls a carton of eggs out of the fridge. She watches him crack several into a bowl and start scrambling them with a fork. The way his muscles flex as he makes even the smallest movement is fascinating.

"Sure," she murmurs as she watches him make her scrambled eggs. What is it about this taciturn and mysterious man that has her so knotted up? Is it a Florence Nightingale thing? Sure, she wants to fix him. Help him figure out what's going on in that brain. But that's not the only thing she wants to do for him. Broken or not, she wants him in her life. He entered her orbit less than forty-eight hours ago, and already she can't imagine her world without him in it.

Guys have cooked for her in the past, trying to impress her with domestic skills. But she gets the feeling he's not trying to inspire admiration. He just wants to feed her. Something about him screams provider. When she bought them Mexican food the day before, he refused to eat until she was full. Only after she sat back and patted her stomach with a little sigh of contentment did he methodically eat everything at the table. He was starving but denied himself until she was sated.

On top of his eagerness for her to eat, he pays attention throughout her rambling monologues. He doesn't mind when she talks and talks. He never looks impatient or upset. Never interrupts her. And it never feels like he's pandering to her when he nods and smiles. He seems like he's enjoying their one-sided conversation. Sometimes his eyes stare off into the distance, telling her he's not listening to her words. But the moment she stops talking, his gaze shoots back to her. Even if he's not paying attention to what she's saying, he's soaking in her voice.

And isn't that damn romantic?

One thing is for certain, his treatment of her is so unlike any other male she's ever encountered. If she's not in love yet, she will be soon.

She watches his naked back move as he pours the eggs into the hot pan. She doesn't know why he seems to always take his shirt off, but she isn't going to complain.

She's so busy ogling Eli that she almost doesn't catch Ash's knowing expression out of the corner of her eye and blushes. Her life has certainly gotten rather interesting very quickly, and barring the violence of the previous night, Steph can't imagine changing a thing.

CHAPTER 7

Loping through the forest, Eli easily avoids the patrols around his cabin. If Richard wants to catch him, he's going to need to do more than put a few grizzlies in the woods. But then again, Richard thinks brawn and power are the most important assets a shifter can have, so the smaller shifters get overlooked and dismissed.

Coyotes would've noticed him sneaking through the woods. One of the small Arabian or Great Plains wolves in the clan would have scented him out the moment he got within miles of his cabin. Honestly, he should be grateful that Richard is so willfully ignorant. It makes Eli's job of stealing into his own home that much easier.

Thankfully his maned wolf gives up control without a fight and he's able to shift soundlessly at the back door of the cabin. He's not surprised by the sight that greets him when he walks in. The place is in shambles. Every piece of furniture has been reduced to kindling. Pillows and bedding litter the floor in small ripped-apart chunks. Everything easily broken is destroyed, and the rest of his possessions have been scattered around.

He never locks his door, not that it would make much of a difference if he did. Richard would've just broken the door down too. At least they didn't break any of the windows, so nothing came into the cabin to start nesting in the mess.

Already feeling anxious to get back to Steph, Eli hurriedly sifts through the wreckage. He salvages a few changes of clothes, his favorite knife, and a necklace he inherited from his grandmother. The image of Steph wearing the necklace and nothing else fills his mind, making his movements uncoordinated for a moment.

Need to get back, his wolf demands and pushes for control of their body. With a hiss of pain, Eli just manages to keep the wolf down.

Stop it, he reprimands the wolf.

Need her, his wolf insists, and Eli realizes the mental images of Steph naked didn't just affect his human side. The wolf is feeling a pressing need also.

Let me pack. These things will make her happy, Eli insists and focuses his wolf's attention on the necklace in his hand. The wolf grumbles but calms down. Apparently, Steph's now the key to controlling his wolf. And if he's honest, controlling his human side as well.

When she soothes his temper with her power, he experiences a peace he hasn't known since he was a child. Since his mother died. When her warm power washes over him, no stress, no fear, no worries, and no clan politics are waiting to rip him apart. His world becomes nothing but her and the wholly unique experience of perfect calm.

When he declared "mine" in front of Ash, it might have been said in haste, but the moment the word was out of his mouth it felt much too right to take back. For once his wolf and he are in total agreement. Steph is his, whether she knows it or not. It might take time to convince her to Heartmate with him, but he's not worried. Wolves can be patient when they're stalking, and his wolf is already showing signs of being willing to do anything to keep Steph.

He thinks about all the stories his grandmother told him—tales about how his grandfather wooed her with gifts and deeds. They'd run for miles in the woods, chasing each other, playing, and flirting in their animal forms. Steph might be human, but he's confident he can still woo her. He can learn what humans like.

For a moment he worries about revealing his animal side, but he suspects that once she loves someone, her loyalty is absolute. Hopefully, once she loves him, she'll be able to overlook the fact that a demented and powerful maned wolf lives inside of him.

I can keep her safe if you let me free, the wolf taunts him. *Stop being weak. You know we need to rule.*

Shut up, he answers the wolf without much heat. He knows the animal is right. If he wants to keep Steph in his life and keep her safe, he's going to need to let the beast out to fight. By the looks of recent events at Falls Tavern, probably sooner rather than later.

That means the wooing needs to start happening now. He needs her to love him before the violence starts, before the fights find him. He's under no illusions. Either the Lowell clan or his own will find him, and then Steph will see him for the monster he is.

Yes, his wolf all but purrs. Fighting is the wolf's favorite thing.

Not my only favorite, the wolf interjects, and an image of Steph's smiling face floats through his mind again.

Cursing under his breath and trying to keep his dick from getting hard, Eli finishes packing the few things he wants to take in a small canvas bag and goes out the door, closing it firmly behind him. He gives his body up to the wolf with a focus on the bag so the wolf knows it needs to come with them.

Obligingly his wolf grabs the bag in his big muzzle and trots off, once again easily avoiding the shifters on patrol and covering the distance back to Steph's house with an easy loping gait. When her bright yellow house comes into view, one word seems to surface in the wolf's mind, surprising Eli with its intense satisfaction.

Home.

The last thing she expects to find when she gets home from running errands is Eli working frantically in her backyard.

All three dogs come trotting up to her as she steps out the back door, but Eli doesn't stop working.

With the pickaxe broken, he's using a shovel to break up the ground. Yesterday he'd only just gotten started in the corner of the yard she designated for the herb garden, but now it looks like he's almost done. She gives herself a moment to admire his muscled form before clearing her throat to get his attention.

Pausing, he rests the head of the shovel on the ground and leans his body against the long handle. As usual, he's shirtless and shoeless. Sweat is pouring down his face and chest, soaking the top of his jeans. His intense green eyes flow over her as he smiles, freezing her in place. The man is just too beautiful for words.

"You're home," he states with a smile so wide his eyes crinkle. "Good."

Shaking herself out of her stupor, she gives him a big smile in return. "I picked up some clothes for Ash from a mutual friend and got some groceries to tide us over," she explains.

His smile disappears. "You promised," he growls out.

"Our friend Emily lives near my work, absolutely opposite direction as Ash's place," she explains quickly. "And I dropped by the little mart down the street. I never crossed over into the forbidden lands, I swear!" With exaggerated movements, she makes an X over her chest and then holds three fingers on her hand up with her thumb holding her pinky down across her palm. He has no idea what either of those motions mean, but she's grinning the entire time so they must be human gestures of honesty. His scowl disappears, and a small smile edges his lips.

"That's good," he affirms. "Hungry?"

"Are you asking me if I'm hungry or telling me you're hungry?" she asks with a little laugh. "I'm not hungry. I'm still full from that giant breakfast. I didn't even need to eat lunch. But I could make a sandwich to tide you over, if you'd like. Ash should be home soon, and we can all sit down and have dinner together."

He nods and lets the shovel drop to the ground. "Sandwich sounds good. Shower?"

When he reaches her side, she turns to walk with him into the house. "You go get cleaned up. I'll put a plate together for you."

With a grunt and a nod, he heads toward the bathroom with Grey right at his heels as usual.

Stacking two sandwiches together, she grabs a couple of beers out of the fridge and carries everything to the backyard. It won't be dark for several hours, and the temperature is just perfect for a pleasant afternoon meal around the empty firepit. Maybe tonight she'll get a nice fire going and the three of them can hang out around it. That thought makes her downright giddy, and she finally admits to herself that she's been a little lonely. She should've tried harder to find a roommate. But she'd been so hopeful that Ash would eventually move in that she never took the search for a roommate very seriously.

With Ash and Eli here, the house feels full in a good way—full of laughter, friendship and warmth—the way it should be.

"I should make the best of it while I can," she murmurs to herself as she pops open her beer and takes a sip.

"Make the best of what?" Eli asks as he drops down to sit next to her on the lounger. He showered and changed pants, but he's still not wearing a shirt or shoes. His leg is pressed against her, and his bare torso is so close she could easily just reach over and run her hand over all those delicious muscles.

"I was just thinking how nice it is to have people in the house," she admits. "I'm not used to living alone."

"Dogs," Eli points out as he manages to eat almost half of a sandwich in one bite. Maybe she should have made three instead of two.

"I love them, but their conversational skills could use some work," she replies.

"Low bar," Eli grunts, but it takes a moment before Steph understands what he means.

"Yup, you're a regular chatterbox compared to them," she agrees with a laugh. Eli swallows the last of the first sandwich and picks up the next one. Yup, next time she'll make him three. Or maybe four, just to be on the safe side. "I know I've said this before, but you're doing amazing work here. I'd like to pay you for your time."

"No."

His answer doesn't surprise her at all. While he's staying with her, she'll just try to buy him things he might need to pay him back for his labor.

"Don't need anything either," he mumbles around a bite of food.

Taken aback, Steph stares at him. "Did you just read my mind?"

Now it's his turn to laugh. "Read your face."

Chuckling along with him, she gives a little shrug, "Yeah, no one's ever accused me of having a poker face."

They lapse into silence as he finishes the second sandwich and pops open his beer. He downs half of it in one go, and Steph starts doubling the amount of groceries she plans to purchase on her way home from work the next day.

With a content sound, he leans back and puts one arm behind him on the lounger to support his weight.

"Do you know you're doing it?" he asks her out of the blue.

Confused, she tilts her head at him. "Excuse me?"

"The thing where you calm us, do you know you're doing it?"

A flash of unease goes through Steph. She's never talked to anyone about her gift, and the fact that Eli figured her out so fast makes her wary. "I'm not sure what you're talking about."

When a push of fear hits her, she automatically reacts by forcing her gift against it. The moment the two meet the fear disappears, and Eli gives her a satisfied look.

"That," he states simply.

There seems to be no reason to prevaricate so she nods. "I know I'm doing it, but sometimes it's just instinct, not anything I mean to do."

"You're powerful." He gives her a considering look. "Your parents?"

"As far as I know, they can't do it. And I don't think they know anything about it. I didn't start noticing it happening until after puberty, and it was subtle back then. By the time it was more powerful I was in my twenties and could control it, mostly."

"Same here," he admits. A thrill goes through her. He's like her. He's the first person she's ever met that's like her. And it doesn't seem to bother him to talk about it. She barely controls the urge to just start blabbering about her experiences with her gift and fire a zillion questions at him.

"You feel different," she starts tentatively, making a conscious effort to control her urge to talk too much.

Giving her a small, sad smile, he continues. "You're calm. I'm not. Feels like I'm out of control sometimes."

"Like the power has a mind of its own?"

"Yes. It wants to take over my body and just run wild. Run on instinct. Attack. Attack or run, but mostly attack. It's hard to control."

"That's got to be exhausting. Mine isn't like that." She's not shocked. She's been feeling his dark power for days now, the edge of violence swirling around him off and on but never directed at her.

It's funny. She always assumed others out there had gifts, but she thought they'd be like her, influencing others toward positive emotions. But Eli's gift seems to be centered around aggression.

But is he so different from her? There was a time when her gift wasn't about being positive. It wasn't about helping anyone, and the result was horrifying.

"Tell me," Eli demands. "Tell me what happened to put that look on your face and that color in your aura."

"This one time my gift was like yours. It took over." She wants to shudder at the memory but pushes it aside and forces a smile. "It was a long time ago. I've never felt out of control since." She can tell he wants to ask more, but a single look keeps him quiet. A small dip of his head is all he does to tell her he's letting her skip it for now, but he's not letting the topic go.

"You're very skilled." His tone is admiring.

"Thanks, but it can be exhausting. Sometimes I want to shut it down. I don't want to influence those around me. But if I fight the impulse and try not to use it, I feel pain." She rubs her chest thinking of the few times she tried to suppress her gift and almost ended up passing out from the agony.

His eyes widen at her admission. "It feels like it's trying to rip out of you?"

"Not quite like that." She thinks about it for a moment. "It's more like a burning sensation deep in my chest. But as soon as I use my gift it goes away. And of course, there's the added bonus that I get to feel whatever I'm helping other people to feel—joy, calm, or peace. It's nice." She pauses, trying to put into words what she experiences. "It just bothers me that I can't turn it off. Not that I want to turn it off permanently or anything. But…"

"But it'd be nice to rest," he finishes for her.

"Yeah, that's a good way to put it. It'd be nice to have a break. To not care for a little while."

"That's why you talked to me. You had to." His expression is a strange mix of hopeful and resigned. He doesn't want the reason she approached him in the park to be only because of her power.

"I think my gift is why I was able to see you, but I wanted to talk to you for a lot of reasons. My gift urging me was only one of them." Relief crosses his face at her words. He looks away from her and focuses on the empty firepit.

"You help others. It's a good power." His admiration is clear.

"What about you?" she asks, eager to find out anything he might be able to teach her. "You're like me, but you seem to be able to control it better."

Eli shrugs. "I'm not like you."

"I get that your power feels different than mine, a bit like a mirror opposite, but that just makes us two sides of the same coin. Are your parents like you?"

"My dad is like me," he concedes but doesn't add any more details.

Steph bites her lip and decides to pull a few more teeth. "You asked if it feels like it's trying to rip out of me. Does your power feel like it's trying to rip out of you?"

With a grimace, he nods. "All the damn time." Leaning forward, he runs his hands over his face, huffing out a heavy breath. Practicing patience, she waits, letting him set the pace of the conversation and decide if he wants to talk more.

It's torture!

"I'm broken," he finally says with a long exhale, his face hidden in his hands. "My wo—I mean my power is constantly trying to take over. It claws at my insides and demands to be let loose. My dad can control his, but mine won't be controlled. It's a beast and a monster." His voice is weary, resigned.

"That's got to be hard," she says with real sympathy, and then she thinks about all her interactions with him. "But you can't be that out of control." When he frowns at her, she elaborates. "Think about it. Except for a few times I know you deliberately used it, you haven't lost control since I've known you."

"I'm different with you." He looks up to meet her gaze and not only are his eyes glowing, but his stare is intense and needy. "You steady me. You make me stable."

Feeling much too warm under his gaze, she looks away and makes a little humming sound. "As I said, we're just two sides of the same coin. It makes sense that we might balance each other out."

A soft, sexy sound comes out of him. "I like your power better," he murmurs, his voice low and husky. A little sliver of power slides over her, very similar to a warm hand lightly brushing her skin.

"There are some definite benefits," she allows, more relieved than she cares to admit over the change of topic. She's not sure she wants to be responsible for keeping anyone steady and stable. "I've never gotten a speeding ticket." That makes him bark out a laugh.

"Deviant," he accuses, and she bumps his shoulder with her own in retaliation.

"Don't be jealous," she teases. He tries to bump her back but puts a little too much force and almost knocks her off the end of the lounger.

"Shit, sorry!" Hastily he grabs her around the waist and hauls her against him. "Got you," he breathes but doesn't let her go. He brings his face down and nuzzles it against her throat. "You smell good."

"You do too." Her voice is a croak. The entire side of her body is pressed up against him now. Even though they're separated by at least one layer of clothing, she can feel heat radiating from him. Her arm curls around his lower back, pressing against the toned flesh. As if her hand has a mind of its own, it slides down under the waist of his pants.

When he opens his mouth and nips at the skin of her neck a flash of lust shoots through her. Without consciously thinking about it she drops her beer, turns her body to face him, and reaches for him with her other hand.

Her palm lands on his bare skin, rubbing over the firm planes of his abdomen. Bringing his big hand up, he traps her smaller one. Slowly he draws it down until it's resting on the small bit of hair just above the waistline of his pants. Then, to her disappointment, he stops and just keeps her hand trapped there.

"I like the power inside you, but I like your outside too," he whispers and leans closer.

Giving in to the frantic urging of her body, she pushes her face toward his, meeting him halfway for a kiss. His lips are hot on hers and she opens her mouth with a little moan.

After doing her fair share of casual dating and occasionally moving the relationship into the bedroom, she's been disappointed more often than not. For a little while she thought she might be asexual. But not any longer.

They're only kissing, and neither of them has touched anything that a bathing suit would cover, yet her panties are soaked. He ends the kiss and pulls back just far enough to see her face. His pupils are so dilated the green is all but gone, and his face is heavy with lust.

"I can smell you," he tells her, awe in his voice. "You want us. You know about my dark beast, and you still want us."

One of his hands moves up to cradle the back of her head, and he resumes the kiss with more force and aggression. It doesn't even occur to her to fight his hold. She flows against him. Tugging her hand out from under his, she climbs onto his lap. She can feel his erection under her. Good god, he feels huge! For a brief moment she worries about his size, but then all thoughts float out of her head as he cups her breast through her shirt. She's wearing an old sports bra today, deciding on comfort instead of support. She isn't dressed for backyard seductions.

From now on, always wear the pretty underwear, she thinks as his hand gently squeezes her breast, his thumb running over her nipple. All thoughts of clothes, sexy or not, disappear. Her entire focus is on his touch. She needs two things to happen right now: both their clothes need to come off and more touching!

Starting with her shirt, she doesn't even manage to get her fingers closed around the hem before he captures her mouth for another kiss. Her palms end up resting on his pecs and she lightly digs her nails in. His pecs jump a little at her touch.

Breaking off the kiss, she giggles, "Ticklish?"

Growling he brings his hand up and digs his fingers into her side, making her squeal. "Ticklish?" he mocks, making her laugh.

Suddenly his face becomes serious. "I want you." It's clear to her that he's asking for permission.

She swallows and nods. "I want you too." Reaching down she grabs the hem of her shirt again and this time successfully pulls it up.

Then a cheerful voice calls out from inside the house, freezing her in place with her shirt bunched around her head.

"I brought home pizza for dinner!" Ash calls out. Steph struggles to pull her shirt back down.

Eli moves quickly. Standing up, he places her on the lounger and then strides off with a low rumbling growl to the far corner of the yard. He's almost there by the time Ash opens up the back door.

"There you are. Come and get it!" Ash disappears back into the house with all three dogs hot on her heels. Even Grey. There's no such thing as canine loyalty with the smell of pizza in the air.

Steph can't move for a moment. All she can do is sit there stunned. One moment she's about to have what she's pretty sure is the best sex of her life and the next moment Eli's walking away. He moved so fast that she couldn't even follow his motions. Is that part of his power?

With a little shake of her head, she stands up and straightens her clothes. Does the lust show on her face? She can feel herself blushing. God, she feels like a teenager again.

"Eli?" she calls out and walks across the yard. He's standing, leaning against the wooden fencing, his chest heaving with his rapid breathing. She approaches slowly. "Eli?"

"Need some time," he growls out. If he turned to face her, his eyes would probably be glowing bright green right now. Checking in with her gift, she doesn't feel any danger coming from him. That gives her the courage to move forward and touch his back.

"We are going to continue this later," she says confidently. He takes a few deep, shuddering breaths, and then straightens up. Slowly he turns, and Steph finds out that she was right: his eyes are glowing an incredible green.

"Promise?" Eli makes that one word sound more like a threat than a request, and she laughs.

"Just try and stop me," she challenges as she leads him into the house.

CHAPTER

8

"When are you going to become a real adult and put your TV on something besides old boards and cinder blocks?" Ash teases as she reaches for another slice of pizza. "And speaking of furniture, isn't this the same couch we had back on Cedar Street? It was old back when we lived together. Now it looks like it belongs in a frat house. You need to get all new stuff."

"New stuff costs money," Steph retorts around a mouthful of gooey pizza. "It took all my savings for the down payment on this place. Any spare cash has gone into fixing the plumbing and then the roof. Buying new furniture was low on the list."

"Are you still working at that same construction company?" Ash asks, and Eli's ears perk up. He's been wanting to know where Steph works but didn't know how to broach the subject without coming off as too forceful.

"It's a towing company. Larson Towing," Steph corrects her with a laugh. "And yeah, I'm still there."

"Where?" Eli asks, trying not to let his tension show.

"It's over by the river in the industrial area," Steph explains. "Garrick Concrete is right next to us. They have that giant sign you can see from the highway."

Ash gives him a knowing look. "It's still in the neutral area," she assures him.

"Neutral area?" Steph asks and Ash looks everywhere but at her.

"Uh, you know, places that don't get a lot of traffic," Ash adlibs badly. "Eli doesn't like people."

"That's true," he says. "I don't like crowds at all."

Steph's brows furrow with confusion. "But you guys said my place is in neutral territory too. And the park is super busy."

Ash blanches at her words, and Eli sighs. Neither one of them is particularly good at prevarication. He goes with his strength, which is schooling his face into a blank expression. Ash decides to double down with the original lie.

"There aren't that many people here during the day. Not like my place or my work. Those areas are super crowded all the time, especially now that the new pizza place opened just down the street. Have you tried their pizza yet? It's almost as good as Pizza Dan's pizza," she leans forward and pats the top of the pizza box on the coffee table. "But no real crowds around here when everyone's at work or school. You're in a nice quiet neighborhood. So that's what we're talking about. Quiet places. Not a lot of loud people. Eli doesn't like loud people."

Out of steam, Ash gives up talking and just looks at Steph with a hopeful expression. Eli turns his gaze to Steph, interested in the woman's reaction. She's much too smart to believe Ash's pile of poorly constructed lies, but how she handles it has the potential of being amusing.

Scrutinizing Ash with narrow eyes, Steph tilts her head slightly. "You suck at poker."

Puzzled, Ash's smile dims a little. "I hate poker. You know that."

"Because you suck at it. The reason you're so bad at it is because your face is an open book."

Realization dawns and Ash flushes with embarrassment. "Eli really does hate crowds," she repeats stubbornly.

"I know he does. And I also know it has nothing to do with whatever you guys are talking about when it comes to neutral areas. But for right now, I'm going to let it go. I'll let you guys have your super-secret squirrel club. But at some point, one of you is going to have to tell me what's going on."

Taking Ash's hand in her own, Steph waits for the woman to look up before talking. Eli can feel the echoes of the power she's using to calm and comfort the coyote. "And no matter what, I'm here for you. I don't care if it involves the mob, FBI, or Jehovah's Witnesses. I've got your back. As long as you know that, I won't press you for answers. I'll just wait for you to tell me. Understand?"

Tears pool in Ash's eyes even as she snorts out a laugh. "Even if it involves dentists?"

Steph gives a mock shudder of revulsion. "Even then." Her expression sobers. "You're like family to me. You know that. Right?"

"I know. Sometimes I wish I liked tacos so we could get married."

"You don't like tacos?" Eli asks, mystified. Who doesn't like tacos? Both women look at him and burst out laughing.

"Please don't explain it to him," Ash stage-whispers to Steph. He gives up and pretends to glower at both of them. That just makes them laugh harder.

After their merriment finally dies down, Steph picks up another pizza slice. "Okay, Ash, as my current roommate and health coach, it's going to be your job to keep me from eating any more pizza after this slice."

"As if I could keep you from pizza without potentially losing one of my limbs." Ash scoffs.

Deciding he wants back into this conversation, and not as part of the comedic relief, Eli clears his throat. When both women are looking at him, he raises an eyebrow at Steph. "You drive tow trucks?"

Before Steph can respond Ash pipes up. "No, she doesn't drive the trucks. You're like a secretary. Right, Steph?"

"Really, Ash?" Steph sorts out a laugh. "You only lived with me for a year, but you still don't remember where I work or what I do? I'm the office manager. I do the schedules, billing, and the rest of the organizational and paperwork stuff."

"But you answer the phones, so it's a little like a secretary," Ash teases.

Steph gives her a playful shove. "Nice to know you're still a brat."

Feeling envious of their easy banter Eli tries to join in. "Girly job in a manly business." Both women snort out a laugh, and this time Steph raises an eyebrow at him.

"I can tow if I need to. The owner had me train and take thc tests the first year I worked there so I could pitch in if we're short on drivers, which happens more often than I'd like. You can put away that attitude, Mr. Manly Man with the pretty muscles."

Grinning, he raises an arm and curls his bicep, making Ash hoot with laughter. He smirks at Steph. "You think my muscles are pretty?"

"From the smell of her, she thinks all of you is pretty," Ash blurts out with a giggle, but when Eli snarls, she freezes. Among shifters that sentence wouldn't raise any eyebrows, but Steph's human so Ash's words make her blush and sputter indignantly.

"What's that supposed to mean?" she squeaks out.

"Uh," Ash looks back and forth between Eli and Steph, her eyes wide and frightened with the smell of fear pouring out of her. All the earlier teasing and cheer are gone in an instant. His anger at Ash's thoughtless words brings his wolf close to the surface. His beast is ready to burst out of his skin and attack, even though Ash's coyote is hiding so far inside the girl, she almost smells human.

"Eli, quit making those noises," Steph demands and then turns her attention back to Ash. "Fess up, girl, what are you talking about?"

"Perfume," Eli mutters, just managing to swallow down his snarl and his wolf. Ash latches on to his excuse with both hands.

"You put on perfume today," she stammers out. "You know, made yourself all nice for Eli."

How did this girl live with Steph an entire year and not give anything away? It must be because he's present. It's hard to remember to stay secretive when you're relaxed with another shifter present.

"Oh, right," Steph blinks a few times. "I forgot what a great sense of smell you have. Well, as long as you're not telling me I stink or something."

"No, never." Ash shakes her head adamantly and then shoves half the slice of pizza in her mouth, pointedly turning her attention back to the TV. "I love this movie," she mumbles around the bite of pizza. Steph shakes her head and gives both of them an indulgent smile.

"You guys are ridiculous," she huffs out a little laugh. "Eli with all his noises and you with that amazing nose of yours."

As she settles down to watch the movie with a slice of pizza, Eli hides a wince. The wolf is still rampaging to get out of him. His skin feels too tight, and his veins are on fire. Between Ash interrupting them in the backyard and his anger raging so suddenly, his wolf is too disturbed to settle. This is one of the things he hates the most about his animal. One moment everything is fine, and the next moment the wolf is ripping him apart to get out.

He needs to change. Ash can smell the wolf heavy on his skin and keeps casting him sidelong glances, her expression apprehensive. He could ask Steph to use her magic to soothe him, but he worries she'll feel his wolf because it's so close to the surface. Better just to isolate himself for a while to let the wolf run and then put his human skin back on once he's calm again.

"I need to go for a walk," he bites out abruptly, startling Steph. Ash doesn't move, instead rolling her eyes to watch him stand up and stride out the front door.

"Eli?" Steph calls, scrambling to get off the couch and follow him, but he's already out the door and down the street before she even gets to her porch. "Eli?"

"He probably just needs to burn off a little extra energy," Ash calls out from inside. "I'd give him space if I were you. He's not good at being still for too long. You know some guys are like that. Come back in here and finish watching the movie with me."

He's in the nearby woods by the time Steph calls out one last time. Relieved she didn't try to follow, he strips out of his clothes in preparation to give his wolf control. By the time

Steph disappears back into the house and closes the front door, his long-limbed maned wolf stands in the shadows, watching her close the door with needy eyes. The human part of him wants to go back and cuddle Steph. Well, maybe do more than cuddle. But his wolf won't let him have his human skin back so soon.

Need to run. Hunt. Fuck, his wolf demands as they start loping through the woods.

I'll give you the first two, Eli negotiates. *But if we want to keep her, we need to woo her. You know how it's supposed to be. If we want a female, we have to give her things. Build her a den. Show her we can provide for her and the pups.*

For the first time he feels the wolf give in without further protest.

Run, the wolf demands. *Run and hunt. We'll provide for our female when we get back.*

That we can do, Eli promises as they catch the scent of deer. The wolf gives chase and Eli gives himself over to his animal half.

Eli hasn't returned by the time the movie is over. Ash helps her put away the leftover pizza and then stays up to sit on the couch to talk. It's nearly midnight before Steph gives up on waiting up for him and heads to bed. Yawning, Ash is more than ready to follow her example and call it a night.

As usual, Mesa and Terror join her in her room, but Grey refuses to leave his vigil at the front door. Even with the promise of treats, the scarred pit bull can't be persuaded to join her in the bedroom. With a sigh, Steph leaves her bedroom door open in case either Grey, Eli, or both decide to join her at some point in the night.

So much for a night of hot sex, she thinks ruefully as she curls up in her soft bed. Of course, she's not sure she's comfortable doing any kind of bedroom gymnastics with Ash just right across the hall.

No, it's probably better that Eli took a long walk to cool off. Ash said she might be working late tomorrow. That'll give her and Eli some alone time. They can go back to exploring what they started in the backyard.

If Eli comes back.

She has no idea what time it is when she wakes up to the sound of Grey whining. Stumbling out of bed she finds him sitting at the back door. When she enters the kitchen, he rolls his head toward her, paws at the door, and whines again. Assuming he needs to lift a leg on one of her newly planted bushes, she opens the back door only to find Eli, naked and asleep on the lounger. It's dark so she can't see much detail, but Grey trots right up to him, climbs on the lounger with incredible dexterity for such a large, square dog, and settles down across Eli's legs.

More amazing than Grey's Mission-Impossible-like scaling of the lounger and Eli is the fact that the big man doesn't stir as his legs become a dog bed. It's probably a testament to both Grey's stealth and Eli's fatigue. Even relaxed in sleep, Eli looks wrung out. Whatever he spent the last hours doing managed to exhausted him.

"I'm glad you came back," she whispers, picking up a blanket from the ground next to the lounger and spreading it out on Eli's chest, pointedly ignoring the rest of his nakedness. "I was worried."

Giving the pit pull a quick rub behind the ears, she murmurs, "Keep an eye on him. Okay, Grey? I'll take over the duty tomorrow night." Walking back into the house, she's unaware of Eli's half-open eyes or the brilliant smile that curves his lips the moment her back is turned.

CHAPTER 9

Yawning, Steph accepts the stack of paperwork from Billy.

"Late night?" he asks with a grin.

Smiling, Steph gives a little shrug. "Just couldn't get to sleep. You know how it goes."

His face is instantly sympathetic. "Hell, yeah, I know how that goes. You can call me, you know. Any time. Just to talk, nothing else." His voice is gruff, and Steph feels touched by the concern of the normally reclusive driver.

"I'm sure I'll sleep tonight, but I'll call if I need to talk," she assures him. "And you know it goes both ways. You've got my number too. I'm as good a listener as I am a talker."

Before Billy can respond, Seth pokes his head into her office. "Yo, Steph, you need to talk Sal down. He's about ready to kill Chris."

"Again?" Steph scrambles out from behind her desk. Billy is already out the front door by the time she gets there. Following the sound of shouting, she and Billy round the building to find Chris and Sal facing off next to one of the smaller tow trucks used to pick up cars and smaller pickups.

"You're doing this on purpose!" Sal screams at the much taller and broader Chris.

"Stop being such a whiny old bitch," Chris shoots back. Four other men are lounging around, watching the drama and not moving to defuse the situation at all. Resisting the urge to roll her eyes, she shoots them an annoyed glance that every single one of them ignores. She can almost guarantee they're busy placing bets with each other.

"Guys," she shouts as she puts herself between Sal and Chris. "Let's all calm down." Although verbal fights are common among the drivers, in all the years she's worked at the towing company, she's only seen them result in a physical altercation twice. That helps her feel confident to put herself in the path of danger.

Of course, even if she's afraid of getting hurt, her gift is practically screaming at her to help the men. Sal's anger batters at her, hot and consuming, as if she's standing too close to a raging fire. Chris's frustration and mounting anger hits her too, but it feels more like being pelted by pebbles. If she lets this confrontation go on, she knows the two will end up throwing punches, and the emotions coming off them will start stabbing at her.

"Get the fuck out the way," Sal yells at her. "This is between me and Chris. Motherfucker left a dirty truck. Again!" Shifting to the side, he stabs a finger in the air at Chris. "You always fucking do that!"

"And I told you I didn't use this truck all week," Chris shoots back, his voice deepening and becoming more guttural. For some strange reason that reminds her of when Eli gets upset and his voice changes.

"You're on the roster for this truck," Sal accuses. "It has to be you."

"This is about a dirty truck?" Steph asks, trying to divert Sal's temper from Chris to answer her questions.

"The cab is full of trash and stinks like old food and smokes. I don't like that, and he knows it. He does it just to fuck with me," Sal tells her, his voice still loud but at least he's not screaming.

"You don't listen too well. Do you? Have you lost your hearing, old man? I was in number four yesterday, not this one," Chris yells back at Sal. The anger coming off the bigger man is now hitting Steph with the same heat and ferocity as Sal's emotions.

In the past she's tried to use her gift on two people at the same time, but it's only worked when she's been able to touch one or both of them. Knowing it's probably useless to try without putting a hand on at least one of the men, Steph unleashes her gift anyway. She focuses it out in a circle around herself. She feels it encounter Sal, who's slightly closer to her. The man grunts and takes a step back, but he doesn't appear soothed at all. When her power runs up against Chris, she ends up staggering.

Hired only last month, Chris tends to be quiet and keep to himself. Her interactions with him have been limited and brief to the point she thought he might have some social anxiety.

Now, not just his voice reminds her of Eli but the way he feels as her gift brushes up against his aura. He flares with power, pushing back at her with enough force to make her wince. With a little gasp she turns her full attention on Chris and speaks without thinking.

"Stop that right now!" she demands. Steph can count on one hand the number of times she's used her gift to hurt rather than pacify and relieve. But she reacts instinctively to the harsh power battering against her. She sweeps aside whatever natural resistance he has to her and twines her power around him, pulling it hard until she sees him visibly gasp from pain. She didn't mean to make it so painful, but she so rarely uses her gift in this way that she's clumsy with it.

Chris's eyes widen before he drops his gaze and cranes his neck to the side. His power withdraws, and she watches him flinch as he pulls it back into himself.

Relieved by his compliance she banks her gift, relaxing as the agony it was causing her stops immediately. Using her gift that way doesn't just cause pain to the person she focuses it on. It hurts her as well. She doesn't know if it's because her gift wants to help, not hurt, or if it's just not the way her gift was designed to operate.

Either way, she's glad to bring out the part of her that alleviates distress instead of creating it. With her entire attention on Chris, it's easy to coax her gift over the large man, soothing the hurt she caused and easing the anger that was overwhelming him moments ago. He opens to her and she watches a real smile form on his lips as the tension in his shoulders relax.

"You think this is funny, asshole?"

She's so focused on her interactions with Chris that she doesn't even notice when Sal steps close to her until he's yelling at Chris from right behind her.

Turning toward Sal, she's not prepared for him to be moving past her, fist raised and face flushed with fury. Without thinking, she reaches out a hand to put it against his chest, trying to get him to stop. Her gift is still entwined around Chris so it takes her precious seconds to pull it away from the younger man and bring it to bear on Sal.

Impatient to get to Chris, Sal bats her hand aside, causing her to stumble and almost go to her knees. With a startled cry she attempts to regain her balance only to get shoved again by Sal. "Goddamn it, woman, get out of my way!" Sal's second shove knocks her down to her knees. Gravel digs painfully into her skin, and she struggles to gain her feet again.

This is too much for the men lounging around, and she hears them start to move toward the three of them, calling out for Sal to back off and calm down. But it's much too late.

"Don't touch her!" Chris roars and rushes forward, his body a blur of movement.

She doesn't see what hits her in the back and sends her flying just as she's getting to her feet. She lands face first on the gravel, crying out from the pain of the impact. The right side of her face feels intensely painful for a moment and then goes blessedly numb. A quick assessment tells her nothing's broken, but the sounds almost on top of her indicate she needs to move. Instead of trying to get up, she rolls over to find that Sal is just about to step backward right on top of her. Before she can get out of his way, his foot comes down on her ankle and agony shoots up her leg.

Hearing her cry out again sends Chris into a fury. He physically picks Sal up and tosses the man away from her as if he weighs no more than a child. Sal lands with a crash onto a bunch of flagging signs kept out for guys to grab if they need to shut down a road. He disappears into the collapsed pile of wood and plastic. They all freeze, staring wide-eyed and silent at the pile where Sal is lying motionless.

A faint groan tells them all he's still alive.

Everyone moves at once. Ignoring Sal, Billy, Chris, Carlos, Seth, Martin, and Alex hurry to her side and all start asking her if she's okay at the same time.

"Back up, guys," she wheezes out, and they all move away about half a step except Chris. The man's shaking badly, his face anxious and frightened. He leans in close to her.

"Don't be mad," he whispers to her, and she looks at him quizzically.

"Isn't that my line?" she asks with a grin and watches the big driver's shoulder hunch.

"Just don't hurt me like you did before, please," he begs.

"No," she mutters, feeling ashamed of her earlier actions. She must've caused him a lot more pain than she realized to elicit this level of a fear response. "I don't—"

"Chris, dude, give her some breathing space," Martin says as he grabs Chris's shoulder and pulls him back.

"How about a little help up?" she asks, holding out her hand. Eagerly Chris shrugs off Martin and grasps her hand. With no apparent effort, he hauls her to her feet and then steadies her when new pain hits her ribs. She suspects she'll have a collection of colorful bruises there later.

"Can someone check on Sal?" she asks, clutching Chris's arm to keep herself steady.

"He's fine," Oscar calls out. Looking over she sees Seth and Oscar pulling Sal from the pile. He appears dazed but moves without trouble.

"I guess we should take him to the ER," she murmurs, but before she finishes that statement, Sal is stumbling back toward her and Chris. All the guys move quickly to block Sal.

"Time for you to go home," she tells Sal grimly. The string of curses directed at her makes any sympathy she might have had for the driver completely evaporate.

"You've been given multiple warnings," she says the moment he stops talking to draw a breath. "And this altercation was one hundred percent your fault. You're fired as of right now. You'll get your last paycheck in the mail."

All the guys look at her stunned, except for Oscar who's been with the company even longer than she has. He just grins and mumbles, "About damn time."

"You can't do that!" Sal sputters, but she just raises an eyebrow and gives him a smile that's more teeth than warmth.

"Just try and come back tomorrow and see how that goes for you," she challenges.

"John Scott owns this company, not you. He's the only one who can fire me. Not some dumb office broad," Sal spits out.

"When was the last time you saw John Scott?" Oscar's quiet question gets everyone's attention.

"Shit, I haven't seen him in months," Martin mutters.

"Steph hired me. I've never even met the guy," Carlos points out.

Chris nods in agreement. "Yeah, me too."

Sliding his gaze over to Sal, Oscar gives him a satisfied grin. "Steph runs this place. Has for years. Last time I heard anything, John was in the Virgin Islands sipping Mai Tais with his wife."

"St. Martin," Steph corrects with a little malicious grin. "He's on St. Martin right now."

"I'll call him," Sal threatens.

"Be my guest," Steph offers and then looks to the guys. "Can all of you make sure he cleans out his locker and leaves the property?" She meets his gaze, her eyes hard. "If you come back here, I'll file assault charges against you."

"Fuck you and fuck this place. It was a shitty job anyway," Sal yells, shoving Oscar away from him and limping to the small area of the building that houses the break and locker rooms. All the guys trail after him except Chris, who pulls his arm out of her grasp to curl it around her for better support.

"Do you need the hospital?" he asks, but she shakes her head.

"Just get me back to my desk." Without any further prompting, Chris helps her limp back to her office. Once she's settled in her chair, he brings her a can of cold soda and two icepacks—one for her face and the other for her ankle.

"Is it that bad?" The right side of her face is throbbing now and feels hot and swollen to the touch.

"Yeah, sorry," Chris says with a wince. Although it hurts, Steph chuckles.

"You need to learn to lie to a girl," Steph chides.

"Uh, you look great?" he says with raised eyebrows, making her laugh and then groan and clutch her side.

"Shit, sorry!" He reaches out to steady her, but she waves him off.

"Don't worry about it, nothing broken, just bruised all to hell," she assures him, but he gets a peculiar look on his face.

"Yeah, about that bruising. Could you make sure he knows it wasn't my fault?"

Flummoxed, Steph eyes him with her brow furrowed. "What?"

"Eli," Chris says. "Could you make sure to tell him this wasn't my fault?"

"How do you know Eli?" Steph asks.

Now it's Chris's turn to look confused. "He's staying at your place. Right?"

"Yes, but I haven't told anyone that. Are you a friend of his?"

"No, I've never met him in person," Chris confesses.

Steph's mouth gapes wide. "Then how do you know. Wait, are you friends with Ash?"

"Ashley Bridge is at your place?" Chris's eyes go wide. If Steph didn't know better, she'd think the man looks panicked. "I shouldn't know that. I wish you hadn't told me that."

"If you don't know Ash and you haven't talked to Eli, how did you even know Eli was at my place? What aren't you telling me, Chris?"

"I… uh… don't you…" he stammers and finally just shrugs. "Ask Eli?" The statement comes out more of a question than anything else, and Steph just barely keeps herself from screeching like a fishwife from frustration.

"Great," she mutters. "Another member of the super-secret squirrel club."

"Squirrels?" The look of utter bewilderment on Chris' face makes Steph smile despite her pain and annoyance.

"Yeah, apparently there's a club and I'm not a member," she teases. When he tries to protest that nothing is going on, she waves him away. "I'm okay. Just get back to work."

With a slow nod, Chris backs toward the office door. "Call me if you need anything, yeah?"

"Sure, right," she says tiredly and then slumps down in her chair and closes her eyes. In only three more hours, she can go home and pretend none of this ever happened.

Her throbbing face tells her that's probably not an option.

CHAPTER 10

While Steph's at work, Eli spends the day building a wooing gift for her. While they were at the nursery on Saturday, she'd looked longingly at the examples of various water features displayed at the front of the business. After she left for work, it didn't take much persuading to get Ash to drive him to the same nursery.

She also paid for the specialty tub and various other things he needed to build a small water feature. He promised to pay her back, but she waved him off and told him not to worry about it.

But he's determined. At some point he'll have access to his cash, and he'll make sure Ash is paid back and he contributes to the cost of housing and feeding him. Steph needs to know he can be a provider. He still winces at the fact that she thought he was a bum.

Determined to create the perfect wooing gift, Eli labors furiously all day.

Using the items he had Ash buy and the rocks he uncovered in the yard, he creates a water feature complete with a small waterfall. Standing back, he admires his work. It looks a little bare now, but once the plants start filling out, the pond and waterfall will look perfect. He knows Steph is going to love it.

With time still left before she gets home, he turns his attention to an old stump that needs to be dug up. The sound of her car in the driveway interrupts his work. He tosses the shovel aside and hurries into the house. After spending the whole day without her, both he and his wolf are eager to be back in her presence. Entering the living room through the kitchen, he arrives just as she kicks the front door closed behind her.

The sight of her battered face sends his wolf howling and clawing at his skin.

"Who?" His voice has stopped, and the growl of his wolf echoes in the small room. She eyes him warily.

"It was an accident," she mumbles as she walks past him to the kitchen. The entire right side of her face is swollen and bruised, but he can tell by the way she's walking she has more injuries than just what he can see on her face. Her eyes are dull with pain and her voice is soft and tired. This lethargic female bears little resemblance to his normally lively and vital Steph.

Without another comment he strides to her and picks her up, ignoring her little gasp. Effortlessly he cradles her high against his chest and carries her to her bedroom.

"I appreciate the romantic gesture," she murmurs dryly, "but I don't think I'm up for any kind of sexual exploits right now."

"Rest," Eli grunts. His wolf is calming at the idea of caring for their injured female. Neither he nor his animal are interested in sex at the moment. If anything, the wolf is demanding he curl up at her side and lick her wounds until the tight pinched look of pain is gone from her face.

He sets her gently on the bed, watching with worry. When she relaxes against her pillows with a bone-weary sigh, it guts him.

"Meds?" he asks.

She points without opening her eyes. "I've got Tylenol in the bathroom medicine cabinet."

He finds the pain reliever, fills a glass of water and makes an icepack with a towel and a bag of frozen peas. Returning to her side he pushes the pills and water on her. He waits impatiently for her to swallow them and then takes the glass away and settles the ice pack gently on her face.

With that done, he tugs up her shirt to see the rest of the damage. He hisses with anger when he sees the bruises running up her right side. Leaning closer, he catches a whiff of a human male and a male bear shifter on her clothes. They're faint but there. Both men had their hands on her today, and one or both of them must be the reason his female is lying in bed covered in bruises.

"Who touched you?" His voice is dropping and becoming more guttural, a sure sign he's about to lose his body to his wolf.

She doesn't meet his eyes. "There was a misunderstanding at work." She tries to tug her shirt back down but Eli doesn't let go. "I tried to break it up, and I accidentally got knocked down."

He gently draws her shirt over her head and then brings it to his nose, parsing out the scents. All kinds of smells are common in offices and places with industrial vehicles, but he needs to pick out the more subtle smells of the human and shifter. That way if he manages to run across them, he'll know who they are.

Out of nowhere he feels her warm power curl around him and his wolf whines. His heart slows, and his rage calms. With a grunt he drops her shirt and settles down on the bed on her left side, careful to keep from jostling her.

"Everything's fine," she promises. "I'm a little battered, but I was hurt much worse last year when I was walking across the street and got tangled up with a tourist on a bicycle. Besides, I got even. I fired the guy who knocked me down."

He knows it's better to let her rest and keep her from worrying about what he might do, so he gives her a brief grin. "You showed him who's boss. Huh?"

"Hell yes, I'm the boss," she grins back. "He was a pain in the ass anyway, but now I'm going to need to find another driver. We're already short one because Manuel's wife just gave birth and he's home caring for the two of them." She shuts her eyes and gives another sigh. "I hate it when I have to tow. I like working in the office better."

"I wish I could help." He can barely drive a car because his wolf hates being in such small confines or he'd offer to work for her. Not that he knows anything about tow trucks or the towing business, but he'd do anything to relieve some of her stress. That makes him think of something.

"Be right back," he mumbles and makes his way out to the living room where she dropped her purse. He finds her cell phone and stares at the screen. It takes him a while before he remembers the number to the gathering house. Someone is always there, and they should be able to put him in touch with who he's looking for.

"Hunger Valley Guided Tours," a familiar voice answers the phone.

"Mason," Eli grunts, and there's a brief pause before Nikki starts talking.

"Eli, is that you?" she whispers. "Shit's going crazy here. Where are you?"

"I need to talk to Mason," Eli tells her, ignoring the clear sound of panic in her voice.

"Well, fuck you too," Nikki grumbles. "The whole world's burning, but hold on, everyone, Eli needs to talk to Mason."

"Nikki," Eli growls out a warning. His tone makes her Iberian wolf produce a little whine.

"Fine," she mumbles. He hears movement and then Mason's clear voice.

"You working right now?" Eli asks.

"Eli?"

Great, he gets to play this game again. Why can't people just answer questions? "Yeah. You working right now?"

"You know the hauling gig is seasonal, winter only. I'm off until November," Mason answers. His voice is full of questions, but he knows better than to ask.

"Go to Larson Towing tomorrow morning at eight. You're gonna work there for a while," Eli tells him.

"Not that I wouldn't be glad to take orders from you," Mason states hesitantly. "But you're not the clan leader. I can't just—"

"The business is in neutral territory and not owned by a clan," Eli interrupts him. "It's a job, not clan business."

"Sure, I guess I could always use the extra cash," Mason agrees. "You should—"

"Good," Eli grunts and hangs up. Satisfied he's helped to solve one of Steph's problems, he returns to her room. She's fallen asleep so he takes a moment to survey the damage to her body. If she was a shifter, she'd already be halfway healed.

"Why a human?" he mutters to his wolf. "They're so fragile. Why couldn't we pick a timber wolf? Or a grizzly?"

For once, his wolf doesn't have an answer.

Once again, Steph wakes to the smell of food. A girl could get used to this.

With a little groan, she sits up in bed. Her face and ribs took the brunt of the fall and feel horrible, but the rest of her isn't too bad. Rolling her foot around she finds her ankle doesn't hurt at all. No point in lounging around in bed if she can walk. Time to stop moping over a few bruises and investigate whatever smells so delicious.

She starts to stand, moves too fast, and ends up falling back on the bed. She's still bouncing on the mattress when Eli seems to appear in front of her. "You're awake."

Grinning at him, she reaches out a hand and lays it on his muscled chest. "Have I told you how much I love your aversion to wearing shirts?"

He grunts at her touch and then barks out a laugh at her words. "Hungry," he insists, reaching down to pull her to her feet. She wants to tell him she's hungry for more than food, but her stomach growls loudly enough to make Eli frown. So she already knows she's not going to win that argument. With a scowl, he urges her out of the room and to the kitchen.

In short order she's sitting at the kitchen table with a bowl of stew in front of her. "This is good," she comments around a mouthful. A loaf of soda bread also sits on the table so she rips off a chunk and dips it into the stew. "Where did you get this? I need to know."

"Made it," he says through a mouthful of bread. She knows it can't possibly be flattering to have her mouth hanging open, especially full of food, but she can't help it. Eli catches her look and snorts out a laugh.

"I like to eat, and I don't like people," he points out. "So I learned to cook."

"You just officially became my most favorite houseguest," she murmurs appreciatively. "Stay as long as you want."

The look he gives her is hard to interpret, but his tone when he pronounces, "I plan to," makes her blush.

"Hey," Ash says as she comes breezing into the kitchen, "I thought I was your favorite house guest."

Looks like Ash isn't working the late shift after all. So much for Steph's plans for sex tonight.

"Eli made it," Steph says, pointing to the pot. Ash grabs a bowl and fills it from the steaming pot on the stove. Eli gives a little growl, and Ash freezes, looking over at him with wide eyes.

"Shhh," Steph soothes him, sending a little tendril of her gift to rub against him. His face relaxes, and a brief smile flits across his lips. "She can have some too. There's plenty."

Looking up at Ash, she gives the woman a welcoming smile. "Join us at the table. The stew is amazing!" Ash looks like she's about to comment on Eli's behavior when she gets her first good look at Steph's face.

"Holy shit! What happened?" Ash says, placing the bowl full of stew on the table and leaning over to better examine the damage.

"Would you believe I tripped?" she asks dryly.

Straightening up, Ash drops into a kitchen chair. "No, you're pretty graceful for a hu—" A warning sound from Eli cuts her off, and Steph just rolls her eyes. They'll tell her what's going on eventually, but until then this is damn annoying.

Ash rallies and continues. "You're pretty graceful. Did you trip in a pothole or something?" Shoving a big spoonful of stew into her mouth Ash makes an appreciative sound. "Is this venison?" Eli grunts and starts eating out of his bowl.

"You're home early," Steph comments, trying to divert the conversation from her face to anything else. "Everything okay?"

"It's a slow night so Clive sent a few of us home. I volunteered because I didn't want to be there when they closed." She gives a little shutter and focuses on her food.

Reaching out, Steph takes Ash's hand in her own. "Are you scared those men will be waiting for you to get off shift?" Ash just nods and Steph can tell the woman is upset and trying not to show it. "In that case, from now on, Eli and I will pick you up after work."

"You will?" Ash says, looking up and giving her a hopeful smile.

"We will?" Eli grunts, looking less than thrilled.

"Yes, we will," Steph tells him. "Or if you don't want to come, I guess I can just go alone."

"We'll go together," he agrees with a resigned grumble.

"Tell me what happened to your face?" Ash asks. "Because I gotta be honest, that's not a good look for you."

Laughing, Steph shrugs. "A couple of the guys got into an argument, and I got between them to break it up. Ended up getting shoved to the ground." She's telling them all about the altercation when a knock at her front door sends all three dogs into a barking frenzy. Steph raises an eyebrow at her two house guests, "Did you guys invite someone over?"

Both shake their heads. Ash looks pale and anxious, and Eli looks annoyed. Steph doesn't trust either of them to answer the door so she gets up and pins them both with a look.

"Stay here." Ash nods, but Eli gets up and follows her to the front door. Steph shoots him a warning look as she gets to the door, but he ignores her.

Giving up, she glances through the peephole, revealing a visitor she's not expecting at all. She looks back at Eli and orders, "Behave," before swinging the door open to reveal Chris standing on her porch. The guy looks worn out and a little battered.

"What are you doing here? What happened?"

He opens his mouth to answer, but she hears a distinct sniff behind her and then Chris looks over her shoulder. Spotting Eli, he casts his eyes down and cants his head to the side, just like he did to her earlier in the day.

Eli pushes past her. "You," he growls out.

"I didn't do it," Chris yelps, backing away and stumbling down the steps. Eli stalks forward, keeping pace. "I threw Sal away from her. Tell him, Steph. Tell him I didn't hurt you!"

Rushing out the door and down the steps, she grabs Eli around the waist and holds on, ignoring the protest from the bruises on her torso. Eli stops moving and puts his hand on hers, trying to extract himself from her hold without hurting her.

"He helped me," Steph insists and pushes her power at him. It meets his cold, furious barrier and bounces back at her, making her cheeks flush with the effort.

"Damn it, Eli. Listen to me," she says, finally losing her patience and pouring power into her gift. She smothers him in warm, calming waves and feels him stiffen before relaxing slightly.

Giving Chris his back, he turns in her arms so he can look down at her. His expression softens. "You're very good at that," he grunts out. "Maybe too good."

She grins up at him. "I can do even better," she whispers. She strokes her power down his chest like a hand.

His eyes widen and a grin flits across his face before he pins her with a mild glare. "The guy who hurt you is named Sal? What's his last name?"

"No way. I'm not going to play that game," she says with a little shake of her head. "Sal's been dealt with. Right, Chris?"

"Steph fired his ass, right in front of all the guys. Outside of a good beating, it was the best punishment possible," Chris calls out from behind Eli. "Besides, he's not… uh… one of ours. We should probably just let it go anyway."

Eli bends his knees and then picks her up. She gives a little squeak of surprise but then wraps her arms around his neck and her legs around his waist. He turns to face Chris with her in his arms.

"Lowell clan," Eli grunts out.

"Right now, I'm not sure," Chris answers. Steph cranes her head around so she can see Chris's face. Although he's at least six inches taller and a lot bulkier, he's acting intimidated by Eli.

"Be nice," she whispers in Eli's ear.

"Civil," Eli counters, and she has to fight a smile.

"Fine, be civil," she agrees. "I'll be nice for both of us." She wiggles until he lets her down, but he doesn't let her out of the circle of his arms.

She turns awkwardly in Eli's arms to face Chris and gives him a reassuring smile. "What are you doing here?"

He glances up at her and then shifts his gaze back down to the ground. "I can't go home."

"It's Clyde," Ash volunteers from her spot on the porch. "He, uh, might be mean to Chris if he crosses over Pine Ave."

"Who's Clyde and why is he being so horrible to you and Ash?" Steph asks. No matter what, she's going to the police tomorrow. She can't let these people continue to be harassed by Clyde and his cronies. Lowell might be a small town with an equally small police department, but she's sure Sheriff Miller will be able to help.

All three fall silent at her question, and she knows she's not getting any answers any time soon. With a huff, she pulls herself out of Eli's arms and takes a few steps toward Chris. Eli steps to one side of her and Mesa moves to be on her other side. Neither man nor dog are making welcoming sounds. Chris backs away from her, casting wary looks at Eli and Mesa. Irritated, she grabs Eli's hand.

"He took care of me after I got knocked down," she tells Eli. "He got me ice and made sure I was comfortable. He's welcome in my home." Then she looks down at her softly growling dog. "Mesa!" The dog looks up at her with an equally exasperated expression, as if saying, *I'm just trying to keep you safe, stupid human!*

"Friend," she insists to the dog and points to Chris. With obvious reluctance, Mesa moves to greet Chris. "Just hold out your hand," she instructs him. Mesa sniffs Chris's hand and then turns and trots back to Steph's side. She's no longer growling, but she's none too happy with this new development. Eli and Mesa have a lot in common.

"Why don't you join us for dinner?" Steph invites.

Chris nods and gives Eli a wide berth as he steps toward the house.

"Come on in," Ash invites from the front door and then turns to lead him to the kitchen. Grey, who watched everything unfold from a nice comfy chair on the porch, jumps down and trots over to Eli.

When the pit bull leans against Eli's legs, he smiles down at the square-headed dog. "Were you ready to back me up?" Grey doesn't respond, just lets his tongue loll out and his head thump against Eli.

"Fun's over," Steph says as she tugs at Eli's hand to lead him back inside. "I'm still hungry!"

"Terror!" Ash's cry makes them hurry. Inside the small kitchen they find Ash holding an unrepentant Terror, his face covered in stew and his stubby tail wagging furiously. Looking down at the table, Steph finds her bowl empty. Holding out her hands, Ash wordlessly hands the naughty terrier to Steph for a quick clean at the sink and then temporary banishment to the backyard.

By the time she's ready to sit back down at the table a fresh bowl of stew is waiting for her. Looking around she sees Ash grinning, Chris looking amused, and Eli fighting a smile.

"Well, there's a reason I named him Terror," she jokes and digs into her food. That prompts everyone else to start eating. Considering how big Eli and Chris are, she's amazed everyone fits at her tiny table.

If I get any more visitors I'm going to need to invest in a bigger table, she thinks. *Or a bigger house.*

Ash, Chris, and Steph talk about the towing company and Sal. Ash cracks up at finding out that Steph is basically in charge of the whole thing. "Well, if I can hire, it makes sense that I can fire too," she points out, amusing Ash to no end.

Throughout the meal, Eli sits quietly listening. He's not scowling or growling. If anything, his expression seems perplexed, as if he's not sure how he ended up at a table surrounded by happy chatting people. He notices she's looking at him and raises an eyebrow. She gives him a grin and tilts her head considering.

"Everyone thinks you're this big mean, vicious guy," she tells him. "But you're just a big, old teddy bear."

Chris clears his throat, "No, Steph, he is dangerous." She looks over at Chris who's staring at his bowl and canting his head to the side again. She finally realizes what Chris's action reminds her of. When he moves his head to expose his neck, deliberately making himself vulnerable, it's like a wild wolf showing submission to another pack member.

"Stop it," Eli grunts. "I'm not going to hurt you for talking or looking at me."

"Right, sure," Chris says with a quick nod. "I've just heard a lot of stuff, you know? Then I heard about you facing off with Clyde over at the tavern. I figured you were here to take over."

"I'm not taking over anything," Eli mutters. "I just want to be left alone."

"Are you guys in a gang?" Steph asks. That would explain the abuse, violence, and fear. It would also explain why some areas are neutral because don't gangs have territories? Wait. Does that mean other gangs are in the area too? Rivals? How could her little adorable town of Lowell be harboring not one but several brutal gangs? And how has she never noticed?

Everyone at the table goes silent with her question as all of them are staring at her wordlessly. Eli's expression is blank, Ash looks like she's trying to puzzle something out, and Chris very slowly nods his head.

"Yes?" Chris does the question-answer thing again. Even though she's never dealt with a gang herself, she's watched enough documentaries to know it can be a death sentence to leave a gang after being initiated. And it's becoming more and more apparent that the three people at her table are all mixed up in a war between rival gangs. It almost sounds like Eli's in line to be a leader of some kind.

"We can't talk about it," Eli tells her flatly. His tone and expression tell her this conversation is over.

Waves of fear waft off of Ash. Chris is afraid also, but his fear is tempered with resignation. With Eli, she doesn't feel anything at first but then a wash of emotions hits her—anger, anxiety, despondency, but most of all fear.

Unlike Ash and Chris, the fear isn't for himself. It's for her.

Her gift flares in her chest, demanding she act to help the distressed people around her. Chris and Eli are sitting the closest so she grabs a forearm in each hand. She lets her gift flow into them, soothing and warm. Chris lets out a heartfelt sigh. Eli's expression doesn't change, but his tense body does relax fractionally and the frantic energy inside of him quiets. Because she doesn't have direct contact with Ash, her gift takes a little longer to work on the woman sitting across from her.

Finally, the tension lines bracketing Ash's mouth relax, and her eyes close as she takes a deep breath. Buzzed from using her gift, Steph lets go of the men and returns her attention to the stew. The other three follow her example and resume eating.

They all eat in companionable silence for a little while until Steph judges it as a good time to talk. "I want all of you to stay here," she tells them without looking up. "I'm in neutral territory. Right?" Chris nods his head. Ash gives a small tentative, "Yes," and Eli stares at her disapprovingly.

Ignoring Eli, she forges on. "I know you guys don't want to involve the authorities yet. I won't say anything either for now. But I want everyone to stay safe. If staying here can help with that, then all of you will stay here." They all nod and look relieved until she starts talking again.

"You know, if you guys are involved in some kind of gang turf war, we're going to need to get help. I think the FBI has a gang task force. Maybe we can get them involved."

Eli snickers and when she looks over, he smirks back. "You watch too much TV," he tells her simply.

Mildly embarrassed, her face flushes.

"You don't understand, Steph," Ash tells her with wide sincere eyes. "Clyde's just waiting. He's going to come after us. Chris, Eli, and me. But if we stay here, he'll come after you too. He'll hurt you. Bad."

"We need backup," Steph counters. "None of you should take this Clyde on by yourself. You're not vigilantes. But, for right now, we'll all stay here. Strength in numbers and all that," she declares and ignores the grumpy sound Eli makes. "Chris, you get the couch. It's a little small for you, but it's better than the floor. Then we can ride into work together tomorrow. You can stay here as long as you need. Stay until we figure out how to deal with Clyde."

"You don't go near Clyde," Eli admonishes, and both Chris and Ash nod their heads in unison.

"He's a murderer," Chris mutters, and Steph jolts at his words.

"Do you have proof?" she asks.

"Not going there," he says quickly. "But you need to listen to Eli. Clyde is just evil." He shoots Eli a wistful look. "Someone needs to replace him."

"You guys could've gone over to Hunger Valley," Eli comments. Hunger Valley is the next town over, but the way Eli uses the name, it must also be the territory for the rival gang not run by Clyde.

Both Ash and Chris look crestfallen. "Richard refused us." Chris's tone and body language scream despondent. "Point blank told me none of the Lowell members are allowed to join Hunger Valley. And none of the other clans in the area are willing to risk war with Clyde by accepting any of us either."

"We're trapped," Ash murmurs.

Slapping a hand to the table, Steph gives them her most stubborn look. "No one is trapped! Not on my watch. I promise we'll figure this out. I'm going to keep you guys safe. If I have to sell my house and we all move, that's what we'll do."

All three of them regard her with stunned expressions. "You would sell your house and leave Lowell just to help us?" Chris asks.

"A house is just a building, and a job is something you do to earn money so you can buy groceries. People are more important. If selling my place and moving all of us away is the only way to save Ash, it's a no-brainer. Maybe I'll even open up my own towing business somewhere," she gives Chris a cocky grin. "I know a driver who'll probably work for me."

"Always," Chris promises fervently.

"What about me?" Eli asks softly, his eyes blazing with insecurity.

"Honey," she drawls as she leans over and brushes her lips over his. "I'd never leave my chef behind! You're coming with me even if I have to tie you up and throw you in the trunk of my car. Just try to say no, and see where it gets you." His eyes blaze with a whole new emotion and he grabs a handful of her hair, holding her head still as he ravishes her mouth.

By the time they come up for air, Chris and Ash are gone. She can hear quiet voices from the living room, telling her the two are probably watching the news.

"I'd never run away from you," he breathes into her ear.

A naughty expression covers her face. "Does that mean I don't get to use ropes?" Eli groans and nips at her neck.

"Don't tempt me, woman," he mutters. "I'm trying to woo you." Then he pulls back so she can see his serious expression. "I'll keep you safe. I promise."

"Let's work on keeping everyone safe," she pleads. He gives an almost imperceptible sigh and rests his forehead against hers.

"I'll try." A sliver of power runs down her body as if his words are a promise backed up by his gift. "I'll try very hard."

CHAPTER

11

"I'm Mason," the giant man declares as if that should explain everything.

"Hi, Mason," Steph responds as she stands up. Sitting just isn't an option with this big guy looming over her. She's never met anyone as tall or as pale as the man standing in front of her. No, pale doesn't cover it. It's more like he's translucent. Staring at his neck, she tries to see veins.

If he has albinism, it would show in his eyes. Right? Looking up she finds herself fixated. He doesn't have the pale blue or gray eyes normally associated with human albinism. His eyes are so dark she can't quite tell where the pupil ends and his iris begins. It's a bit unnerving and it takes her a moment to realize she's just staring at the guy's eyes.

Clearing her throat to hide her embarrassment, she offers her hand over the desk. "Welcome to Larson Towing. What can I do for you?"

She watches as her hand is swallowed by his. It's a relief when he doesn't try to do the macho grip-too-hard handshake. As they shake, his nostrils flare and he drops her hand like he's been burned. Taking a hasty step away, he almost knocks over a chair. She can honestly say that's the first time she's intimidated a guy with a handshake.

Fidgeting, he drops his gaze to the floor and tilts his head to the side, exposing his neck just like Ash and Chris have done. What does it say about her that the move doesn't even make her blink anymore?

"Let me guess," she murmurs. "You're one of Chris's friends?"

"Chris?" Confused, Mason meets her gaze for a second but then drops his eyes back to the floor. "I don't know who Chris is. But I'm here to work. Eli sent me. Told me I'd be working here for a while."

"Oh, you're friends with Eli?"

With a snort, Mason doesn't look up. "No one's friends with Eli."

"I beg to differ," Steph's voice is tight. "I consider him a friend."

"Then you're brave as hell or foolish as fuck," Mason mutters. Then he must have realized he spoke out loud because he pales a little. Considering how colorless his skin is already, that's a feat. "Don't tell him I said that."

A real smile breaks across her face. "Don't worry. I'll keep you safe from Eli."

"She will too," a voice from the doorway says. Mason turns, giving Steph a view of Chris standing in the hall just outside her office. "He was gonna charge me last night, and she just grabbed him and stopped him."

Mason turns to her with wide eyes. "He didn't maul you?"

"Uh, no." What kind of things has Eli done in the past to earn this level of fear? "Is he an enforcer for your gang?"

"Gang?" Mason echoes confused.

"She thinks we're in a gang," Chris tells him, and they exchange meaningful glances.

"I guess that's not far off," Mason concedes.

Chris nods thoughtfully before pointing a thumb at his chest and then a finger at Mason. "At least between Lowell clan and Hunger Valley clan."

Done with their meaningful glances and vague conversation, Steph clears her throat to get the men's attention. "I thought you were on your way out to Harfit to pick up the Ford?" she asks Chris pointedly.

"Carlos was closer after he dropped that Beamer off," Chris tells her. "I came to ask if truck four was running." Chris jerks his head to indicate Mason. "What's he doing here?"

"That's what I'm trying to figure out," Steph says and can't help the small, exasperated sound that comes out of her mouth.

"Eli sent me. Said you needed a driver," Mason explains, and Chris jerks a little, his face showing hopeful startlement.

"Did he already—"

"Nah, man," Mason cuts him off. "Not yet, anyway. But maybe soon. We all hope, you know?" His words make Chris deflate a little.

"We need him here more," he mutters.

"He's one of ours," Mason says aggressively. "If he takes over, it will be for us. Not your fucked-up band of sadists."

Familiar with the effects of testosterone and the male penchant for fighting, Steph steps around the desk and grabs Mason's arm, using her gift to calm him. Then she shoots Chris a warning glare.

"That's enough out of both of you." Within the first year of working for Larson Towing, Steph created her "authoritative" tone. It's a combination of a mother's warning and a boss's admonishment. She's perfected it over the years and watches both men stiffen at her words. Then, almost in perfect unison, they both drop their gazes and crane their heads to the side, exposing their necks.

"Chris, truck four is working, so you can take that out. Danny's shop needs a tow so call them to get the details," she instructs.

"Sure thing, boss," Chris says. Then as he turns to leave, he gives Mason a spiteful look. "Even if you get Eli, she's ours." Then he's gone before she or Mason can say anything.

Making a small, annoyed sound, she lets go of Mason's arm and regards the massive male in front of her. She gives him a gentle look.

"Do you want to work here?" she asks, and Mason's expression conveys shock.

"Yes?" Just like Chris, his word is as much a question as an answer. Do these guys go to some class that teaches them to talk like this?

She tries a different tactic. "Let's try that again. If I promise Eli won't get mad if you say you don't want to work here, can you answer that question without the question mark included?"

Flashing her a real grin, Mason nods his head. "I'm not working right now and could use the money."

"Next question: Are you licensed?"

Nodding, Mason digs out some folded and crumpled paperwork from his back pocket and hands it to her. She looks through it and then sits back behind the desk. Taking a cue from her, he slumps down in one of the office chairs. The chair groans a little but holds. She looks through the paperwork, pleased to see that all his requirements are up to date.

"Well, I'm not going to lie. I'm down a couple of drivers and could use the help," she explains as she starts putting the forms together and handing them over to Mason with a clipboard. "Start filling these out, so we can get you in the system and get you moving."

By noon she's got Mason in her system and out with one of the trucks. Even with his help, they're still scrambling. With a resigned sigh, she grabs a set of keys and heads out to hop in one of the trucks as well. Movement out of the corner of her eye catches her attention just as she exits the building.

Stopping, she takes a careful look around the yard, wondering why her intuition is screaming at her. Fear isn't what's curling up in her gut; rather it's a strange kind of anticipation.

"You can come out," she calls, wondering if she's being paranoid or delusional—perhaps both. It's called paranoid schizophrenia for a reason after all. When Eli steps out from behind a pile of old tires, she breathes out a sigh of relief. Not insane but maybe a little stalked.

"What are you doing here?" she asks as he draws closer to her. Without thinking about it, she wraps her arms around him. He smells perfect and, as usual, he's only wearing pants with no shirt or shoes. He doesn't even wince as he walks across the gravel lot. That man must have feet of iron.

"Needed to check on you," he explains and warmth spreads through her.

"Aww, I missed you too," she murmurs. "Thanks for sending Mason over. He's been a real asset."

He sounds out one of his familiar grunts that could mean anything from, "You're welcome," to, "I'm about to kill someone." Resting his cheek against the top of her head, he holds on to her as if she's the only thing in his world that's solid. They stand like that in contented silence for several minutes before Steph reluctantly pulls away.

"I've got to go pick up a car," she explains, holding up the truck's keys. She can tell by his expression he's not happy about that.

"Where?"

"There was a one-car accident over on Apple Street. A senior citizen put her car into a ditch. She's fine, but I need to pull the car out and haul it to the shop," she explains and if anything, his face gets even more severe.

"No."

Her hands go to her hips, and she cocks an eyebrow at him, "Let's nip that attitude in the bud. This is my job. You don't get to tell me what to do at my job." She considers that statement and then shakes her head. "You don't get to tell me what to do anywhere. You can ask. We can discuss. But you don't get to order."

"Fine," Eli gripes, and she can tell that wasn't the "F" word he wanted to say. "I'll go with you."

Opening her mouth to refuse, she stops when she feels a wave of fear come off Eli. He's not being possessive. He's scared for her. "Let me get you a shirt and some boots," she says instead. "Stay here. I'll be right back." Before he can say anything else, she runs back into the main building, grabs one of the company shirts they use as a uniform, and a pair of spare heavy-duty rubber boots all the guys carry in their trucks in case of chemical spills.

Returning, she hands him the shirt first, which he reluctantly pulls on. When she hands him the boots, he holds them for a moment, eyeing them with disgust. Looking up he sends her a pleading look.

"Rules," she states firmly, crossing her arms over her chest.

With an irritated grunt, he puts his bare feet into the rubber boots and then grimaces. Steph bites her lip to keep from giggling at his discomfort. With him properly attired, they get into the truck and head out.

The wreck is only twenty minutes away, and Steph is relieved it's a straightforward job. Once they get there, she positions the truck and tells Eli to sit on a nearby stump. He grumbles but follows orders. It doesn't escape her notice that he's vigilant, scanning the area around them with intense focus as she drags a cable to the rear of the damaged vehicle.

After hooking a tow cable to the car, she scrambles back up the embankment to the truck and then hits the electric winch to pull it out of the ditch. Once it's on the shoulder, and she's sure it won't slip back down the embankment, she unhitches the cable. Repositioning the truck until it's lined up with the back of the car, she lowers the flatbed section to the ground just behind the car's rear bumper. It doesn't take long for her to hook up the car and neatly winch it onto the flatbed of her truck.

Once the bed is back in position and the car appropriately secured, she turns her attention to Eli. He's grinning at her, and she's momentarily startled by his proud expression.

"What?" she asks. He stands up from the stump and strolls over to her. When he's right in front of her, he reaches out and curls a hand around the back of her neck. His skin feels warm on hers, and she can't tear her eyes away from his.

"That was hot," he murmurs as he lowers his lips to hers. She doesn't even think about the fact that anyone could pass them on the road and see them making out or that she needs to get back to the office to answer calls and coordinate the drivers. Helplessly, she opens her mouth and falls into Eli's kiss.

This kiss is just as good as the one they shared in her backyard, and she melts against him. She's sweaty and grimy, but Eli doesn't seem to care. He slides a hand under her shirt and rests it on her lower back. The feel of his callused fingers on her bare skin sends a shot of lust through her. Slowly he runs his hand up her back until he encounters the back of her sports bra. With no hook to unlatch, she's taken completely by surprise when she feels a little snap and the sports bra comes loose.

With a gasp she pulls out of his arms and crosses her arm over her chest. "What did you just do?"

His face is all need and lust, and instead of answering, he reaches for her. She steps back again, shaking her head violently.

"No way, buddy," she pants, holding out a hand to stop his forward progress. "We need to get this car dropped off and get back to the yard."

"You liked it," he accuses. He jerks his head toward the nearby woods. "No one is there. Come with me. I'll find us a nice soft place." His tone is both demanding and pleading.

"We are not horny teenagers who need to sneak off into the woods for privacy," she retorts hotly. His incredulous look reminds her about Ash and Chris back at her house. "Right, we could use some privacy, but now's not the time for…for…"

"Fucking?"

Face turning beat red, she glares at him. "For making love," she counters, and this time he blushes. It's a fascinating transition to watch. His face goes from dominant and aggressive to bashful.

"Would it be?"

Blinking, her brows furrow. "Would what be?" Did she wander into an existential debate in the middle of a teenage make-out scene?

"Would we be making love?" Ah, now she understands. Smiling at him, she holds out her hand and waits for him to take it.

"Yeah, we'd be making love," she assures him. "I don't just go around fucking guys. I'm picky. Right now, you're it for me Mr. Growly."

A wide, satisfied smile covers his face. Letting go of her hand, he grabs her up in a bear bug and starts walking toward the woods. Feet dangling, she laughs and slaps him lightly on the arms as she protests. "Eli, no!" He stops moving and gives her a begging look. "Put me down! Bad Eli!" she admonishes, making him chuckle.

"You're talking to me like one of your dogs," he says as he sets her down.

"If the shoe fits," she mutters and squeaks when he gently smacks her backside. Throwing him an amused smirk, she points back to the truck. "March! No more letting our hormones do our thinking." Relenting a little at his disappointed expression, she grins. "I'm sure we can figure out how to get some alone time later. Okay?"

He rubs his hands over his face and gives a little growl. "Fine!" His tone sounds angry, but the energy coming off of him is sexual and playful.

Without another word he turns and strides to the passenger door of the truck. His back is stiff and his expression thunderous. Trying to get her breathing and arousal under control, she heaves herself into the driver's seat.

Once she's seated, she turns her attention to her loose sports bra under her shirt. Sliding one strap under the shirt and over one arm, she takes it off without removing the shirt by pulling the whole thing out through the other sleeve. She examines it, surprised to find Eli somehow cut right through the narrow area at the back. Well, it was old anyway, so he probably tugged a little too hard on a weak spot. She needs to go clothes shopping.

And remember to wear her sexy underwear. Every day.

The fact that she has someone in her life to appreciate her sexy underwear makes her feel lighthearted and happy along with horny. It's a great combination of emotions.

Without another comment, she tosses the ruined garment down on the seat between them and puts the truck in gear. She does her best to ignore Eli as she drives, but it feels like the truck is filling with pheromones. Do humans even give off pheromones?

The lust ricocheting through her body is making it hard to concentrate, and when they finally get back to the yard, she's a nervous wreck. Oscar is there, pulling out of the gate with one of the other flatbeds. They stop driver side to driver side in the entryway.

"Hey, boss, a minivan broke down over at the DQ," he explains as he gives Eli a curious look. "Who's your friend? Another new hire?"

"This is Eli, and he's staying with me for a few days," she says and then feels herself blushing. Oscar's eyes go a little wide with surprise.

"Is that right?" he murmurs. "Nice to see you with a friend. Even this one." He puts the emphasis on *friend*, making her feel like she's facing down a nosy parent rather than a coworker.

"No comment," she mutters to him with a frown.

"She's important to us." Oscar's expression turns concerned as he addresses Eli. "You know what this means. Right?"

Eli gives Oscar one quick nod. "I know what needs to be done."

Giving Eli a hard look, Oscar frowns. "If you don't step up, we will."

"Stay out of it, firewood," Eli spits out.

"As long as you clean house, puppy dog. The way the local clans are being run is starting to bother the rest of us." Both men are glaring at each other now.

"Firewood? Puppy dog? You guys do realize those are some weird insults. Right?" They both turn their attention to her.

Oscar's expression softens as he talks to her. "You know, I thought you'd end up with one of us. Not his kind."

Eli scowls deeply and hisses out an angry breath. He mumbles something too low for Steph to hear but knows it's not complimentary toward Oscar.

That's it, she's had enough!

"His kind? The rest of us? What are you guys talking about? What the hell is going on? Oscar, how do you know Eli?" She demands, her voice much higher pitched than she likes, but she doesn't seem to have any control at the moment. "Tell me right now how you know each other! Is it a gang thing? Are you in the gang too? Tell me!"

"Easy, Steph," Oscar says, eyeing her warily. "Eli will explain."

"Well, he hasn't yet," she retorts crossly.

"Go," Eli orders the other man.

"I don't take orders from fur faces," Oscar snaps out coldly.

"What the hell, Oscar?" she just about screeches. "You're never this rude or this…" Oscar cuts her off, his tone kind but firm.

"I'm sorry, Steph, but Eli will have to explain it all. I've got to go." Oscar turns his attention back to his vehicle and drives away, ignoring Steph's demands for him to stay and explain everything. Eli grunts with satisfaction as Oscar disappears out of sight.

"You better be downright talkative when we get home," she threatens as she finishes pulling into the towing company's yard. "Or your next grunt might be your last."

CHAPTER 12

Eli doesn't speak for the rest of their time at work. Once she's back in the office he tries to sit, but his constant fidgeting makes her banish him outside. She catches him prowling around the yard through her window but concentrates on work instead of giving in to the urge to go out and talk to him. She can tell something's agitating him but damn if she will act the soothing role she falls into so often. If he wants access to her gift, he can damn well fess up to whatever's going on first.

The drive home is also made in silence and Steph finds herself fuming. It's rare for her to experience this level of frustration, but she decides to embrace it. She can count on one hand how many times she's truly lost her temper, but Eli's right on the edge of finding out how bad it can be when a normally easygoing and cheerful person rampages.

By the time they pull into her driveway she can't wait to get Eli into the house so she can start yelling at him and demanding answers, but a stranger on her porch derails that plan.

Standing stiffly with his arms stuffed into his jean pockets, the stranger eyes her front door with a combination of concern and fear. He's a tall, slim black man, and his lean, muscled frame exudes confidence as he raises his hand to knock at the door. His long dreadlocked hair is held back in a high, thick ponytail and he's wearing an old shirt and jeans, but no shoes. He must belong to the same shoe-hating club as Eli. She doesn't recognize him, but because of Ash and Chris, she assumes this stranger is showing up at her door because he too is in some kind of trouble.

Eli unfolds himself from her car before she's even shut off the engine and aggressively strides toward the stranger. "Leave."

Not a friend of Eli's apparently.

"I need help," the stranger declares as he turns away from the door to face Eli. Before Eli even gets to the porch, the stranger is holding out his hands, as if to fend Eli off. Then he drops to his knees and slants his head to the side. "Please, Eli," he begs. "Please listen to me."

Steph struggles out of her car, her irritation at Eli forgotten as concern takes its place. Strong emotions make her clumsy, and Eli is already on the porch before she's even clear of the driver's seat.

"Get up," Eli barks out, and the man flinches but doesn't move to get to his feet. "Get up and get out!"

"Not until you hear me out." Steph hears the determination in his voice now as she hurries to the porch, worried about both Eli and this stranger. Eli casts her a reproving look.

"Go inside," Eli orders, making her temper flair.

"You go inside," she counters and knows that doesn't make any sense, but she's just too annoyed at the whole damn world to care. "This is my house and my porch, so guess what? That makes this guy *my* guest." She turns to face the stranger and forces her face into a semblance of a smile. "My name's Steph Garmin. Welcome to my house."

The guy eyes her cautiously and offers her his hand, but he remains on his knees. "Troy Desta," he says as they shake. It feels odd to her to shake hands with a man on his knees, but if working at the towing company has taught her anything, it's to go with the flow. Having Eli in her life is just reinforcing that concept.

"What can I do for you, Troy?" she asks in a conversational tone.

A smile ghosts across his face. "I need to talk to Eli and maybe not be grievously injured in the process." His words are casual, his tone teasing, but the tension in his body and his constant glances over at Eli tells her this man is intimidated as hell. Just like Chris.

"Well, he's not much of a talker," she gripes, and this time Troy laughs.

"Truer words," he says under his breath.

"Troy?" She hears Ash's voice and looks over to see her friend carrying a bag of groceries from the street. Her eyes are wide and startled.

"Ash!" Now Troy does get to his feet and runs to her. Ash drops the bag and flings herself into Troy's arms.

"I was so worried," he says as he hugs her tightly. "I heard Clyde gave you to Glenn and you got away, but I couldn't find out more without making people suspicious."

She clutches at him fiercely. "Steph and Eli saved me."

Troy places her on the ground but keeps his arms around her. He turns them both so he can regard Steph and Eli, both still standing silent on the porch. "Anything I have is yours. Anything. You saved my heart," he states simply, and Steph feels tears gather in her eyes.

"That's so romantic," she whispers and glances over at Eli just in time to see him roll his eyes. Then he catches her glare and shrugs.

"Words are sound. Actions are more important," he tells her defensively.

"Whatever," she mutters. "Come on, you two," she calls out. "Let's get this show in the house before Mrs. Leland calls the cops on us for being dramatic in public or something else equally stupid."

Laughing, Ash pulls out of Troy's arms, grabs the bag of groceries in one hand, and then takes his hand in her other. He grins at her as she tugs him up the steps and into the house. Eli sighs aggressively, and Steph casts him a chiding look.

"You're on thin ice with me right now," she warns him. "I'm annoyed and horny, not a good combination."

His whole demeanor changes as his face lights up, and his eyes gleam. "I can fix that last part."

"Leave it to a guy to focus on that," she mutters with an unwilling grin forming on her lips. "Inside, big guy. Let's sort out our latest guest."

Ash, Troy, and Eli quietly converse in the living room as she stows the groceries Ash brought home. Then she puts together a simple meal of bread, veggies, and cheese onto a few large trays. Mesa is tense and won't leave her side, but Terror seems to be in love with all the company, especially after Chris gets home and goes out into the backyard to play Terror's favorite game of fetch. As usual, Grey sticks to Eli's side, refusing to be moved even for his doggy dinner in the kitchen.

"You know I buy your kibble," Steph reminds the big pit bull who just looks at her with mellow, content eyes as she drops his bowl of food between his front feet. "A little loyalty would be appreciated."

Sitting on the couch snuggled against Troy, Ash laughs. "Eli seems to be gathering followers whether he wants to or not."

Making an annoyed sound, Eli shoots a warning glare at her, but her smile doesn't change. If anything, it gets brighter. "Oh no, I'm not intimidated by you anymore, Eli Colton. I see you now for who you are."

With a gesture at Steph, Ash giggles. "Steph's tamed the beast."

"I never set out to intimidate people," Eli grumbles and swallows half his beer in one swig.

"To be fair, all the fights went looking for him," Troy says. "He never tried to incite a single battle."

"I didn't know that," she murmurs and now her smile dims a little. "You honestly don't want to be clan leader. Do you? Or an enforcer?"

"Or a guardian or anything," Eli continues. With a grunt, he stands up and heads into the kitchen. "I just wanted to be left alone." They hear him set his empty beer bottle on the counter and go out the back door, Grey's nails clicking on the floor at his side.

Everyone is silent until the back door clicks shut. All eyes are on her when Chris taps her on the shoulder. "You should go check on him."

"He's had it rough for a while," Troy says. "And it's going to get a lot worse before it gets better."

Knowing better than to demand answers from any of them, Steph stands and follows Eli out to the backyard.

The sky is just starting to get dark now with only a few bright stars visible. Eli is sitting on the lounger, looking up at the darkening sky, and she can feel the tension flowing off of him as she sits down next to him. For some reason it reminds her of the first time she approached him in the park.

"I know you can't tell me what's going on," she says softly. "But if you ever want to talk about anything, I'm all ears."

He glances over at her, his eyes bright in the fading light. "I don't like talking," he reminds her.

Grinning, she wraps an arm around him. "Then we can just sit here and breathe."

"I like it when you talk."

With a little chuckle, she tilts her head to rest it against him. "It's one of my talents."

"Tell me about your family," he demands.

"There's not much to tell, I'm afraid. My mom was in her early forties when she got pregnant with me. They never planned on having kids, so I was an unwelcome surprise." He scowls, and she rubs a hand over his back. "They weren't mean or anything. They never raised a hand or voice to me. I guess the best way to describe it was that they just weren't very interested in raising me. The woman next door had three kids. They were a tight and loving family. I ended up spending more time over at the neighbors' than at home. Elenore, the mom, just folded me into their group. Dan, their dad, always included me in the family outings. I grew up feeling closer to them than my parents. Mom and Dad never said anything, so they were just probably relieved that I wasn't under foot."

"They sound cold."

"That's not a bad way to describe them. Cold and distant, even with each other. They worked, had hobbies, and did the bare minimum required to take care of me. Looking back, I think the only reason they got married was to combine wealth so they could have a comfortable upper-middle-class life. I watched a documentary once about royalty and marriage. They reminded me of one of those medieval noble families, marrying for gain instead of love." She goes quiet for a moment, thinking about her detached, unloving parents.

"What happened when you grew up?" he asks, bringing her back to the present.

"The summer I turned eighteen they gave me a little cash and an old car and asked me to leave. That was it."

Looking aghast, Eli hauls her into his lap. "They kicked you out?" With a small sigh of happiness, she wraps her legs around his waist and her arms around his neck.

"They didn't kick me out. If I'd raised a fuss, they would've let me stay longer, but I was tired of living with them anyway. I was eager to go. Elenore and Dan offered to let me stay with them so I could attend the local community college. I stayed with them for a year, took some classes, and got a part-time desk job with a construction company. The next thing I knew I was working there full-time and quit going to school."

"Do you regret not going to college?"

"Not really," she admits. "Some of the classes were fun, but I'm not good at theory, and that's what college mostly felt like. I like being out in the world and doing more. College isn't for everyone."

"True," he agrees. "How did you end up with the towing company?"

"Well, the company was on the small side so I got to wear a lot of hats. It kept me busy, and I learned a lot. After a couple of years, I was an assistant project manager. Then the owner of that company died, and the kids decided to sell it. I knew John Scott because he hauled heavy equipment back then. He and I interacted a lot on that project, and he asked if I'd come work for him after the kids sold the company. I've been at Larson Towing ever since."

"How long?"

She thinks for a second. "Almost ten years now. Last year John started traveling with his wife and just left me in charge of everything. I love it."

They sit in silence for a little while; then he asks another question. "Do you ever see your parents?"

"No." When she doesn't say any more. Eli doesn't push.

"Sorry," she finally says. "I tried for years to have a relationship with them, but they just weren't interested. It hurts to think that these two people, who should love me, aren't interested in even having a conversation with me. I've struggled with it a lot over the years. Even went to therapy," she gives a small, bitter laugh that doesn't sound at all like her. How did this conversation turn so maudlin? "But someday I'm going to have a big loving family of my own. For a while I wanted to marry a guy who had a ton of family so I could just be part of his family. But I seem to have a hard time keeping a guy interested." He squints at her, as if considering her words.

"Fools," is all he says, making her laugh and pulling her out of her dark thoughts.

"I like the way you think," she declares gaily.

Running a hand up her back, he gives her a decidedly salacious look. "I like the way you feel." The backdoor squeaks. Neither of them moves to look.

"We're hungry," Ash announces. "We're going to walk to the sandwich shop and then eat in the park. And we're going to take the dogs."

That makes Steph feel guilty for abandoning her guests. "I can cook."

"Nope," Ash says, popping the P in the word. "You guys just hang out and have some nice alone time. Grey," she calls out to the pit bull lying on the stones next to Eli's big feet. "Get over here!" The dog gives Eli a pleading look while laboriously getting up.

"Go," Eli says softly. With a huff, the dog shuffles off to Ash.

"We're going for a walk," she reprimands the dog in a teasing tone. "Not torture, silly mutt!"

They listen to the sounds of the three getting ready to leave along with the dogs. There's friendly arguing over who gets to lead Terror and who's stuck with the aloof Mesa. In the end, Chris gets Terror. Ash is the only one Mesa will mind, and Troy leads the morose pit bull. They make a loud, happy group as they file out of the house, leaving quiet in their wake.

"I wonder why they didn't invite us along," Steph murmurs, feeling mildly hurt. Maybe they wanted to discuss all the things they can't talk to her about. Being excluded is one of the things she hates the most, but she tries to be understanding. Hopefully, at some point, one of the four of them will trust her enough to tell her what's going on.

"We can join them," Eli offers.

"I don't want to bother them. Besides, I don't want to force my company on anyone. Some people find my chattiness a little much." And isn't that just all kinds of painful? Memories of her parents constantly telling her to quiet down or to stop talking filter through her mind.

A warm hand cups her cheek and forces her to look up. Meeting Eli's warm gaze, she attempts to keep the hurt out of her expression.

"They aren't rejecting you," he tells her softly. "They're giving us time alone together. They know I'm wooing you."

"Oh." Her mood lifts as Eli's words sink in. "Wooing me, huh? Does that include sex?" Instantly his body tenses, and lust flares across his face.

"It can."

Grinning, she wiggles a little on his lap. "Then let's start wooing properly!"

CHAPTER

13

Expecting Eli to just pick her up and start ravishing her, she's unprepared for the way he freezes with his eyes on her. Lust still dominates his face, but now it's tempered with concern. "I want to make this good," he confesses. Awww, he's nervous. That's the most adorable thing Eli's done so far.

"Don't be worried. I'm already turned on," she assures him.

"You'll tell me if I do something you don't like?" he asks, his apprehension clear.

"I promise to communicate loud and clear," she gives him a cheeky grin. "I'm good at communicating. To demonstrate, let me tell you how much I love your aversion to shirts." She runs her hands over his bare chest, and his muscles tense under her touch. He makes a small approving sound as she gently digs her short blunt nails into his pecs.

"You like my body?"

"Honey, anyone who doesn't like your body is blind," Steph declares confidently.

"I only care that you like it."

"You're so damn hot that I'm flattered that you like me back," she admits.

"Does that mean I can take off your shirt?" The excited look on his face is so typically male she snorts out a laugh.

"Absolutely!" Sitting up, she grips the hem of her shirt and pulls it off over her head. She never put another bra on, so now she's naked from the waist up. She pauses, letting him look at her in the dim light. Fighting the urge to cover herself, she clears her throat. "I'm not lean and muscled like you," she starts to say, ready to apologize for her soft body, but Eli's growl cuts her off.

"Perfect." He cups one of her breasts in his callused hand, running a thumb over her nipple. His soft touch makes her entire body flare with hunger.

"More."

Gripping her nipple between thumb and finger, he squeezes until she's wiggling against him. He backs the pressure off and then does it again. When he brings his other hand up to her other breast, she blows out an explosive breath. The sensation of his fingers on her nipples is lancing lust through her system.

Undulating her pelvis against him, she arches back and moans. Wanting him to move his hands lower while continuing to touch her breasts creates a conflict that robs her of speech. It's not helping that on top of what his hands are doing to her, his gift is pressing against her, pushing inside her. She lowers her defenses, and heat blossoms inside her chest as his power flows through her. In response, she thrusts her gift into him.

Head dropping back, his eyes closed, and he moans. "Yes, like that. Please, just like that."

It must feel as good to him as it does for her, so she presses more of her gift into him, just as he's doing with her. The heaviness of his power makes her breath catch, and excitement rockets through her system. Wetness floods out of her sex, and Eli's nostrils flare.

"You smell so damn good," he breathes. "Everything about you is much too perfect."

With their powers so entwined she can feel the truth of his words. His emotions are all flooding into her, enhancing her desires. It's becoming difficult to figure out where her sensations end and his begin.

When he lets go of her breasts she whimpers, but then he wraps powerful arms around her and stands up. Pivoting in place he gently lays her down on the lounger and tugs off her sturdy work boots. Then he practically rips her jeans off, making her gasp from the violence of his movements. His hands are shaking with need as he shucks off his pants, adding them to the growing pile of discarded clothing.

She gets a quick look at his erection as he kneels between her legs. The thing is a monster! Is it even going to fit? Then he runs a finger through the curls at the apex of her legs, and thinking isn't possible any longer.

Large fingers explore her sex, finding that little nub of nerves that aches to be touched. Sparks of power flow between them, crashing back and forth as he touches her. Moving her hips hard against his hand, she silently demands more. He doesn't comply. Opening her eyes to meet his gaze, she finds a devilish expression on his face as he teases her sensitive flesh.

Deciding two can play this game, she rears up and reaches for his engorged cock, but he grabs her wrist before she makes contact. A sound of protest comes out of her mouth, and she tugs at her trapped hand.

"Not yet," he whispers.

"But why?" she whines. "You're touching me!"

Without answering her, he ducks his head down and sucks her nipple into his mouth. His rigid cock presses against her leg while his other hand languidly explores her sex. His touch is still too light. Straining against him, she raises her hips to press against his shaft while trying to increase the pressure of his fingers.

Making a sound of pleasure deep in his throat, he bites down just enough to force a strangled scream of pleasure out of her. She never thought biting could be a turn-on, but Eli's proving her wrong about a lot of her prior notions about sex.

Letting her hips slam back down on the lounger, she sneaks her other hand between their bodies, wrapping her fingers around his erection. He hisses out a breath and freezes. Experimentally she runs her hand from root to tip, enjoying the long, hard, smooth texture of him.

"I need this inside me," she whispers.

"I need you to come first." His words start as a demand but end in a plea when she drags her hand lower to cup his heavy balls and gives a gentle tug. "Oh fuck. Do that again."

Laughing with delight, she does, and his eyes just about roll up into his head. His breathing is irregular, and she can feel his fast heartbeat throbbing in the thick veins of his cock as he rubs it against her leg. Letting go of his balls, she grasps his thick length and squeezes.

"Stop!" he cries out, and she jerks away, worried she hurt him. The moment she's no longer holding him, he uncoils. Grabbing her ankles, he practically throws them over his shoulders and dives his face between her legs.

"Oh no," she protests. "Don't do that!"

The one time a guy tried to go down on her she was so self-conscious she couldn't orgasm. Besides, she should shower first, or at least wash up with a cloth before he does anything there. Pressing her hands against this shoulder she tries to move him away. "Let me…" she starts to say but then his fingers are there, parting her labia to the cool night air. Before she can register the sensation, his mouth is on her, sucking and licking at that little bundle of nerves.

Pleasure explodes inside her. She doesn't have time to be self-conscious. She's too busy crying out as his mouth tortures her and his magic thrusts into her, letting her know very clearly that he's enjoying the taste and feel of her. He slips his fingers into her in a restrained demand, undoing her.

Normally her orgasms are slow to build and pleasant when they flow over her. There's no slow build here. This one nails her with a force she's never experienced before. It slams through her, forcing all the air from her lungs and the blood from her brain. Everything in her tenses as if jolted by electricity. She wants to scream. She wants to pull away. She wants to force his head down harder. She wants everything all at once.

If she could form words, she might be able to convey something, but her thinking brain is offline. She's all sensations right now. His mouth and fingers keep working on her until she lets out a pleading sob. "Stop." Only then does he look up. The proud smirk on his face makes her smile back.

Unfurling from between her legs, he kisses his way up her body. When he's in the perfect spot, she wraps her legs around his lean waist, pleased to find her limbs are still working.

"Your turn," she whispers and leans her head forward for a kiss. She can taste herself on him and decides she likes it.

"And your turn again."

Huffing out a laugh, she wants to argue with him that there's no way she can come again after that powerful orgasm. She might not be able to do anything for a while. The nerve endings in her body don't seem to want to fire correctly.

The broad head of his shaft nudges at the entrance to her sex. The look on his face is questioning, and she realizes he's asking for permission.

"Please." That's all he needs. He pushes inside her slowly, letting her adjust to his girth. The guy isn't small, but there's no pain and when he's fully inside, it's glorious. They both gasp at the sensation.

"You feel amazing," he murmurs, his voice strained.

"You too."

"I can't," he moans when she moves her hips a little. His pelvis is pushing against her sensitive clit in the most delicious way, but she wants more pressure. "Don't move or I can't control…" he begs, but she wiggles her hips and his control snaps. Thrusting into her, he sets a pace she'd normally find too harsh and bruising. But with him, it's perfect. Every time he pistons his length inside, he rubs her clit. When she tightens her legs around him, the pressure shifts just a little so part of his flesh rubs back and forth over her.

The orgasm she was sure couldn't happen hits her hard. Startled, she bows under him, clawing at his shoulders as he comes too. Gasping and shuddering, the power crashes back and forth between them, heightening their pleasure. She might have thought she'd had good sex before, but she was wrong. Earlier partners have nothing on Eli or this earth-shattering sex she just experienced.

"Good wooing," she chokes out between gasping breaths. Eli looks as wrecked as she is by the pleasure. When he snorts out a laugh, it makes their connected bodies move and causes her sensitive flesh to send a jolt of sensation through her. They both convulse and moan.

She should be worried about the fact that he didn't wear a condom. She should be concerned that she just slept with a guy after only knowing him a few days. But her brain refuses to rouse itself enough to be concerned. Some deep part of her knows Eli is the one for her. Something in him speaks to something in her. He's the right person at the right time.

"We can figure everything out tomorrow," she mumbles and lets her eyes drift shut. Her heartbeat is returning to normal, and all she wants to do is stay like this with Eli wrapped around her.

When he slides his softening cock free of her body, she makes a small protesting sound, but he doesn't leave her. Somehow, he manages to fit them both on the lounge chair, her body cradled tightly against his. She drifts to sleep, feeling warm, protected, and cared for.

CHAPTER 14

Eli succumbs to sleep not long after Steph, both he and his wolf content to be cuddling this wonderful woman. It's a novel experience for him. His wolf rarely lets him sleep with another person so close, and never if they're touching him. But, as with so many other things, his wolf is different around her. Within him, his beast gives a derisive snort and stays silent, letting Eli enjoy a dreamless sleep.

He wakes up to the sound of everyone returning. The night sky is bright with stars, and the waxing moon is just starting to rise in the sky. Even before Terror hits the backyard to patrol his favorite places, Grey is at his side, examining their figures by poking his nose at the blankets. He gives Eli's face a little lick and then settles down on the stones next to the lounge chair.

Not ready yet to talk to anyone, Eli remains still and listens to the other shifters talk as they move around the house. None of them come out to the backyard, and they leave the back door open so the dogs can come and go from the house at will.

Hours later his body starts protesting the way he's forced to twist so they can both fit on the lounger. He needs to at least move Steph to a bed, but he hates to part with her.

Can we sleep inside tonight? His wolf is quiet, and a thrill of shock goes through Eli. His wolf is never mute. Even when it doesn't use words, the beast is always flashing emotions or images at him. But it's doesn't do mute acceptance of anything. Ever.

Finally, the animal responds, languid and content. It sends pictures of Steph, face tense with passion as she orgasms.

Good mate. Stay with mate.

Did Steph screw his wolf into submission? The thought makes Eli smile. It appears his wolf has no issues sleeping inside for the night. With great care, he wraps Steph up in a blanket and picks her up. She murmurs something but doesn't come fully awake. She just snuggles against his chest with a soft smile. She appears just as content as his wolf.

Chris is in the living room, stretched out on the sofa and fiddling with his phone. When Eli walks in carrying Steph, the grizzly looks up and then back down at his phone, making sure not to make eye contact with Eli. Normally he'd want to growl at the bear shifter to cut out the deferential protocol, but right now he's just too content to bother with being annoyed.

He can hear the quiet voices of Ash and Troy filter through the guest room door as he maneuvers Steph through her bedroom door. Setting her down on the bed, he tucks her in. He wants nothing more than to snuggle down in that bed with her, but he doesn't want to dirty her sheets. His wolf protests when he steps out of the room.

I need to shower. Our mate will like it if I'm clean. The wolf grumbles but quiets down.

She comes half-awake as he turns to leave. "Join me," she murmurs sleepily.

"Shower, then I'll be back," he promises her. "Go back to sleep." He moves back to her side, gives her a slow kiss and a nuzzle on the cheek, and then stands back up. She's already fallen back to sleep with a satisfied smile on her face.

He hurries from the room, eager to get cleaned up and back in bed with Steph. The guest room door opens, and Troy emerges. That makes Eli's smile disappear and his wolf wakes up. His beast doesn't snarl or demand his body, but he's tense and ready in case Troy thinks to do anything more than talk. Eli's mostly sure Troy would never attack him, but after so much time with his father's violent tendencies, he's always on guard.

"Can we talk?" Troy asks. Eli wants to say no, but knowing Steph would want him to be civil, he manages to keep from growling. He just wants to shower and join Steph in bed, not have a heart-to-heart chat with an Ethiopian wolf. Sensing his mood, Troy glances over his shoulder and back to Eli. "Please? It's about Ash. She's my mate."

Those words make his wolf sit up with interest, his aggression retreating. Since Steph walked into their lives, his wolf is a lot more drawn to the concept of mates. Old memories of his mother and father have been floating into his head at odd times, brought forward by his wolf looking for examples on how to be a good mate to Steph.

Richard, his father, is a horrible example of a good mate, but Troy, with his steadfastness and honor, will make an excellent mate for Ash. Troy's parents were wonderful together and provided a good example for their son.

Thinking about Troy's father makes Eli wince. He likes Troy but hasn't talked to him in years. He grew up with the Ethiopian wolf, and when they were younger, they spent a lot of time running the forest together. That was before Richard killed Troy's father during a challenge. Too ashamed to face his friend, he retreated into the woods and has become angrier and more bitter over time.

When he saw Troy on the porch, his first thought was that this clan member was out for revenge. He couldn't challenge Richard, but he could hurt Eli through Steph. It never occurred to him that Troy would be there for any other reason than revenge. That's Richard's doing. The man taught Eli to look for hurtful motives behind all interactions. It's one of the reasons he retreated from his clan. He couldn't figure out who to trust. It drove him and his wolf crazy. It became easier to just forgo talking to anyone.

Now Eli's faced with the disconcerting realization that not only does Troy not want revenge, but he needs Eli's help. Everyone either wants his protection or his death. Except for Steph. The amazing person that is Steph wants nothing from him. If anything, she wants to give things to him—a home, food, comfort, her body.

His wolf grumbles at the delay in returning to Steph, but he knows she'd want him to talk to Troy. Ash is important to her. And Troy is important to Ash, so he ignores his wolf and focuses on Troy.

"Fine," Eli grunts out and all but stomps down the hall and into the backyard. If he's going to have an uncomfortable conversation, he's not going to do it trapped inside the house.

Grey pads outside with them, settling down at Eli's feet the moment he sits on the lounger. Troy paces a little but then flops down into a chair.

"I love Ash," he states. "I'd do anything for her. I'd die for her."

"The whole star-crossed-lovers thing didn't go well for Romeo or Juliet," Eli points out dryly. "Dying for her probably means she'll follow not long after."

"You don't think I know that? I don't want anything to happen to her. If things keep going as they are, I'm dead, and she's either dead or given to Glenn. You know what that bastard will do to her?" Troy's expression turns haunted. "I've heard stories. He had a girl for a couple of years, an Iberian wolf named Mandy. She tried to run once. He caught her and locked her away in his house. We don't know what he did to her, but no one saw her for months. When he did finally let people see her, she was just a shadow of herself. Ash says after that, the girl just gave up and stopped eating. Managed to starve herself to death. He did that to her, Eli! He tortured her so badly that she decided to die a slow, lingering death instead of staying with him. Ash is torn up about it, but she couldn't do anything. None of us can do anything. We're not powerful enough to challenge Clyde and no nearby clan will take a Lowell clan member in. As long as Clyde is clan leader, Glenn and the others can abuse and kill without repercussions."

"Not my problem," Eli says quietly. The moment the words are out of his mouth he feels like shit. Steph would never say anything like that. His mate would never abandon anyone in need. She's one to put herself right in the path of danger to help others.

"You're the only one who could help," Troy forges on, pretending Eli didn't say anything. "You're a maned wolf. You could easily beat Clyde in a challenge for clan leader." Troy punctuates his words with a finger jabbed in Eli's direction. "Lowell clan is sick, and Hunger Valley clan isn't much better.

Clyde needs to go, and you're the only one strong enough to challenge. Leave the Hunger Valley clan. Take over here. I'll follow you. Help run everything. It won't all be on you."

"I can't, and you know why," he states simply and watches Troy deflate. Frustration and anxiety roll off Troy who gets up to pace in front of Eli.

Troy knows better than anyone what Richard will do if Eli tries to leave the Hunger Valley clan. Eli might not have any friends in the clan, but that doesn't mean he wants to see anyone hurt because of him. Richard thinks nothing of killing off the entire family of anyone who dares challenge him. Tired of being challenged, Richard started a policy where he executed the family of anyone who lost a challenge to him. That meant a challenger didn't just risk his or her own life but also those of their close family. The new policy made the challenges all but disappear.

That's the reason Eli left Hunger Valley territory. His father won a challenge and decided Eli needed to start acting as his second. It was Eli's job to kill the family of the last challenger who lost to Richard. Eli ran instead.

He always believed his father tried to do right by the clan, but how could anyone kill the innocent? Damien's wife and kid didn't do anything wrong. Hell, the kid is only eight. Out of all the measures Richard takes to keep his clan safe and in line, Eli rejects this one he most. A family shouldn't have to pay for a lost challenge. It should only be between the men in the challenge circle. But not only is Richard unwilling to relent, he has repeatedly called Eli weak and a coward for not following commands.

The wife and the child might die, but Eli won't be the one doing it.

"I'm sorry, Troy. If I go against Richard like that, if I try to take over a neighboring clan, he'll do something to stop it. Something…" He doesn't need to end that sentence. Richard's reputation is well-known to them both. He sees utter defeat on Troy's face. He knows the expression well since he sees it in the mirror often.

"Fuck," Troy mutters as he drops down to sit on the edge of the firepit, burying his face in his hands. Even though he's nowhere near as sensitive as Steph, he can feel the abject fear and desperation rolling off Troy. "We don't have any choice. We're going to have to run, Ash and me. We're going to have to run and try to survive, just the two of us."

Both he and Troy know the couple will be dead within the year if they try to do that. Clyde won't let that kind of insult stand, and no other clan will give them protection.

Grey whines and Eli looks down at the usually quiet pit bull. Big soft eyes look up at him, reminding him that more is at stake than Ash and Troy. Chris is in danger too.

And Steph.

She might be human but that won't keep her safe from Clyde. Richard might be willing to leave her alone, but Clyde would see her defiance as a personal affront. Only one thing will keep Steph safe.

The repercussions are going to be horrific, but Steph is worth it.

"I'll challenge and kill Clyde." His sudden declaration after the earlier refusal makes Troy jerk with surprise. It takes the Ethiopian wolf a moment to comprehend what Eli's saying, but then a tentative smile forms on his face.

"When you take over as clan leader for Lowell—"

"No."

"No?"

"I won't be clan leader." Eli just manages to swallow down a snarl. "I can't be a clan leader. My wolf," he stops talking because if anyone knows how out of control his animal is, it's Troy. "Besides, like I said, Richard won't stand for me to take over. It'll have to be someone else."

Crestfallen, Troy shakes his head. "It won't work if you don't take over. Too many powerful and twisted people are under Clyde. He gathered them when he took over. They're his enforcers and guardians." Troy gives a mocking laugh. "Guardians. Sorry excuse for protectors. It's good this territory doesn't have a rogue vampire problem because those guys would probably turn tail and run if faced with anything worse than a scared clan member."

Dropping his face back down into his hands, Troy makes a sound halfway between a snarl and a whine. "If you don't take over as clan leader, Ash and I are still doomed."

Looking up, he narrows his eyes at Eli. "And your precious Steph will still be in danger."

Without thinking about it, Eli stands up and grabs Troy by the throat in one fluid motion. Troy grabs Eli's wrist to try and relieve the pressure on his throat, but otherwise he doesn't fight the hold.

"You know it's true," Troy wheezes out, just barely able to breathe past Eli's grip on his throat. "If you don't take over as clan leader, she's dead. Either kill Clyde and take over, or he kills her. Or maybe the next fucked up clan leader kills her. Either way, she's dead."

"We'll leave," Eli declares, dropping Troy back to his feet. Troy takes a few gasping breaths before talking.

"Good luck," Troy retorts. "To get her to leave her job and her house, you'll have to tell her about us. About the clans and everything. And from what I know so far, she's not the kind of woman who's going to walk away from our troubles. They might not be her problems, but no way will she let others suffer if she can do something about it." Troy jerks his arm out to encompass Steph's little house. "Look at what's going on here! She hasn't turned a single one of us away. Not you. Not Ash. Not Chris. And not me. This house is so full of shifters it might as well be a gathering house, but it's not owned by the clan. It's owned by a single human female who's got more heart than brains."

"Shut up," Eli growls, but it's a half-hearted protest. He knows Troy is right. He's starting to wonder how Steph didn't run afoul of Clyde and his cronies sooner. The woman is an absolute danger to herself.

He longs for his little cabin. If he thought he could get away with it, he'd kidnap her and isolate them both. He can't imagine anything much better than having Steph's undivided attention without the distraction of so many clan members trooping into her life. Or her job potentially taking her into dangerous clan territory if she's called to tow a car outside of the neutral areas between clans.

The feeling of a new shifter's presence approaching the house makes Eli tense and freeze. His wolf snarls inside of him and claws to get loose. Troy goes still also and turns to face the direction of the new arrival, taking a deep breath in through his nose. His eyes go wide, and he glances over at Eli. "Uh, shit, I think we might have another guest."

Feeling much too aggressive to bother decoding Troy's words, Eli bounds around the house and through the gate, bursting into the front yard just as a hulking figure is about to take a step onto the porch. The figure starts to turn, but Eli is on him. He doesn't bother checking his momentum as he hurdles the porch railing and barrels into the big guy, knocking him to the ground with a flying tackle. The man goes down face first into the grass with a cry of surprise. The smell of polar bear fills his nose as the shifter under him roars and starts shifting. His wolf clambers to get loose, overjoyed at the chance for a real fight.

"Eli, *no!*" Troy yells and grabs him by the neck, trying to drag him off the intruder. Eli pushes his power at the smaller Ethiopian wolf. With a cry of pain, Troy lets go and backs away as if he's been burned.

"It's Mason!" he shouts out. "Eli, that's Mason!" Troy's words penetrate Eli's aggression, making him realize he's about to hurt one of his own clan members.

The porch lights come on, and Ash runs out the front door and into Troy's arms as Steph stumbles after her, taking in the scene on her lawn with eyes still dazed from sleep. She's naked with a blanket wrapped around her. He watches her try to understand what she's seeing.

Rubbing a hand over her face she regards Eli and then the man under him. "Do I even want to know what's going on? Is it too much to ask that a girl can have a little uninterrupted shut-eye after the most amazing sex of her life?"

Her words make everyone stop moving. Ash laughs, and Troy hides his smiling face in her hair. Chris, who's filling the doorway, snorts. And Eli looks at her with interest.

"Amazing?"

Shooting him an incredulous look, she cocks a hip. If she didn't have to hold the blanket around her, she'd probably put her hands on her hips as well. "You're sitting on some poor guy, grinding his face into the dirt, and that's what you focus on?"

Sitting up, he shrugs his shoulders. "Yes."

"Get off me, you mangy wolf," Mason grumbles, his voice deep and distorted as he keeps his bear from erupting out of his skin. Feeling guilty, Eli pulls himself off the polar bear and steps away.

With a snarl, Mason rolls onto his back and glares up. Eli offers the polar bear a hand to help him to his feet, but Mason ignores it in favor of staying on the ground and continuing to glare.

"Some thank you," he grounds out. "I go help your girlfriend and guess what happens? Richard finds out and threatens to challenge me. What the fuck do I do, Eli? This is your fault, and you need to fix it."

"Mason?" Steph calls out as she steps closer. "What are you doing here? Who's Richard?"

The sigh that comes out of Eli is so loud everyone around him flinches except for Steph. She just fires up her strange power and sweeps it over everyone, soothing and calming them. Mason stops glowering and gets to his feet, eyeing Steph with new interest.

"That's handy," he murmurs. And new. Eli's not sure she's been able to affect so many all at once without touching anyone before. Either she's been holding back or she's getting stronger. By the stunned look on her face, this increased power is a surprise to his little human as much as it is to the rest of them.

We did that, his wolf crows.

Shut up.

The wolf pouts. *But we did. And when we form a Heartmate tie with her, all of us will get stronger.*

"She does that a lot," Chris tells Mason. "Although not usually so strong. It's great, though."

Uncomfortable with this discussion, Steph takes a step toward Mason. "Are you in danger too, Mason? Are you in their gang? Do you need a safe place to stay?"

Shifting his gaze back and forth between Steph and Eli, as if he's not sure which one of them he needs to get permission from, he nods. "I need a place to stay."

"It's going to be okay," she promises him and another wave of comforting power washes through all of them. A strange look crosses her face, but is gone quickly. "Unfortunately, I don't have a couch or bed to offer you."

"Do you still have that air mattress we used when friends stayed over at the old apartment?" Ash asks, and Steph looks over to her small garage.

"I'm pretty sure I do." She takes in Mason's size. "It might work, just barely. You might need to sleep diagonally though. We could push the couch back and move the coffee table to the garage. It's going to be a little crowded, but we can make this work." Then she gives everyone a hard look. "I get dibs on the bathroom first thing in the morning," she declares. Then without another word, she turns and sweeps back into the house.

"Did she just accept another house guest?" Troy asks as he and Ash take a step closer to Eli. "It's almost like she's acting like a clan leader herself. A real one. The kind that cares about the people under them."

"Too bad she isn't a shifter," Ash murmurs wistfully. "You know, I've heard that really powerful witches can turn someone into a shifter. Maybe we could—"

"Don't," Eli growls, and Ash squeaks a little at the aggressive power he pushes at her.

"I was just thinking out loud. I'd never do anything without talking to Steph about it," she says quickly, taking shelter behind Troy.

The Ethiopian wolf glares at Eli. "Stop it. Ash didn't do anything wrong and you're being an asshole."

Knowing Troy is right, Eli reins in his temper and looks over to Mason. "He threatened you because I asked you to work for Larson Towing? It's not even in Lowell territory. There's no conflict."

"He found out about Steph," Mason warns him. "He knows you're attached to her. He has no idea what she can do, though." Eli can tell Mason is impressed by Steph's power. But then again, who wouldn't be. Humans just don't have that kind of ability. "But he knows she's human. He's angry, Eli. You know Damien's wife and kid are still alive. He's waiting for you to come back and do your duty. He officially made you his second at the last clan gathering. Now everyone's whispering that you might change things. He won't stand for you to refuse him much longer, not if he thinks it makes him seem weak."

Looking to the northeast toward Hunger Valley territory, Eli lets a frustrated growl rumble out of his chest. Although he knew it was inevitable that Richard, the Hunger Valley clan leader, would find out where he was, he'd hoped it would take longer. Eli feels a strong sense of dread fill him. Everything is going to come tumbling down around him sooner rather than later.

Probably reacting to the frustrated energy coming off him, Ash makes a small, distressed sound.

"Easy, baby, it's okay," Troy coos to her, pulling her into his arms and holding her tightly to him. "Everything's going to be okay now."

"I doubt it," Eli mutters. The others cast him dark looks, but no one disagrees with him.

CHAPTER

15

The door to Steph's office faces the main lobby area and is almost always kept open. Because they don't have a receptionist, she needs to be able to see if anyone comes in. However, if she's distracted it's common for her to not even notice anyone has entered until they're standing right over her desk.

And that's exactly what happens when she looks up to find a stranger looming over her, silent and scowling. A jolt of fear goes through her. She pushes her chair back and stands to give herself a little more room between them.

"I didn't hear you come in."

"Obviously."

He doesn't say anything else, just keeps glowering at her. Tentatively she reaches out with her gift only to feel a power very similar to Eli's push against her. Anxiety skitters through her, and she involuntarily takes another step back, coming up hard against the wall behind her.

The man doesn't move, but his intense eyes follow her with the same glowing color as Eli's. That's not the only thing that's similar to Eli. This stranger's hair might have gray in it, but the color interspersed with the gray is the same as her lover's, and they share the same nose. This man is too old to be a sibling, so the only conclusion is this man must be Eli's father.

And he doesn't appear happy at all.

"What do you think you're doing?" His voice is all aggression and disapproval.

Giving him an experimental smile, she tries a little humor. "Right now, I was entering invoices in the billing program. If you mean in a wider context, I'm just trying to live a good life."

With one powerful, violent sweep of his arm, he sends everything on her desk crashing into a nearby wall. The computer monitor makes a particularly gruesome sound when it hits. That's going to leave a mark.

With a growl very similar to Eli's, he leans forward, placing his hands on the desk.

"You will never be welcome in my clan," he grounds out and she's not sure, but it seems like his canines are abnormally long. "Getting control of my son will get you nothing but pain and death."

She really should just stay quiet. It's the wisest course, but Steph can't help herself.

"Intimidation, check. Destruction of property, check. Threat of injury and death, check," she pretends to check things off an imaginary notepad as she talks. "Looks like you hit all the highlights for being an abusive asshole. Congratulations. We'll mail you the trophy."

His muscles start to bunch, and she's pretty sure he's about to leap over the desk to get to her when a snort of laughter makes the enraged man turn around with a snarl. Realizing her big mouth was about to get her hurt, Steph feels all kinds of relief to see Eli standing in the office doorway, arms crossed over his chest, regarding the man between them with a cold smile.

"What are you doing here, Richard?"

Is this the man who kicked Mason out? One of the gang leaders? And he's Eli's father! No wonder Eli's so dark and angry all the time. This guy screams child abuser. Poor Eli.

"I don't know what you think you're doing, playing house with her, but it ends now."

Eli saunters into the room. As he moves forward, his father steps aside until the two men are facing each other in front of her desk. "You don't have that kind of authority over me."

The rage coming off of Richard is so strong Steph can feel it pressing against her skin. "I'm your fucking clan leader. I have all the authority over you. You'll do what I tell you to do!" That last sentence is delivered with a roar. Eli doesn't flinch or change facial expressions, but she can feel him bracing himself for something.

"I'm going to join another clan," Eli pronounces softly. An immense sense of purpose is attached to those words. Eli is determined to go against his father, and it's a sure bet no quarter will be given from the irate Richard.

"Let me guess. You're going to take over the Lowell clan. What are you going to do with her while you lead that group of degenerates?" Richard scoffs. "You aren't willing to do what it takes to keep control of a clan. You don't have the stomach to do the kind of things that will keep this cow from being eaten by the rest of the clan." Without looking, he points at her. She never thought someone could point violently, but Richard has a knack for it. He's probably talented at doing everything violently.

Can someone violently brush their teeth?

"Really?" Steph turns her attention to Eli who's regarding her with a quizzical expression, and she realizes he's picking up her thoughts because she's stopped shielding from him. Since the mind-blowing sex the night before, she's felt him in her head like a warm presence. Sometimes she'll catch feelings or images from him. The reverse must be true, and he's catching some of her random thoughts.

She gives a little helpless shrug. "Sorry. My mind goes to strange places sometimes."

Their little banter doesn't make Richard particularly happy.

"You will obey me!" Fury fills the room, so strong it makes Steph choke a little. In a knee-jerk reaction, she lets loose with her power. She not only shields herself from the stifling effects of Richard's violent energy, but she also thrusts power at him, forcing his anger back while pouring calm into him.

That's another thing that's happened since last night. Her gift seems to have gotten inordinately stronger. Instead of being a soft energy ready to be gently deployed, it now feels like a powerful current inside of her, eager to be unleashed. Before now, using her gift required focus to work, but now she needs to concentrate to keep it from deploying without her consent.

As her gift hits him full force, Richard jerks like a live wire touched him and staggers back half a step. After he straightens back up, he regards her with interest, like she's a dog that just did an unexpected trick. "That explains a lot."

"No," Eli cuts in, stepping between Richard and her, forcing the older man to take several steps toward the door.

"I understand now," Richard murmurs, a cold calculation on his face. "You're cleverer than I gave you credit for, son. I haven't felt that kind of power in a long time. What an unexpected weapon."

"She's not a weapon," Eli grounds out, taking another menacing step. Richard holds up both hands with a smile on his face. A moment ago, he was so angry his rage could peel paint, but now he's smiling. Steph knows her gift didn't cause it. At least it's not because she used her gift to make him feel happiness. He's smiling because he's decided she's valuable now.

"Not a weapon yet, but there's so much potential. We'll speak on this later. I'm going to see if I can contact an oracle over this. Don't concern yourself with Damien's family. That's of little importance now. Concentrate on keeping her. Don't leave her side, and don't let Clyde anywhere near her. Don't do anything until you hear from me." He turns his attention to her, his smile changing to a sneer. "Obey my son or everything will go very badly for you." Before she can react to his threat, he's gone, striding casually out of her office as if he didn't just threaten to kill her.

Charming.

"Are you okay?" Eli asks, coming around her desk and crushing her in a hug. She doesn't complain, just wraps her arms around him to return the embrace.

"That was unpleasant," she mutters and feels Eli huff out a laugh against her neck.

"Understatement."

"I'm sorry."

"Why are you apologizing? It's my fault he's here."

"Because no kid deserves that as a father," she states firmly with a little shudder.

"You have no idea," he agrees fervently. "Is it time to go home yet?"

Glancing over at the clock, she nods. "If any day calls for closing ten minutes early, it's today. I could use a drink. And Ash promised margaritas."

Ash's margaritas are potent. Evidence of that is the gently snoring Steph in his arms. After dinner, they all settled in the backyard around the firepit with a big pitcher of margaritas. Eli and Troy stuck to beer, but the bears like the sweet concoction as much as Ash and Steph.

One thing becomes obvious quickly, humans—or at least Steph—are more susceptible to the effects of alcohol than shifters.

"She's out," Ash declares with a giggle, snuggling into Troy's arms. "I remember once we had a party, and Steph fell asleep right in the middle of it. I sometimes forget how easy it is to get humans drunk."

With a grunt, Eli shifts so her head is resting on his shoulder. She makes a small sound and curls one of her hands into his shirt, nuzzling his neck with her face. The move sends a zing of pleasure through him. His wolf sighs with contentment.

Finishing off the rest of his drink, Mason holds the empty glass out to Chris. The grizzly obligingly refills Mason's glass from the pitcher. Sipping his sweet drink, Mason looks around thoughtfully. "Steph needs a bigger house."

"Or fewer guests," Eli counters with a growl. To his surprise, no one flinches or even looks uneasy at his growl, instead they grin at him. He casts a questioning glance at Troy, but Ash explains.

"Hard to be scared of the big, bad maned wolf when he's cuddling one of nicest, sweetest people I know. Steph would never let you kick any of us out."

"I never thought I'd see you and your wolf getting along so well," Troy murmurs. "I was sure the two of you would rip at each other until Richard had to put you down."

"What do you mean?" Chris asks, pouring the last of the pitcher into his glass and looking disappointed when the glass ends up only half full.

"Do you have to talk to your bear?" Troy asks Chris, who looks flummoxed.

"Talk to my bear? I don't understand."

"Let's say you want to stay human, but the bear inside you is pushing you to change. Do you have to talk to your bear and ask it to calm down?"

"That never happens." Chris shoots Eli a thoughtful look. "My bear and I are the same. His instincts and my instincts mesh. Is it different for maned wolves?"

"Not for maned wolves, just me," Eli grunts out.

"Eli has to negotiate with his wolf all the time," Troy explains.

"I fight with the fucker," Eli corrects, making Troy laugh.

"Right, you fight with your wolf. The two of you rip at each other until one of you gives in. It happens sometimes to the very powerful shifters. Their animal is almost like a second personality inside of them."

"That has to be horrible." Ash gives him a sympathetic look. "No wonder you're so grouchy."

"I'm pretty sure having Richard as a father is enough to put anyone in a permanently bad mood," Mason points out.

"Richard showed up today," Eli tells them. "At Steph's work."

Mason jerks at the news. "I swear I didn't tell him you were there."

"I know you didn't."

Breathing out a sigh of relief, Mason swallows down more of his cocktail. "But how did he know you were there?"

"He was there for Steph, not me."

"That's not good," Troy mutters. "Did he…"

"He felt her power," Eli confirms, making all the faces around him go from surprised to anxious.

"At least that means he won't want to kill her," Mason says. "She's much too powerful to get rid of. Right?"

"Trust me, you don't want to be considered useful to Richard," Troy answers. "It's better to be inconsequential and ignored. It's almost as bad to be considered useful as it is to be perceived as a threat."

The maned wolf inside Eli suddenly sits up and takes notice of something out in the woods beyond the neighborhood. Eli lets the conversation flow around him as he stretches out his power to try and figure out what got his attention. When he homes in on what his wolf sensed, he curses silently to himself.

Abruptly standing up, he passes the sleeping Steph to Mason. Surprised and alarmed, Mason awkwardly accepts the small human. "I'll be back. All of you stay here." He points at Mason. "You hold her and keep her safe. But no extra touching."

"Never," Mason agrees quickly as he arranges Steph in his arms. She stirs, mumbles something with a little frown, and then goes right back to sleep.

"Eli what—" Troy starts to ask, but Eli's not listening anymore as he strips and shifts. Chris and Ash gasp at the sight of his shifted form. Before they can utter a word about his wolf, he's already cleared the six-foot fence without issue and is covering ground with a long loping stride.

He finds his father waiting for him in a small clearing. The tree canopy makes the woods dark, but his wolf eyes easily pick out the familiar figure, leaning against a tree and staring off into the forest.

Richard doesn't look at him when he steps into the clearing. "Took you long enough."

Shifting, Eli regards the man with glowing eyes just like his own. "Go away."

With a laugh devoid of humor, Richard finally turns to face him. "That's not an option, son. But I have to admit, I'm downright proud of you. I talked to the oracle in South Dakota, the one that lives in Sioux Falls. Your human is powerful. Very powerful. The oracle said she can be Heartmated by one of us.

That means you could control her. With her power on top of your wolf, no one could stand against you."

In the past, when power was far more important than love or equality, only one partner Heartmated to the other, making that person vulnerable and subservient. Except for people like Richard, couples now form Heartmate ties to each other, so power is shared and neither has an unfair advantage.

The idea of having a single-sided Heartmate tie with Steph turns his stomach. It would effectively enslave her, making her nothing more than a puppet he could control.

"She's mine," he grounds out. His wolf is howling to be let out. To battle Richard for supremacy. To eliminate any threat to Steph.

"I'm not arguing that," Richard states coldly. "But you need to get moving and Heartmate her soon. If not, I'll take her, or maybe give her to one of the guardians. But make no mistake, she's joining our clan. She's too valuable to be left on the table for anyone to snatch up. I don't know what she is. The oracle didn't know either. But power is power."

With a roar, he moves to attack Richard when a dozen dark figures emerge from the woods.

"You want to challenge me, boy?" his father asks, drawing himself tall. "You want to be clan leader of Hungry Valley clan?"

Shuddering from the effort, Eli banks his power. The last thing he wants to be is anyone's clan leader. He's already going to need to challenge and kill Clyde and then figure out what to do with Lowell clan. Adding Hunger Valley clan to his burden is incomprehensible.

Besides, challenging Richard is a foolish idea. He might be decades older than Eli, but he has the power of the clan ties to pull from during a challenge. Even though clan leaders aren't supposed to pull power from the clan ties, everyone knows they do it anyway.

Eli is strong, but he might not be strong enough to defeat Richard. Clyde with his weak clan ties shouldn't be a difficult challenge. Richard, with his level of power and his penchant for finding an opponent's weakness, is a hard man to kill. Of course, sneaking up and killing the old wolf in a surprise attack is out of the question. He never travels without his entourage of enforcers and guardians. Paranoid wolf.

No, he's not paranoid because everyone does want him dead—even his own son.

"I didn't think so," his father drawls, taking Eli's reluctance to issue a challenge as cowardice.

"Now Heartmate the bitch and get your asses back into my territory. Seeing as you have your emotions all twined up in her, I'll give you a few days to make it nice. But get it done or I'll send my boys to collect her, and I won't be nice about it."

With those words, Richard turns his back on Eli and strides off into the dark woods. The enforcers and guardians fall in step behind him.

Couldn't we kill just one of them? Eli's wolf whines. Watching all the men disappear into the darkness, Eli realizes that in the end, he's going to need to kill a lot of people to keep Steph safe.

Don't worry. We'll probably be killing someone very soon, he tells his wolf. *We can only hope Steph won't hold it against us.*

CHAPTER 16

Kiss her.

For perhaps the hundredth time that day, Eli snarls silently at his wolf. *Shut up.*

Touch her. She's so close. Just touch her. His wolf is whining now. The beast started the day demanding and then cajoling; now he's whining.

She doesn't like it when we distract her at work. That manages to make his wolf back off for a bit. As much as both he and his wolf need Steph's touch, he doesn't want to upset their mate either. They're sitting in one of the chairs in the reception area of her work, staring out the window and wishing the day was over. Impatient, his wolf started getting louder about twenty minutes ago and now is being incessant.

As if sensing his rising discomfort, Steph is suddenly there, standing in front of him. It's notable that his wolf has him so distracted he didn't notice her get up and walk to him. She hugs his head to her chest and runs her fingers through his hair. He's not sure what he likes better, the feel of her nails on his scalp or having his face nuzzled between her perfect breasts.

"We're almost done here," she soothes him. His wolf quiets inside of him as Steph's scent fills his nose. "Do you think you can last another forty minutes?"

Fighting the urge to grab her and drag her into his lap he nods his head. "I'm hungry too."

"You're always hungry," Steph counters, stepping away from him. The loss of her touch hurts, and his wolf whines again.

"Shut up."

"What?" Steph starts at his snarl, and he feels his face get hot.

"Sorry, that wasn't at you. It was… me. I'll just take a quick walk around the building." Feeling embarrassed and more out of control than a teenager, he leaves the office and strides to the back of the building. A nice area has a little grass and a large tree to provide shade. Ignoring the bench, he opts to plop down on the grass instead. Falling back with a frustrated sigh, he concentrates on the sensation of cool damp grass on the bare flesh of his back.

It doesn't help. Agitated, he stands back up and starts pacing along the back fence of the property. He's not sure why, but his wolf is unsettled. It started the moment he woke up this morning, forcing him out of the house and into the woods. Shifting, he ran until dawn broke and he felt calm enough to return to Steph.

She was just getting up when he came into the house, naked, starving, and horny at the sight of her in a small bathrobe. The horniness changed to aggression when Mason stumbled in begging for coffee and gently knocked into Steph. Ready to rip his head off, he snared, startling both Mason and Steph. With a frown, she banished him from the kitchen, ordering him to shower and cool off.

The aggression calmed with a cold shower but didn't go away. Seeking out danger with his magic got him nothing. All he can feel is Steph in the office and Chris in the front of the yard cleaning off one of the trucks. Maybe he's just reacting to his father's threat from yesterday. Richard's words have been weighing heavily in his mind.

He needs to sit Steph down and tell her everything. Talk her into Heartmating him. Talk her into accepting him despite his fucked-up family, the clan, and the violence. He needs to figure out how to keep Steph safe and help Ash and Troy. No matter what, he's going to need to kill Clyde.

That part worries him the most. Not the challenge. There's no way that Clyde stands a chance of winning a formal challenge. But what happens when she sees him kill? He might be able to keep the challenge from her, but at some point she's going to see him kill someone. Especially if they end up becoming Richard's second.

Can she handle that part of him, or will she walk away? The thought of her walking away makes his heart beat wildly as fear grips him.

We make her stay with us. Make her accept us. His wolf is resolute.

We can't make *her do anything. She would be miserable.*

The wolf goes back to whining. *Want her.*

That's an understatement. They don't just want her; they need her. Without Steph, his skin always felt too tight, the world felt too loud and intrusive, and his control over his wolf tenuous. With Steph the wolf is calmer, it negotiates with him, and the world feels muted and manageable.

Peaceful. That's what she does for him. She makes him feel peaceful. The word didn't occur to him immediately because the last time he felt it was back when he was too young for his father to bother "training" him. His mother made his life peaceful. Until she died, she sheltered him from the worst of Richard. After her death, his father's aggression toward his vulnerable son went unchecked.

Well, he isn't vulnerable any longer. He's become so much stronger and more stable with Steph. Maybe, after Heartmating, he could challenge Richard and win. Then he could open up Hunger Valley clan and accept Lowell refugees.

"Eli?" Steph's soft voice calls out to him from the front area.

Practically running, he sprints to the front of the building. Steph is standing there with her purse and a big smile. "There you are. Ready to head home?"

"More than ready," he grumbles and grabs her up in a hug.

Laughing, she kicks her dangling feet a little and then pats him on the shoulder. "Put me down and let's get going. You're hungry. Remember?"

Keeping her held tightly to his chest, he starts walking. He doesn't set her down until they're right next to the car. Face flushed and eyes sparkling she playfully shoves him away from her.

"Well, that's one way to sweep a girl off her feet. Now get in before I leave you here and you're forced to hitchhike home."

Stopping just outside the yard, she puts the car in park and gets out. She's the last to leave so it's her job to lock the heavy wrought iron gate behind them. Hopping back into the car, she steers it in the opposite direction of home. One questioning look from him makes her grin and explain. "I don't feel like cooking and we have so many people to feed right now. Sometime soon we're all going to need to figure out some kind of grocery and cooking schedule. But for now, I ordered Italian for everyone because I feel like having pasta tonight. I didn't ask because so far you eat everything."

Grunting, Eli casts her a sidelong glance. "True. I'm not a picky eater." He's even swallowed down the occasional field mouse when he's been out in the woods for days on end.

"And that's one of the things I love about you."

Love.

A spike of awareness goes through him, working with the agitation he's been fighting all day. Does she mean that, or is she just using it as a figure of speech? It's probably not real, and he's reading too much into it.

She means it.

Shut up! His wolf doesn't say anything else, but it does hum with pleasure inside of him. His wolf has no doubt that if she doesn't love them now, she will very soon. The human part of Eli isn't so confident.

Delicious smells emanate from the bags of takeout in the back seat of Steph's car, making Eli's mouth water and his stomach growl. He's so eager to dig into the food, he doesn't pay much attention to the strange SUV parked in front of

Steph's house until he's out of the car and heading up the drive holding several bags.

The smell of unfamiliar bears hits him. Turning to face the SUV, he watches as three grizzly bear shifters get out. He doesn't recognize them, so they must belong to Clyde. Ignoring Eli they walk to the house. Curious, he sends a small tendril of magic at them. In unison, they all stop walking and look at him. The three of them have similar facial features, probably brothers or cousins.

One of the grizzlies smirks at Eli. "We're just here to collect a wayward clan member. None of this is a concern of yours."

"Who are you people?" Steph tries to walk past him to confront the grizzlies, but Eli easily steps in her way so she bumps into his back instead. With speed, he sets the food down out of the way and turns to her.

"Don't go near them," he warns her. "I mean it. Don't get close to any of them no matter what happens."

"Yeah, do what your little doggie tells you to do," one of the grizzly taunts. All three bears laugh and start walking to the house again. A little gasp makes him look up to the porch. Ash is standing there, pale and gripping the porch railing with white-knuckled hands.

"No," she whispers, staring at the grizzlies with a horrified expression.

"Yes," the first one says, his eyes gleaming with malice. "Been out all over looking for you. Clyde's going to be pleased when we come back with you in tow."

Taking a stumbling step back, Ash wraps her arms around her waist and shakes her head violently. "No, please no."

"You knew you couldn't hide forever. Now get down here. Right now!" The last words are loud enough to make both Ash and Steph jump. Eli's merely irked by the bear's drama.

"No, no, no." Ash is crying now. Her head hangs low as fat tears fall down her face and her body shakes from fear. Then Troy is there, pulling her against his chest and wrapping her in his arms. He's murmuring to her and glaring at the bears. The scent of a terrified coyote and an enraged Ethiopian wolf fills the air.

"Let go of her," the lead bear commands Troy. "Ashley, get your ass down here."

"She's mine now," Eli tells the bear, pushing Steph toward the house as he talks. "Go inside," he tells her. "I need to deal with this."

"I can't leave you out here to face them down alone." She tosses her purse aside. In one hand she has her can of pepper spray and in the other her clever little folding baton. Pride swells his chest right alongside concern for her safety.

"Mason!" Eli bellows, making the grizzlies jump and growl. Eli gives them an evil grin as the polar bear emerges from around the backyard gate and hurries over. He's eyeing the grizzlies with interest but not fear. Shifted, Mason outweighs a grizzly, and among bears, size matters.

The grizzlies don't back down as Mason approaches, probably sure they still have the advantage because of their numbers. The dumb bears are dismissing Eli as a threat. What was it one of the clan elders used to say? That's right, stupidity should be painful. He can't wait to make some idiot bears feel the pain.

When he hands Steph to Mason, she struggles to get out of the bear's hold. "Be gentle with her," he warns Mason.

The polar bear gives a derisive snort. "Tell her to be gentle with me."

Ignoring Steph's protests, Eli turns to the three bears. He points to Steph and Mason. "Mine." He points to Ash and Troy on the porch. "Also mine. Now, go away."

"You can keep the hu… that one, but Ashley needs to come back with us. Her Romeo can stay. And we don't care about those other two either. Glenn is fond of her, though, so she's coming back with us. Don't make us hurt you." The look on the bear's face clearly says he's looking forward to a fight despite his words.

"Fine," Eli says and points to the gate. "Backyard."

In unison, the three bears look at the gate, up at Ash on the porch, and back to Eli. He crosses his arms over his chest. "Either out here or back there. Your choice."

One of the first things drilled into shifters is to keep their existence a secret. The group of them might be able to maintain human form and fight in her front yard, but there's a risk they'll get carried away and shift. Shifting out in the open in broad daylight with humans watching is about as taboo as a shifter can get. Even Clyde with his disgusting behavior as clan leader wouldn't approve of a shifter fight out in the open.

Two of the grizzlies look to the third for instruction. He nods his head. "Sure, we can settle this in the backyard." Pointing at Ash, he growls out. "After this is done, no trying to run or struggle. You're going to be a good girl. Right?"

Finding the grizzly's voice grating, Eli hits him with a shock of power, making the man stumble and his eyes go wide. "Less talking, more walking."

Some of the bears' cockiness dissipates as they eye Eli with more caution. No one speaks as they file into the backyard. Mason sets Steph down, and Eli hears him tell her that she needs to keep out of it or she could end up distracting Eli and getting him hurt. She's grumbling but no longer trying to get to the grizzlies.

Eli faces off with the bears on the large bare patch of backyard that he plans to turn into a nice herb garden for Steph. Troy and Ash come through the back door and join Mason and Steph behind him.

Looking over his shoulder at Steph, Eli sends a little tendril of magic at her. He can feel her in his mind. She's worried for him and scared but ready to jump in and help. If he let her, she'd try and take down one of the grizzlies with her little weapons. He needs to teach her how to effectively use her power as a weapon. So far all she's been able to do is cause discomfort and mild pain. But if she practiced, she could incapacitate a shifter. The skill could keep her alive.

But now isn't the time to have that conversation with her. Now he needs to pay attention to the bears.

He's going to have to shift. She's going to see everything and might run screaming. Fuck.

I love you. Desperation makes him honest. He doesn't expect a reply but gets one anyway.

I love you too, idiot. Her warm love fills his chest, making his breath catch.

Lucky idiot.

He feels her give a mental huff. *My idiot.*

Everything I am is yours. But you need to stay out of this. No matter what happens, stay clear. I need you to be safe. And I need you to know I'd never hurt you.

I already know that. And as long as you're safe, I'll stay safe is all she promises. He can't believe how well they can communicate. He's never heard of any shifters being able to talk like this, let alone a human and a shifter. Just more evidence of Steph's uniqueness.

Carefully, taking in the three grizzlies in front of him, the surrounding backyard, and the distance between him and the house, he shucks out of his pants and calls his wolf as Mason steps forward.

"I've got your back," he murmurs and he pulls off his shirt, preparing to shift.

That's when one of the grizzlies pulls out a gun and squeezes the trigger.

CHAPTER 17

Eli's wolf is paying much closer attention to the grizzlies than his human side because the moment the lead bear pulls out a big handgun, the wolf sends him into motion. Knowing this isn't the time to fight his wolf, Eli lets the animal take his body. Shifting changes his shape so the bullet wings him, taking hair and dermis, but not doing any real damage.

A flash of white shoots by him as he lands against the bear with the gun. Mason must have shifted and taken on one of the other grizzlies.

Because he's got the gun, the grizzly under him doesn't try to shift. Grunting with the effort, he fights Eli's wolf, trying to turn his hand so the muzzle of the gun will point at Eli's head. Reaching out with his power, Eli binds the man's hand, rendering the gun useless. Realizing the weapon is no longer effective, the goon starts to shift into his grizzly form. For a bear shifter, the guy is fast to shift, but it doesn't matter. Closing his large jaws over the man's throat, Eli rips back leaving a massive gaping wound.

Trying to scream, the man flails under him, his shift subsiding because he's too busy dying to finish turning into a bear. No longer concerned about the bear under him, Eli scrambles off the man, ready to face down the next threat. He finds Mason on top of the other grizzly, ripping into the bear with massive claws. Already covered in red blood, Mason is a gruesome sight even before he hits an artery and blood spews across his side as the bear under him gurgles and chokes.

With two of the bears out of the way, Eli looks for the third, his wolf eager to rip out another throat, when he stops cold. Both Troy and Chris face down the third grizzly, but they can't make a move because he's holding Steph. This bear is still in human form. One massive arm is around her chest, pinning her arms to her side, while he holds his hand to her throat with the other. His hand is partially transformed so massive claws are digging into her vulnerable neck.

Her eyes are wide as she looks at him. "Eli? What the hell—"

The bear doesn't let her finish her question. He tightens his hold on her just enough to draw droplets of blood. "Let me pass or I rip her throat open," he demands, taking a step back and carrying her with him. Blood trickles down her throat and soaks into the collar of her shirt. Despite the pain she must be in, she doesn't make a sound. Not surprising is that the expression on her face is more angry than frightened.

Reaching out with his power, Eli finds the bear is wearing some kind of warding charm. It's not that powerful, but in the few seconds it will take him to break it, the bear will have plenty of time to hurt Steph.

Don't fight, my love, Eli begs her. *Just be still, and let me take care of this.*

When she doesn't respond he assumes she's too scared to focus on talking to him.

Shifting effortlessly back to his human form, Eli regards the bear with raging eyes. Troy and Mason gather behind him, waiting for his orders. "Let her go or I'll make your death painful."

Giving a humorless laugh, the bear tightens his hold around Steph's chest, making her gasp from pain. "Back off or I make her hurt before I kill her."

Holding up his hands, Eli takes a small step back. "Just let her go and I'll let you walk out of here unharmed."

"He won't," Chris pipes up from behind the grizzly. The bear gives a small roar and half turns so he can keep an eye on Chris and Eli. "Devin likes to hurt people, especially women.

He'll take her with him and hurt her until she dies. He did that to my cousin." The last few words are a growl because Chris is fighting his change. He must have just gotten home or he would've joined the fight just to kill this bear earlier.

"He killed someone?" Steph asks. Her voice is only a whisper, but all the shifters can easily hear her.

"He's killed many. He likes young women the best. My cousin was only eighteen."

Feeling sick at Chris's words, Eli is struck again by how truly twisted this clan is. Why has Richard allowed this? Between the two of them they could defeat the clan leader and his enforcers, so why has his father let this kind of horrific abuse continue? It's one thing to maintain power with an iron grip, but to allow the torture of innocents is unconscionable.

That thought hits him with a wash of shame as he realizes why Richard let everything remain the same. If there's a perverse and abusive clan next door, no shifter can leave. Richard allows Clyde to abuse his people because it makes Richard's position that much more secure. And Eli let this happen. He stuck his head in the sand, hid in his cabin, and ignored everything.

That ends now.

But before he can fix anything, he needs to get Steph safe.

When he meets Steph's gaze, he's alarmed at how calm her face is. Her breathing is labored from the pressure of the bear's large arm around her chest, but she's not crying and her expression isn't panicked. Then, to his utter shock, she shakes her head as if telling him to keep away.

Power thrills across his skin, and he hears the other shifters gasp as it hits them with more force. Chris goes down on his knees from the strength of it, and a painful coyote howl echoes through the backyard.

"You don't get to hurt anyone anymore," Steph states calmly. Her voice is so soft, even his shifter hearing can barely make out her words.

That's when the bear holding her starts to scream. He tries to let go, but he can't seem to move anymore. Her power builds, but instead of pushing out, it retracts around her and the bear. The bear's arm drops away from her, and he falls to his knees as Steph calmly steps away from him. Her pupils are almost fully black now. The power around her makes her hair flow out as if she's swimming in water. Her shirt billows and small particles of dirt float up as the grizzly seems to melt into the ground at her feet. Then the big shifter starts crying.

"Please, make it stop," he begs.

Eli can't tell what she's doing to him. On the outside, the man doesn't look changed. His skin is whole. No blood is coming from his nose, eyes, or mouth, and Eli can hear his breathing fast but strong.

"Oh no, you don't get mercy now," Steph tells him as she crouches next to him. Her face seems otherworldly as she gazes down at the bear. She looks up into empty air and tilts her head, as if watching something only she can see.

"All those girls, you sack of shit. I can see what you did to them. How does it feel? Do you like all this pain? Do you like the feel of the belt against your skin? Or the fire burning your feet? What's it like to gasp for air as hands close around your throat?" The bear jerks, opening his mouth in a silent scream as she talks. Eli watches, fascinated as marks appear on his skin with her words. The level of power it takes to do something like this is immense.

The fact that a human woman controls this much power is mind-boggling.

And terrifying.

She's perfect. Of course, his wolf would think that.

The bear is convulsing now, saliva bubbling from his mouth as his eyes roll back in his head. With a last shudder, the bear goes still. He's no longer breathing, and Eli can't hear a heartbeat. Steph stands back up, her eyes fixed on the supine shifter.

"Don't worry. I'll make sure you're not alone in whatever corner of hell you end up in. I'm sending all your buddies down there to keep you company."

Powerful maned wolf, son of a clan leader, and dangerous in his own right, Eli's never been intimidated before. But he's not ashamed to admit he's intimidated as hell right now. This small, chatty, overly friendly human just used enough power to light up a small city. On top of that, she used that power to torture a bear shifter to death.

And he was worried she'd be scared when she saw his shifted form…

No one moves as she looks around at all of them. Troy shifted back to his human form, but Mason is still in bear form, looking at her with wide, frightened eyes. It's not often one sees a scared polar bear. When her gaze rests on him, he drops heavily to the ground and cranes his head sideways to show his neck.

Troy and Chris are on their knees, and Eli can tell neither of them are sure whether they should run or try and approach Steph in supplication. Honestly, Eli is wondering the same thing himself.

Out of all of them, Ash, still in coyote form, trots up to her, tail wagging and tongue lolling out. Normally so fearful, traumatized Ash shows no fear when she nudges Steph's hand so it's resting on her head.

Steph gives a little chuckle as she strokes Ash's head and neck. "Ash?" Giving a little affirmative yip, she leans her small sleek coyote body against Steph's leg.

"The rest of you too," she confirms as she looks around and finally lets her eyes rest on Eli. "The snarling and not liking to wear clothes." She gives him a relieved smile. "This explains so much."

With those words she pales and sways as her eyes roll up in her head. Eli is just fast enough to catch her as she collapses.

Standing, he carefully hoists Steph into his arms. Her breathing is even, and her heartbeat is strong. She's probably never used so much magic all at once.

Mason lumbers up to his side and shifts. "Holy shit, Eli," Mason breathes out in awe. "Did you know she could do that?" He ignores Mason. His full focus is on his unconscious mate.

Shifting to her human form, Ash puts a hand on Steph's forehead. "Her temperature feels fine. I think she just wore herself out." Grinning, she meets Eli's gaze. "I knew she had power, but nothing like this. When this gets out, no one's going to fuck with us ever again."

"Or they'll just shoot her in the head when no one's looking," Troy pronounces grimily. "She's not a shifter. There's no Conclave to protect her from that kind of assassination. And she's not a witch with an Assembly or a druid with a Council to keep her safe. She is only a human, and another dead human won't mean much to the Conclave."

Killing among shifters might be common, but they have rules. You can wound with bullets, but killing another shifter with anything but natural powers along with tooth and claw is illegal. According to Conclave laws, killing humans any way you want to is fine as long as it's in an effort to keep shifters hidden and safe. That's the Conclave's number one priority, keeping shifters a secret. Other than that, they have very little to do with clan politics or policies.

"She's mine," Eli snarls.

"Then you need to Heartmate her soon," Troy's voice is gentle but firm. "Because until she's considered part of a clan, she isn't safe. The Conclave themselves might even like to see her destroyed if they found out how powerful she is. I mean, damn Eli, how'd she do that?"

Meeting the eyes of everyone around him, Eli does something he never expected to do. He sends his power out into each shifter. First, he finds their old clan ties and snaps them. Troy manages to stay on his feet, but Mason, Chris, and Ash drop to their knees with low moans.

"Eli?" Troy whispers, his voice rough from the pain of having a clan tie ripped away so brutally.

"Be easy, old friend," Eli murmurs and then sends out his power, slapping new clan ties into the shifters with more force than finesse. Gasps of pleasure ring out.

Troy looks at him with wonder as he rubs a hand over his heart where the tie is probably throbbing with new pulsing energy. Eli has never formed clan ties before. That's something a clan leader does. Something he never wanted to do. But now, the ties quivering with emotion, Eli feels a rush of relief and joy coming at him from the four of them. He expected at least a little anger at his high-handed behavior, but instead all they're feeling toward him is deep, resounding satisfaction.

"You're all my clan now," he declares. "I'm your clan leader. Mason, you and Chris get rid of the bodies. You know what to do."

"Sure thing, Eli." The brilliant smile on Mason's face runs entirely counter to the fact that he was just told to dispose of bodies.

"Yes, Clan Leader." Chris's smile is no less brilliant as he steps up to stand even with Mason.

Looking over at Troy and Ash, Eli issues more commands. "You two stay here. I want a list of the Lowell clan members. Mark who are enforcers and guardians. I need to know numbers. Then I want you to start looking for a place to use as a clan gathering house. I'm probably going to need to start talking to large groups of people." His wolf snarls at that, but Eli just tells him to shut up again. This is his fault anyway.

"Yes, Clan Leader," Ash and Troy say in unison. The four of them hurry off to carry out their orders while Eli cradles Steph gently to his chest.

"I'll keep you safe," he promises her.

Our mate is powerful on her own, his wolf points out with excitement. *She's deadly. Beautiful and deadly.*

And isn't that just the perfect Heartmate for a partially insane maned wolf?

CHAPTER 18

Steph comes awake slowly. Judging by the pain in her head, she assumes she's suffering from a hangover. But then she moves and the pain in her muscles makes her wonder if she fell down a flight of stairs while binge drinking.

Unfortunately, she knows why her body hurts, and it's not from anything as fun as getting drunk with friends and tumbling down a set of stairs. Only one thing causes the unique combination of misery she's experiencing, and that's when she overextends her gift. She's only done it once before when she was attacked and the man tried to rape her. She passed out that time also, but only after the man was dead.

Later the police said it was a freak stroke and she got lucky, but she knew the truth. She killed that man with her gift, and taking a life comes with a price. She never gave that death a second thought. The man deserved what he got. Just like the one who held her hostage in her backyard, the rapist had a long history of hurting people and enjoying it. She has no room in her soul for mercy with those kinds of people. Everyone thinks she's the embodiment of kindness and peace, but what they don't realize is that her attitude isn't all-encompassing.

When her gift gives her the kind of insight she got from her attempted rapist or the man who wanted to take Ash, she can't summon any response but execution by pain. At least that's what she calls it.

She makes these men experience the same pain they caused others but all at once. She feels their brains overload. Their nerves start to fry, their blood gets thick and doesn't want to move through their body, and finally, the spirit flees, no longer able to deal with so much abuse of the mortal flesh around it. Once it's done, all she feels is an intense satisfaction—no regret or guilt. The world is right again, and the scales have been balanced.

Then, of course, she feels fatigue so profound she passes out. This time is a little different than last time, though. The other time she woke after taxing her gift beyond its limit, she was in a hospital. She was vomiting and shaking, and the staff was worried she'd come down with the flu on top of being assaulted. This time she feels wrung out but not sick.

A power is slowly sifting over her, and as she wakes up more fully, she feels along the magic to its source. Without opening her eyes, she strokes the magic and hears a little gasp next to her.

"Warn a girl," Ash grumbles and shifts in the bed behind her. Then the soft magic coming from her good friend flows stronger. It's a warm, laughing power that makes Steph want to giggle and to hug someone tightly.

When she opens her eyes, Eli's face fills her vision. Her smile only gets bigger as she realizes she's curled up against Eli's chest. Ash is a warm presence at her back. She can feel both Eli and Ash's magic kneading against her, seeping into her skin, warming her, and soothing the hurt. It's amazing, and she never wants it to end.

"You scared me," Eli grumbles through his smile. Closing her eyes, Steph burrows her face against his chest, filling her nose with his clean masculine smell.

"Sorry about that. I got mad."

"About that," Ash says as she pops her chin on Steph's side. "You've been holding out on us, girlfriend."

Memories of earlier flood her mind, and she bolts up, almost knocking Ash off the bed. "Bears!" she exclaims.

"Oh my," Mason says from the doorway in a high-pitched voice. The grin on his face vanishes when Steph meets his gaze, her own eyes narrowed.

Warily, Eli sits up while Ash scrambles off the bed and takes a few steps back. They're all watching her with leery expressions, as if they're afraid of her. She points at Mason, "Polar bear?" Mason nods so she turns to Ash. "Coyote?" Ash nods and slides her gaze down.

Then she turns her full attention to Eli. "And what the hell are you?"

"Maned wolf," Eli explains. "I'm one of the rarer types of shifters."

"Shifters? That's what you call yourselves?"

"Well, yeah. But there are subgroups," Ash volunteers. "Troy, Eli, and I are all canines and belong to the Varg. Mason and Chris are Ursa because they're bears. Cat shifters are Doitsoh. In the old days we weren't allowed to mix because they thought children of mixed couples weaken bloodlines. But now we know that's not true so only the most rigid clans keep the groups separate."

"Clans? You guys have been talking about clans a lot." Comprehension dawns on Steph. "Lowell clan. They're shifters. Groups of shifters, not gangs. That's what this is all about. Power plays and disagreements between clans of shifters."

Eli looks both elated at her quick comprehension and fearful of her reaction. "It's complicated."

Huffing out a laugh, Steph swings her legs off the bed. "Find me coffee and pain killers, and start explaining because no one's doing anything else until I understand everything that's going on here."

Ash and Mason scramble to fulfill her request while Eli is suddenly next to her, pulling her into a gentle hug.

"You're not afraid of me?"

Looking up into his worried face, her expression softens. "Never."

"Good," he states simply and buries his face in her hair. She can feel his anxiety draining away as love pulses through their magic connection.

"I love you too," she whispers.

For some reason she hears a whine in her head, and Eli sounds a little snarl into her hair. It takes her a moment to untangle what just happened, but when she does figure it out, she sends a little pulse of affection through their link. The response is an impression of a happy maned wolf face with a lolling tongue and wagging tail. Eli stiffens against her.

"Did you just talk to my wolf?"

"Should I not?" He's silent so long she's worried she broke a serious shifter taboo. Then he's picking her up and swinging her around, clutching her to his chest tightly enough to make breathing difficult until he finally sets her back down on her own two feet.

"Talk to both of us as much as you want. I don't care what you say. But never stop talking to us."

"Well, okay then." She pats his shoulder feeling slightly awkward. "I guess it's a good thing I like to talk."

"Well, that's a whole lot of fucked up." Taking another sip of sweet creamy coffee, Steph eyes the shifters gathered in her living room.

Troy and Ash are cuddled on the blow-up mattress. Eli is on the couch with her. Chris pulled a few pillows off the couch and set himself up on the floor, and Mason pulled a chair in from the kitchen. They're now referring to her house as the gathering house. She's not sure how she feels about that but lets it go for now.

Over the last hour she's received a crash course in shifter society, power structure, and politics. Troy's been doing most of the talking with everyone else except Eli interjecting here and there. Occasionally Eli will growl or snarl, and when he does, a little pulse of affection through their connection calms him.

She enjoys communicating with his wolf. The creature sends her simple messages and only wants affection and reassurance in return. Isn't that what everyone craves? The fact that Eli seems to argue with his wolf just makes her want to soothe both of them all that much more. She can't imagine harboring an animal inside herself that's constantly fighting with her.

"It's not like that for everyone else," Eli whispers to her as Troy takes a break from explaining the power of a clan leader to check his phone. "I don't know why, but my wolf and I have always been like this. Everyone else blends with their animals seamlessly, but not me. Not us." He sounds so mournful it breaks her heart.

"That's probably why I like you so much." She can't see his expression because he's kept his face hidden in her hair this entire time, but she feels his surprise. "It's true. Besides, I'm pretty sure I wouldn't be as content if you only had one personality to talk to. Maybe that's why I've never had a boyfriend last more than a year. I get bored talking to only him." His laugh ruffles her hair. "With two of you to talk to, no one gets bored."

"Anyway," Troy says, putting his phone back down. "Now that Eli's our clan leader, and we have you at his side as a second, they—"

"Whoa. Back up there." Steph holds up a hand, wondering if she just missed something vital. "You just went from explaining that Eli needs to challenge Clyde for clan leader to saying he's already a clan leader. And when did I become second? I'm not a shifter, so how can I even be in the clan, let alone have a place in leadership?"

Although everyone else falls silent and cast looks of trepidation at Steph, Mason starts to explain, blithely unconcerned. "After you killed that bear, very cool by the way, Eli bound us all to him. That makes him our clan leader."

"When you say 'all of us,' does that mean the four of you?"

"Yes," Troy says cautiously. "A clan leader establishes bonds with their clan members called clan ties. There are only four of us now, but after Clyde is dead, the ties of all the other clan members will snap to Eli. That's how a challenge works. If Clyde died of natural causes, or an accident, or anything outside a formal challenge, the clan ties would just snap. It would hurt, and we'd all feel horrible until a new clan leader created clan ties again."

Cupping her hand under Eli's chin, she urges him to look up at her. "Did you clan tie me?"

The reluctant look on his face warns that she might not like what comes next. "Yes and no."

"That's as clear as mud," she mutters and feels his wolf give a little snarl and then whine. Sending a calming touch through their link, she realizes she's been unconsciously soothing his wolf since she first met him. "We developed a type of clan tie right away. Didn't we? I felt your wolf, but I just thought it was a traumatized mind."

"I didn't do it on purpose," he explains quickly and both his and the wolf's anxiety come through their link loud and clear.

"Easy there, you two," she whispers. "I'm not mad yet. Just help me understand, and we'll go from there." Both Eli and his wolf calm slightly.

"The clan tie we have is very similar to what Heartmates have, but it's not cemented yet. We are equals in the bond between us while what I have with the others is more dominant. I can push commands through the clan leader tie, making it difficult for them to say no. But not with you."

"That's the third time someone has mentioned that term, Heartmate. Anyone want to explain?"

"It's the shifter version of marriage," Ash clarifies. "But it can't be broken. It used to be one-sided. The stronger of the pair would wrap the power around the weaker person's heart, making one person subservient to the other. But now it's common practice to Heartmate each other, so both sides wrap their power around each other's hearts and share."

"Share what exactly?"

"Emotions mostly, but some Heartmates can share power too." Ash turns her face to Troy and gives him a little kiss on the cheek. "We've been in love for ages but couldn't Heartmate because our clans don't get along. Now we can."

"I'm going to make sure we have the most beautiful Heartmate ceremony," Troy promises her. "I want it to be everything that makes you happy. I've been saving up so you can order anything you want. Even that dress you like so much with all the crystals on it." Both Ash and Steph sigh at Troy's romantic words while Mason makes a gagging noise and Eli snarls.

"Shut it, you two!" Steph orders and feels a zing of power go from her to Eli and from Eli to Mason. The polar bear yelps and drops his gaze. Then he cants his head sideways to expose his neck.

"Mason, I'm so sorry," she says and shoves a bunch of soothing power directly at him. "I was just trying to zap Eli, not you too."

"You need to ease up," Troy says. He's sitting the closest to Mason. "I can feel it over here, so Mason is probably overwhelmed. Pull some of that back before he ends up a babbling mess."

"So nice," Mason murmurs, his eyes unfocused and his pupils dilated. He sags down in his chair and looks like he's about to slide off. Troy puts a steadying hand on the man's arm to help keep him upright. Pulling back her power, Steph watches the polar bear shifter slowly come back to himself, his eyes refocusing on her as he straightens back up and gives his head a little shake. "That was even better than coyote joy."

"Coyote joy?" This entire conversation feels like she walked into a class only to find out there's an exam that day and she doesn't even know what the subject is.

"Each group of shifters have their own special kind of magic," Troy explains. "The wolves tend to be cunning, so sharing a little of their power helps non-wolves figure things out. To plan."

"My magic, Coyote magic, is happy. We're like Prozac. That's the reason Eli had me cuddle with you in the bed, so my magic could help make you feel safe and happy."

Turning her gaze to Mason, she raises a questioning eyebrow. "What about bear shifters?"

Grinning, Mason taps his chest. "Polar bears, like me, tend to help with confidence. Except for Kodiaks, who are the biggest and when you're the biggest it's hard to be afraid of much. Black bears are on the calm side, so if you're anxious or worried, visiting them helps clear your head and help you find a peaceful center. Every shifter has their special flavor of magic and in a healthy clan we all share."

Turning her attention to Eli, she waits for him to meet her gaze. "What about maned wolves?"

Chris answers for Eli. "They're so powerful they're born to be clan leaders or seconds. Guardians at the very least." Eli nods his head at her.

"I never wanted to be clan leader. I don't like talking to people."

"I never would've guessed," she teases him. "What does my power feel like? Coyote?"

Eli considers her question for a moment. "Your power feels like nothing I've ever experienced before."

"She feels like the Mother," Ash says quickly, as if she's been waiting to say that for a while. "When we do the gathering ceremonies and you can feel the Goddess Mother's presence. That's what Steph's power reminds me of."

Everyone turns their gazes back to her, and Steph shifts uncomfortably.

"Trust me. I'm not an embodiment of any goddesses, Mother or otherwise," Steph says with an attempt at a light tone. "I'm pretty sure a goddess wouldn't struggle with her hair or have mildew in her shower."

Instead of smiling with her, everyone including Eli regards her with sober expressions. "It's true," Eli agrees. "Your power is kindness and light. I feel only the chaos of my power, but with you, I feel balanced."

"The Mother does like things to be balanced," Troy murmurs thoughtfully. Embarrassed by their scrutiny, Steph tries to redirect the conversation.

"We should get back to the real issues at hand. Clyde and Richard? Oh, and I feel like I should point out the fact that I can't be Eli's second because I'm human."

"A human that the Mother blessed," Troy counters, undeterred. "She's touched you with her power, and you're not even a shifter, witch, or druid. That means she meant you to find us. To be with us. To help us. The Mother created you to be one of us."

So much for getting them off that topic.

"There's one problem with that theory. I can't control what I did earlier. It's happened once before, just the same way. Something just comes over me, and it's almost like I'm watching it happen. I'm pretty sure that puts me out of the running of being Mother blessed or whatever."

That confession is supposed to make everyone calm down and drop the idea that she's somehow touched by a deity, but the shifters get even more intense.

"You're not Mother blessed; you're Mother embodied!" Chris croaks out, his eyes wide and scared. His fear is mirrored in everyone's faces. There's even a feeling of being intimidated coming from Eli through their link.

Exasperated, she rolls her eyes. "Guys, it's just me."

"You're you, but you're also a conduit to the Mother," Ash whispers, as if this deity herself is listening in. "Being Mother blessed means she imparted strong gifts to you. Being Mother embodied means you not only have gifts of your own, but sometimes she uses you to keep the balance among her creatures. It's a powerful role and one of the rarest. I've never heard of anyone being Mother embodied in my lifetime, or my parents'."

Shifting on his cushions, Chris looks like he's trying to push his way through the wall to get further away from her. "You're the embodiment of the Goddess Mother, giver of all life and keeper of the balance. The fact that you're here with us now can only mean one thing; she's deemed the clan no longer fit. You're meant to restore balance."

The word balance vibrates through her. The word repeated in her mind both times she used her gift to kill. Could there be something to this Goddess Mother? That's profoundly unnerving.

"You make me sound like an old-school mob boss who needs to take out an opposing mob family." Again, her humor falls flat as everyone's face shows a mixture of respect, fear, and relief.

Sliding his gaze away from her, Troy talks. "You mentioned you did something similar to what you did to the bear shifter once before. What happened?"

They've shared so much with her, so it's only fair she is as open with them. "A few years ago, I left work late because John, the owner of Larson Towing, managed to totally screw up the accounts again. That happened the week before he decided to turn control of everything over to me."

"Smartest thing he could have done," Chris says, earning a smile.

"Darn right! Anyway, the last guy who left the yard forgot to secure the gate and when I was leaving, I was attacked in the yard. The guy hit me from behind and…" A lump forms in her throat. It's a hard memory to talk about, even though it didn't end as badly as it could have for her. Eli's wolf growls in her head, and when she pulses calm down their connection, it comforts her along with the agitated beast.

"You never told me about this," Ash says softly.

"It happened before we moved in together. And, really, I just wanted to forget about it. Pretend it didn't happen. He didn't get a chance to rape me, which was what he wanted. The police later identified him as the serial rapist they'd been trying to hunt down for months."

"What happened when he tried to hurt you?" Eli asks with a shocking degree of calm. Surprised by his restraint, she furrows her brow at him. He shrugs at the implied question. "The guy's dead. Right?" Mutely, she nods her head. "Then I'm not going to get pissed. He's dead, as it should be."

"Huh, well, yeah, I guess. He got on top of me and as soon as he was touching me, I could see all the things he did to all those women. He beat several of them unconscious. It was horrible. Then I wasn't me anymore. It was a little like having an out-of-body experience. After it was all over, I passed out. I woke up the next day in the hospital. The autopsy said the guy died of a stroke. Case closed."

"And the balance is restored," Mason murmurs.

Everyone repeats. "The balance is restored."

"Okay, that wasn't creepy at all," Steph mutters, making everyone chuckle.

"Sorry, that must seem weird to an outsider," Troy apologizes. "For the Goddess Mother, balance is very important. Life and death. Joy and pain."

"My mom said childbirth is the embodiment of the Mother. A woman labors in great pain to bring life and joy into the world. Balance."

"You created balance by ending the life of a man who did nothing but hurt others," Chris adds. "Devin was evil, just like Clyde and the rest of the men he surrounds himself with."

He stops talking abruptly, as if unsure how much more to stay. He looks over to Ash, who shrugs.

"Just tell me, guys," Steph huffs.

"If the Mother has decided to create balance, there's no telling when it will end," Ash states softly. "She could claim many souls before it's over."

Breath catching in her throat, Steph stares at Ash. "That sounds horrifying."

"Have you ever heard the ghost story about the Old West town in Nevada where all the residents just dropped dead one day back in the 1880s?" Troy asks.

Confused, Steph nods. "Sure, Hollowhead. Everyone's heard that story."

"That was the last time the Goddess Mother balanced everything," Troy explains softly. "That we know of."

A spike of fear goes through Steph, and she knows Eli can feel it. Nuzzling her neck, he whispers soothing words to her as his wolf sends her images of dark woods lit by a full moon—probably his version of a comforting thought.

Feeling shaken, she tries to be stern and practical instead of giving in to the part of her that just wants to go back to bed and bury her head under a pillow.

"Let it go, everyone. I'm not this balancing embodiment Mother person. I'm not. Now drop this or no more beer. Let's focus on more important things, like how we're going to keep everyone safe and fed."

"Yes, Second," they chorus, and Steph drops her head in her hands.

"I didn't sign up for this," she sighs.

"Welcome to my world," Eli whispers in her ear and then gives the shell of her ear a little nip. His growl of pain when she zaps him feels highly satisfying.

CHAPTER 19

A plaintive doggy whine wakes her up. Yawning, Steph swings her legs off the bed and searches for her slippers. "I'm moving. Hold your horses," she mutters as the whine sounds again. The click of claws on the floor brings her sleep-crusted eyes up, but it's not Mesa standing in front of her begging to be let out for a late-night bathroom break. It's a maned wolf.

"Eli?" Tail wagging, ears forward, Eli rests his furry head on her thigh and looks up at her with pleading eyes. "Do you need to go outside?" With a yip, he steps back and drops into a play bow, making her smile. Her mind clearing, Steph picks up her phone to check the time. Two in the morning. Eli is lucky tomorrow is Saturday or these late-night antics would get him in trouble. A girl needs her beauty sleep.

"Considering you could just shift back to human form and leave if you wanted you, I'm guessing you want me to join you outside?" When he yips again, she switches on the bedside lamp and finds warm clothes to dress in. Once dressed with sturdy boots on her feet, she follows him through the dark house to the front door. Both Mason and Chris snore loudly as she passes, neither waking up even when she pulls open the front door and slips out into the night with Eli.

Taking the hem of her coat in his mouth, Eli tugs her down the street and toward the woods, his body language everything playful and excited. Once they reach the woods, he lets go of her jacket and runs off, disappearing into the night.

Tentatively, she pushes her gift out until she feels Eli's familiar magic. Eagerly, he returns the push, letting her feel what it's like to sense the night as a wolf. The smells hit her first. So many different fragrances with nuances her mind can't decipher. Then the sounds come to her   rustling leaves she never would have noticed, the chirping of rodents, the movement of tiny feet in the trees or on the ground.

Through Eli's wolf senses, the woods around her come alive. The magic between them helps her keep track of his movements, even though he doesn't seem to make any sound when moving through heavy brush. It also helps her navigate the dark world around her. The moon isn't far from being full, but the thick forest canopy is blocking most of the light. With access to Eli's wolf's sight, she's able to see the narrow path and follows him deep into the forest.

Caught by the sight of an owl swooping down for a kill, she stops in her tracks. The predator is beautiful and almost silent as it swoops down, claws extended. The rat escapes into a tangle of brush and the owl changes trajectory, flying back up into the canopy. She remains standing in place, looking where the owl disappeared and hoping it might fly down again.

Bursting out from a bush, Eli startles a laugh out of her before he bounds off out of sight again. Content to let him run circles around her, she resumes her travels down the dark path, hopeful to see more wildlife. There's no fear in her. Her handsome wolf would never let anything hurt her.

A small gray figure emerges from behind a tree, and she stops walking. As the four-legged animal cautiously eases forward, its form fully coalesces. It's a coyote, head canted to the side and gaze fixed to the ground.

"Ash?"

The coyote drops to the ground and then rolls onto her back to expose her belly. Her tail is wagging and when Steph brushes her power over the coyote shifter, all she feels is happiness. Then another wolf appears, this one looking very much like a giant red fox and not much bigger than Ash's coyote body. This must be Troy, shifted into his Ethiopian wolf form. He drops down next to Ash, nuzzles her until she rolls over, and then gives her a playful nip on the ear.

Like a shot, Ash is off running with Troy right on her heels. Steph can hear playful yips and barks in the woods as the two run. When they cross her path again, Ash is chasing Troy, telling her this is some kind of shifter version of tag.

Then Eli is there, pushing against her leg with his big body. Her mind floods with his wolf's demand for pets. Stroking her fingers through his luxurious fur, she lowers herself until she's kneeling next to him.

"You're a gorgeous beast," she murmurs and feels him preen from her praise. She sputters when he strokes his tongue all the way up her face. "Not sexy," she declares, laughing.

The sound of something large moving in the bushes stops her laughter cold, but Eli isn't reacting with aggression, so she just turns her gaze in the direction of his and waits. Soon a giant white shape appears, covered in leaves and twigs.

When Mason sees her, he grunts and ambles over. Her heart starts racing, the man's shifter form is massive, but when he just noses his snout under her palm, she relaxes and runs her fingers over his head.

Eli gives a little growl, making Mason grunt and draw away to continue ambling down the path. Not long after, a grizzly bear appears and does the same routine of snout under hand. Before Eli can growl, Chris's grizzly form trudges off after Mason.

"I guess the whole gang's here," she murmurs as she straightens up. Eli dashes away, and she starts walking, following the slow-moving bears. Eventually, they come to a clearing. The bears start munching in the berry brambles that curve around one side of the clearing while Eli, Troy, and Ash dart in and out of the clearing, yipping, barking, and raising a general fuss.

Finding a soft bit of grass to sit on, Steph makes herself comfortable and lets the night move around her. Occasionally Eli will come to a stop next to her for a pet, but then he's off again. It doesn't bother her that she can't join in. Her connection to Eli means she feels what it's like to play with them. In that way, she's right there, jumping through the woods and nipping at heels too.

She must have drifted off because when she wakes up, she finds Eli standing there with a dead rabbit dangling from his jaws. Sitting up with a yawn, she accepts the rabbit, barely keeping her gag reflex in check.

"Is this for me? How nice of you," she praises him. The wolf fills her mind with joy at providing for her and promises her something more substantial next time by sending the image of a deer.

"This is perfect," she assures the wolf. "No need to kill Bambi!" Eli's wolf laughs in her mind and sends her an image of the stew Eli made. She works hard on not wrinkling her nose in distaste. Looks like she's already eaten a meal full of Bambi and found him delicious.

"I'm a monster," she states with a chuckle.

Chris scratches his back on a nearby tree as Mason shreds the trunk of another one with his claws, stretching his long white arms high into the tree. Somewhere in the dark she hears Ash howl and then Troy. When Eli joins in, Steph decides to be part of the pack. Turning her face up to the night sky, she does her best to sing along.

Finally, Eli tugs at her jacket sleeve, encouraging her to her feet and guiding her back down the path. Soon the rest of the shifters follow as they make their way back through the woods. At the border, their piles of clothing sit and Steph watches with interest as everyone except Eli shifts back to human form and dons their pajamas. No one's embarrassed by nudity, and she notices none of the men look at Ash below the neck. Considering they must need to be naked around each other a lot, this is probably shifter etiquette.

Once dressed, no one talks as they walk the short few blocks back to her house, but everyone's wearing big, cheerful smiles, and the magic surrounding her feels jubilant. Soaking in the wonderful feelings of the people with her, Steph realizes how fortunate she is to have such an amazing experience. These shifters just shared their world with her, and it's extraordinary.

Eli only shifts after she's back in bed so he can join her, pulling her cold body into his and chafing her chilled skin with his hands. "Thank you," she whispers, sending the feeling through their link as well as saying the words. She feels his sleepy wolf in her mind, thrilled that she enjoyed his woods and his clan.

"My clan too," she murmurs as she falls asleep.

"Your clan too," Eli agrees.

CHAPTER 20

The week has flown by as Ash and Troy gather information, Eli holds Richard off with promises of Heartmating and power, and Steph works her butt off to keep the tow company from devolving into utter chaos. After using her powers to exhaustion, she unknowingly slept all of Thursday and most of Friday. Chris called in telling everyone she was sick and Oscar took over the office in her absence. Cars got towed, vehicular messes were cleaned up, but Steph returned the following Monday to find the kind of disarray normally reserved for hurricanes or tornados.

How did Oscar mess up the schedule and billing so badly when he was only covering her office for two days? Two days!

Now it's Friday again and her week is almost over. Except she's got a house full of hungry shifters and no food left in the kitchen. They've all been taking turns bringing home food, and Steph volunteered for tonight. What should she fix? It needs to be quick and easy.

Contemplating various foods, she answers the desk phone almost absently. "Hi, Steph, it's Chris," the shifter on the line announces. "I just dropped off that rig at the diesel shop. I'm in the big hauler, and I know it's due for service. Do you want me to leave it here for service instead of coming back in?"

"How will you get back here?" She, Chris, and Eli had taken to riding to work all together this week.

"The shop is on Troy's way home. He's going to swing by and get me. Is Eli still there with you?"

"No, Mason had to take him somewhere urgently. Neither one of them told me what's going on, but Mason was tense. Eli was his usual growly self, so who knows how bad it is."

"I'm sure it's just a meeting with someone from the Hunger Valley clan. I wouldn't worry. I'll come back to the shop and ride home with you. I don't want you to be by yourself."

"I'm perfectly safe," Steph states with more confidence than she feels. It's broad daylight and it's unlikely anyone will try to do anything to her in public. Didn't the guys tell her that's one of the strictest rules; no shifting in public? That means she should be safe. "Get a ride home. I'll meet you there."

"Sure thing. Thanks, boss," Chris says and hangs up.

Ten minutes later the answering service they use comes online, so she locks up the office and then the iron gates to the yard. Everyone's already gone, most sneaking out five or ten minutes early. It's Friday. She can't blame them.

The grocery store parking lot isn't crowded, giving Steph hope she'll be able to get in and out reasonably efficiently. If she's hungry, the shifters at home will be starving. That's not the only reason she wants to hurry. The idea of being home and surrounded by her new clan fills her with a wonderful contentment. She's come home to an empty house for too long. Now suddenly, her world is overflowing with friends and it's marvelous.

Grabbing a shopping cart, she attacks her shopping eagerly, tossing items in with cheerful abandon. Only after she's finished stacking meats from the deli does she notice a woman staring at her.

The woman is tall and slim with honey blonde hair and large expressive light brown eyes. She looks to be in her forties, toned and athletic. Her gaze is intense, and Steph starts to feel uncomfortable.

"Can I help you?" Those words bring the woman out of her trance and she takes a few steps forward, pressing herself flush against the front of Steph's cart. Grasping the sides of the cart, she leans over and sniffs.

"It's you," she whispers, her mouth parted in surprise with awe in her eyes.

Steph's about to ask if she knows this odd woman when it hits her. "You're a shifter." Worry trickles through her. She's in a grocery store. No one can hurt her here. Probably. Now she regrets not making Chris come back to the shop so they could ride home together.

"Did the Mother not give you the scent?" the woman asks, letting go of the cart and stepping around. She effectively traps Steph against a cold display behind her. "Touch me so you can know one of your clan members." The woman grabs one of Steph's hands in her own. A soft warm power brushes against Steph. The feel of it reminds her of Ash.

"Coyote," she states softly, making the woman smile. Steph can tell the woman has been tired, sad, and scared for a long time, but she carries hope now, too.

"Yes. We've waited so long for help and now, finally, the Mother sent you." Looking down at the cart, the woman raises her eyebrows at the amount of food. "It looks like clan members are already staying with you. Soon we will have a proper gathering house where many can stay when they are in need and all are welcome. Even before the suffering got bad, we were neglected. All of us are suffering from too little exposure to each other. But now you're here." She beams at Steph.

"I'm not sure I'm what you think I am," Steph tells her as she pushes some soothing power into the woman. The lines of tension bracketing the woman's mouth ease and her brow smooths out. "I'm sorry, but I'm not a shifter. I'm not anything. I'm just human."

"You're Mother embodied," the woman argues. "A gift to all of us. My name's Angela. And you must be Steph Garmin." This stranger knows her name. This, more than anything, freaks Steph out.

"I need to get moving." Steph pushes the cart past Angela. The other woman falls in step with her, smiling and trying to help Steph with her shopping at every turn. Steph's always been an outgoing friendly person, but she's never been treated like a messiah before. She's not a fan.

Once the cart's full and they're in line for checkout, Steph points toward the corner of the store where they met. "Didn't you leave your cart back there?" The woman is texting on her phone but looks up at Steph's question and laughs.

"Don't worry about that. I'll deal with it later. This is more important."

"I can check out on my own. I don't need any help. Honest. You can go do what you need to do," Steph encourages, but Angela doesn't leave. She just starts helping Steph put items on the checkout belt.

"Matty," Angela greets the checker by name. His face lights up when he sees her.

"Hi, Mom!" Oh, well that explains it. Steph starts feeling a little better until Angela practically shoves her forward.

"This is Steph Garmin! This is her!" Matty's eyes go wide, and he pales a little.

"Mom, stop touching her!" he hisses, and Angela laughs.

"She's good. Feel her. Feel her kindness. The Mother picked her for us." Shaking his head, Matty meets Steph's shocked eyes.

"I'm sorry, Miss Garmin. Mom's a little old school. Let me get you bagged up." Turning his attention to his mom, he reaches over the checkout counter and pulls her away from Steph. "Mom, you can't just touch her like that. How would you feel if she did that to you?"

Abashed but still smiling, Angela folds her arms over her chest, resting her hands on opposite shoulders. "He's right. I'm terribly sorry. I let myself get carried away. Matty is a wolf. So clever and cool headed. He'd be a great help when you're ready to deal with clan properties."

"Mom!" This time Matty's voice isn't pleading. It's angry. "You need to stop. Just go. Right now. Don't make me call Dad."

"Fine," she says to her son, her happiness not abated in the least by his censure. "Make sure she knows where we live. She'll want to know where all of us live. I'll put together a list. And cookies. I'll make cookies." She keeps talking to herself excitedly as she walks away.

Matty shrugs and gives her a little smile. "Coyotes, what can you do?" As if that clears it all up, and then he starts bagging her groceries. He works in silence until the last bag is in the cart. "My mom's over-the-top exuberance and complete lack of manners aside, I want you to know how grateful we all are that you're here. When you decide the time's right, we'll all accept a clan tie from you." His words finally help her understand, at least a little, what's going on.

"Oh no, I'm not going to be clan leader. Eli will be."

Eyeing her thoughtfully, Matty ignores the next customer, impatiently tapping on the checkout counter. "Are you sure about that, Miss Garmin? Because from where most of us are standing, it sure looks like the Mother picked you, not him."

"It's not me. I'm going to help him, but it's not me." She tries to hand him cash, but he steps away.

"Your money is no good here," he declares and resolutely turns his back on her to deal with the next customer.

Shocked, she stands there for a moment with her mouth hanging open until she realizes someone's walking away with her cart full of groceries. She hurries after him.

"Hey, that's mine." The man, tall and broad, looks down at her and smiles.

"I know, Miss Garmin. I'm just taking it out to your car for you," he explains.

"Do you work here? How do you know my name?"

"No, ma'am, I don't work here. Just came in to grab some beer. But then I saw you and thought I could help. Which car is yours?"

Reaching out with a tendril of power, Steph touches the man and finds his bear grunting at her with mellow interest. Her small use of magic doesn't go unnoticed because the man's smile widens. "My name's Ernesto," he tells her as he slowly walks her cart out of the building.

Giving up on getting control of her cart and wondering if it's symbolic of her life in general, she points Ernesto toward her car. "But how do you know who I am?"

"We all know," he states unhelpfully.

Someone falls in step behind them and when Steph looks, she finds another stranger, this one a teenage boy with long black hair tied back in a ponytail. He's dressed in the typical jeans, t-shirt, and hoodie, with a backpack thrown over one shoulder. Unlike the majority of teenagers she's met, his face is open and smiling instead of sullen and closed off.

"I'm Dray," he announces and holds out his hand to shake. Automatically she takes it and feels his power curl along her arm, scared and hopeful. Out of habit, she pushes a little soothing magic at him, and the boy's eyes widen and then relax. "Can I come home with you?"

They're at her car now, standing next to her trunk when he says this. She freezes, blinking and silent, unsure what to say when Ernesto tugs at her sleeve. "I need you to open your trunk."

In the few moments it takes her to dig in her purse for her keys, several more people have gathered around her car. When she looks up, she's startled to find them all staring at her with similar expressions of fear mingled with hope. Except for Dray and Ernesto, they all maintain a polite distance, but so many eyes focused on her is unnerving.

"I need to go home," she states carefully, unsure how to handle these people. Several nod their heads while others look disappointed.

"You didn't answer. Can I come home with you?" Dray asks, crowding in next to her. Ernesto carefully piles her groceries in the trunk and more people join the crowd. Now a dozen people are all watching her. Beyond unnerved now, she grabs bags and just chucks them into the trunk without a care about what might get crushed. Once everything's in the car, she slams the trunk closed and faces the growing crowd.

"I'm going home," she declares. "All of you, just, uh, go about your business." They look disappointed, but they all start trudging off as she slides into her car. All of them except Dray, who jumps into her passenger seat.

"You should have an escort," he declares. "Clan leaders always have escorts."

Resigned to having the teenager in her car, she fumbles her keys into the ignition with shaking hands. "I'll drop you off at home," she offers.

"No, I'm coming home with you. Don't worry. I can sleep outside."

"No, Dray, I'm taking you home. I'm sure your parents will be worried. Now just tell me where to go." He doesn't speak as she drives through the parking lot. When she's waiting for a green light to turn left out of the lot, she looks over at him. He's staring straight ahead and crying giant silent tears.

"Dray?"

The light changes, and she's forced to look away and drive. When Dray starts talking, his voice is small and tentative.

"They're dead. Clyde killed them last month and took our house as part of the clan's properties as punishment for Mom and Dad's betrayal. None of the clan is allowed to house me, but I'm still clan so I can't leave."

Shock makes Steph slam on her brakes, causing several cars to blare their horns as they make their way around her. Grabbing the teenager's hand, she pushes soothing magic at him, flooding him with her power. He gasps and his whole body shudders. Then, with a contented sigh, his head flops back against the headrest. The tears are still rolling down his cheeks, but at a slower rate.

"It's going to be okay," she promises. "You're going to come home with me, and we're going to protect you. You're not alone any longer." Letting go of his hand, she tries not to let her anger sully the magic she's pushing at him. Her gift is howling at her to care for Dray, protect and shelter him.

Well, she always wanted kids. It looks like she gets to start with a teenager first.

"I'm a bear," he tells her. "When I'm able to shift I'll be big and strong and I'll be one of your enforcers." She doesn't tell him that his magic feels more like a coyote to her than a bear. But what does she know?

"For now, I need you to be a kid," she tells him.

"I'm not," he counters with a small frown. "There are no kids in this clan. It's too dangerous to be young and helpless."

But you are, she thinks sadly and feels another wave of anger at Clyde and Richard—men who value power more than people.

"Well, that's going to change," she declares. "I might not be your clan leader, but I'm going to make damn sure you guys are kept safe."

CHAPTER

21

Not only is her drive full of cars, but there's not a single spot to park anywhere on the street. Someone must be having a party because her neighborhood is never this crowded. It's probably a birthday or anniversary. *Good for them,* Steph thinks, trying to be charitable as she's forced to double park outside of her house. It's a small inconvenience for someone else's joy.

Her first indication that more is going on than a party is when she notices people milling around her front yard. As soon as she shuts off the car engine, people surround her car, pressing hands and faces against the windows. Dray gives a hiss of fear and shrinks into his seat.

"What's going on?" she murmurs as faces she doesn't know peer in at her.

"They're clan," Dray explains, his face pale and anxious. She reaches over and places a hand on his shoulder, sending a reassuring pulse into him.

"It's okay. I'm not going to let them hurt you." He relaxes at her assurance, but his expression is still mostly worried.

The car doors are locked, but no one's trying to break into the car after finding they can't open the door. Instead, they all just stand there and wait. It's disconcerting.

"Is it just me or does this feel like it could turn into a horror movie?" she mutters.

"It sure ain't a comedy," Dray retorts.

She tosses a grin at the kid. "Good one."

He shrugs nonchalantly at her compliment, but she can feel his pleasure.

Fun dialogue over, she returns her attention to the gathering crowd. "Right, let me make some room for us."

"I could—" Dray starts to say but she shakes her head, cutting him off.

"Don't worry. I got this." Taking a deep breath, she yells out, "Everyone needs to back away." She imbues her words with a little power. They all look at each other and shuffle backward, saying things that Steph can't hear because she's not a damn shifter with super acute senses.

Then she feels Eli, concerned and frustrated. A roar sounds out and the people who only moved a few feet when she demanded they back up all hurry to clear a wide area around her car. Then Eli's there, trying her handle and looking like he's ready to rip the car door off to get to her. Hastily she unlocks the door, and Eli roughly pulls her out of the car and hugs her to his chest.

"What's going on?" she whispers.

"They started showing up a few hours ago," he mumbles. "I just got back from meeting one of my father's guys in Hunger Valley and found them all here."

Fear, concern, uncertainty, and worry all push against her from the crowd of shifters surrounding the car. Her gift screams at her to do something, to soothe these people around her. Giving up, she locks her arms around Eli to pull some power from him and floods the area around her with calm. She hears gasps, sighs, and sobs as she fills these abused clan members with affection and reassurance. As her magic touches them, she feels a slimy dark power that makes her grit her teeth. It has to be Clyde's clan ties and she instinctively wants to rip at them.

It proves difficult to keep her power in check when those abhorrent clan ties taunt her. It occurs to her that her gift wants her to cut those ties, almost as if she's not so different from Eli. His wolf fights with him, and her gift is fighting with her at the moment. Never before has she been forced to work so hard to suppress it. She just barely manages to restrain her power from knifing through every clan tie around her, to cut them like so many strings and bind them up again.

But not to Eli. To her.

No! No, no, no. That's the definition of a bad idea. These are Eli's people, not hers. She can help. She can assist. But she can't just go in and take over. She's human and they need something more. They need Eli.

By the time she shuts down the pulses she's sending out, her hands are shaking with the effort to ignore the demands of her gift. But as she pulls her magic back, every last ugly clan tie is still in place, shackling all of these poor people to Clyde.

Eli sends a pulse through her, making her feel better. Her hands stop shaking, and her breathing eases. Focusing on him, she finds him regarding the crowd with narrow, annoyed eyes. She strokes her connection with him, and he looks down at her and gives a little growl.

"Too many," he grunts, making her giggle.

"As far as you're concerned, three is too many," she retorts. "Why are they here?"

"Begging me to break their tie with Clyde and re-tie them to me," he explains. "At least that's what I assume."

"Can you do that? Should you do that?"

"I can, but it would just be easier to wait until I've killed Clyde. Breaking ties is hard work."

"Murder isn't very nice," she mutters to herself but watches Eli smile down at her.

"Clyde doesn't deserve nice."

"Agreed," she says, pushing her misgivings aside. It's concerning that she's not more bothered by the thought of Eli killing.

The word balance floats into her mind. Clyde's death would be justice and create balance. She might not be a shifter, but she can understand those motivations. "Let's tell everyone to meet at the park and you can talk to them there. Give them some reassurance."

"If I must," he grumbles.

"I'll be right there with you," she promises. With a resigned expression, he looks up at the crowd and clears his throat. He doesn't need to get their attention; all eyes have remained focused on the two of them the entire time. Steph feels herself blushing under so much scrutiny.

"Everyone, go to the park," he barks out, making several people startle and jerk. Huffing with annoyance, Steph speaks up.

"It's going to be fine. I promise. Take blankets or jackets to sit on. Take refreshments if you have them and share if you can. We'll be there soon to speak with all of you." With expressions of relief, everyone eagerly shuffles off, giving Steph a clear view of the front of her house. Ash is standing there, looking amused until she spots the teenager still sitting in Steph's passenger seat.

"Dray!" she calls out and sprints to the car. She wrenches open the door and drags the boy out, hugging him tightly. With only a half-hearted protest, the boy accepts Ash's affection. "I thought he killed you too," Ash murmurs into the boy's hair.

Crying and trying to hide it, Dray hugs her back. "He thought about it and then said I should live as a warning to everyone else."

"You're safe now," Ash assures him. "Steph and Eli are going to make us all safe."

"Why don't you take him into the house," Steph suggests. "I guess he's going to stay with us for the time being. I'm not sure where he's going to sleep. I'll let you figure that out." The coyote shifter nods and starts walking the boy to the house. Chris and Troy appear next to the car.

"Groceries?" Chris asks.

"In the trunk. If you could get them in the house, that'd be helpful," Steph requests as she pushes herself back into Eli's embrace. She's not ready to let go of Eli just yet. He feels like a strong solid anchor in a world that's become strange. They stand like that, next to the car and in the street as dozens of shifters, arms full of blankets, coats, bags, and even a cooler, make their way past and toward the park.

"I'm sorry," he says simply.

"Don't apologize," she whispers back fiercely. "You're working to make life better for all of them. Don't ever apologize for that. Only, make sure they know you're the clan leader. Okay? A bunch of people were at the grocery store, and they all seemed to think I was going to be in charge. I'm not a shifter. I shouldn't be clan leader. I shouldn't be second or anything. I want to help, but I don't want to take any position away from someone more qualified."

He doesn't respond to her words but just holds her tightly. Only when the street is mostly empty does Eli pull back so he can look into her face. "I don't like talking to people," he says and she gives him a puzzled look.

"I know," she says slowly, trying to figure out where he's going with this.

"I don't like it at all. And clan leaders need to talk. A lot. To everyone. A good clan leader forms social ties, not just magical ones."

"You'll do great," she lies without guilt. No matter how bad Eli's communication skills are, he's still going to be a whole hell of a lot better clan leader than Clyde. "Besides, I'll be there to help. I'm good at talking to people."

"I know, that's the point. You'll be second and take care of all the people stuff. I'll forge the ties and organize the guardians. But you do the talking. That kid was crying. I hate it when people cry."

A dizzy spell makes her sway as the blood drains from her head at his words. "No, Eli! I can't be second! I'm not one of you. I'm not even sure what a second does."

"It's like what you do at the towing company, but more. Paperwork, organizing, communicating, all the things you're good at. Think about it," he insists. "They already look to you. Ash, Mason, Chris, they look to you for guidance, not me."

"But they're all here because you're here," she argues.

"No, not just me," his voice borders on harsh. "They're here because of you too." Jerking his head in the direction of the park, his eyes glowing with power and his body stiff, he lets out a little growl. "I'm going to go talk to them. Please come with me." When she hesitates, he snarls and she knows he's struggling with his wolf. She sends her calming magic into him and his expression softens. She feels his wolf, pacing and anxious. Neither of them is thrilled at the idea of being in charge of so many lives.

Well, man and wolf are just going to have to get used to the idea. Stepping out of his arms, she gives him a little shove. She'll support him however he needs, but no way can she be second.

"You head to the park. I'll find a place to park the car and join you there."

"Can we go to the woods tonight?" Images of his maned wolf running through the trees, happy and free, makes her smile.

"If you go be nice to everyone, we'll go to the woods tonight for as long as you want," she agrees.

"Civil," he counters.

Laughing, she nods. "Fine, be civil. I'll be nice for you."

"And tonight, we'll hunt! I'll bring you a deer this time," he promises her, and she manages to keep the grimace off her face.

"I'll make sure to look up recipes," she responds and when his wolf sounds a happy yip in her head, she knows she's doing the right thing. Giving him a playful shove, she gets back into her car and starts it up but doesn't drive off right away. She's captured by the sight of a shirtless, shoeless Eli striding off toward the park, his predatory grace entrancing.

A honk from an annoyed neighbor gets her moving. She ends up having to circle to the far end of the park to find a place for her car. At least the park isn't too big and she can cut across it to get back to Eli and the group. Worried that her absence might be upsetting Eli, she doesn't pay attention to her surroundings as she breaks into a jog. She can just see them all gathering near one of the barbeque areas in one corner of the park.

She is so focused on her destination she doesn't even see the shadow that emerges from behind a tree. When the attack happens, shock paralyzes her, and then she's sliding into blackness.

Swimming back into consciousness slowly and with great effort, she opens her eyes to see nothing but absolute darkness. Her head hurts worse than she's ever felt. Someone must have hit her. How much damage did they do? It takes a strong blow to the head to knock someone out. She probably has a concussion. Is she blind too? Panic threatens, and she works hard to keep it from taking over.

Turning her head a little, she realizes something is covering her head, which is why she can't see. When she tries to bring her hand up, she finds her arms are bound behind her back at the wrists. Her ankles are bound too. She must have been in this position for some time because her shoulders are throbbing and her hands are numb.

Footsteps approach, and she strains to hear anything else. A quiet voice. A door slamming. Muted talking. A car honks in the distance.

Carefully, slowly, she reaches out with her gift to figure out who might be close to her. A shout of alarm. Running footstep. They're coming for her. Trying to push past the pain in her head, she gathers magic to her, ready to push it out to protect herself.

"Shit, she's waking up. Get the drugs in here. Get the drugs!"

"The witch will be here soon."

"But we need to knock her out right now!"

More hurried footsteps. Hands descend on her, roughly flipping her on her back and pushing up the sleeve of her shirt.

Something sharp pricks the soft skin at the bend of her elbow. She tries to concentrate on gathering power. Concentrate on getting free.

Cold washes over her. The power she's trying to gather dissipates and blackness overtakes her again.

CHAPTER 22

Something is very wrong. Not only is Steph not there with him, but something in their link feels off. Dozens of faces watch him expectantly, following his agitated movements as he paces and fidgets. Their gazes only add to his growing unease.

The crowd in front of him is waiting patiently for him to talk. Chris, Mason, and a few others are patrolling the ends of the crowd, making sure humans don't wander in by accident.

Steph said she was just going to park the car and then join him. He knows she wouldn't abandon him or all the people seeking help. He might be inclined to run off to avoid anything he doesn't like, but that's not Steph's style at all. But he could easily imagine her getting sidetracked on the way back. She's so different from him, ready to talk to anyone. One of the shifters probably got scared or started crying and she's helping them. His mate is everything he wishes he could be—open, easy, patient, and with an abundance of kindness.

She'll make a perfect second. She might not be a shifter, but she has the power to back up her position. And, unlike most seconds, she'll have the skills to deal with the everyday issues that can crop up in clans. Elders in need of assistance. Families who need a little help. Young adults acting out. Richard, despite his violence toward any defiance of his authority, always made sure every clan member had shelter, food, and care if they needed it.

The crowd is talking among themselves. Even without clan ties he can feel their desperation for change plucking at him like an incessant wind. Clyde's created a clan of distressed shifters, ready to cling to any hope for salvation. This time that hope is a demented maned wolf who's currently fighting his urge to shift and disappear into the forest.

Thoughts of the forest make his wolf push to take hold of their body. Steph's not there yet, but he needs to get this done before he loses to his wolf and ends up shifting. Where the hell is Steph? They need her! Subduing a snarl, he stands before the shifters and starts talking.

"Most of you don't know me, but my father is clan leader of the Hunger Valley clan. I plan on challenging Clyde for control of the Lowell clan."

"Will you hand us over to your father?" someone asks. He's impressed with the courage of the speaker. He's sure that kind of question would normally get someone violently reprimanded if this meeting was being held by Clyde.

"No," he answers easily. "I'll remain clan leader, but we might join some assets with Hunger Valley clan. They're a strong and large clan, and we might need their help."

"Will you tithe us?" someone else asks. These are the questions he doesn't want to deal with. He's not good with details like money. Suddenly, Troy is standing next to him.

"All clans need to tithe. How else will we take care of the elders or injured?" Troy answers for him.

"Clyde only takes, he never gives," an angry voice shouts out from the back. "You'll do the same."

"I don't want your money," Eli snarls out loudly enough to make several people in the front of the crowd flinch away from him. Their reaction makes him feel guilty. He needs Steph here. He needs her calm. Looking up, he sees Mason not too far away.

"Mason," he shouts out. "Go find Steph."

At his words two things happen, Mason nods and hurries off, and the crowd starts to murmur among themselves with renewed vigor. Steph's name seems to have a strong effect on them, making Eli blink with surprise.

"Who's Steph to all of you?" he asks, expecting someone close to him to answer, but instead they all go silently and blink owlishly at him. Annoyed and already done with this meeting, he snarls again. "Someone talk!"

"She's ours." A boy speaks up. He's standing next to Ash, looking pale and scared but determined. He steps forward. Ash tries to grab him, but he evades her hands. "She was sent to us. She's ours. You're not our clan leader. She's going to be our clan leader. The Mother sent her to us."

Waving the boy forward, Eli is grateful someone in the crowd is willing to talk. The kid looks like he's so scared he's ready to piss himself, but he walks up to Eli anyway. When he comes to stop within arm's reach, he tries to meet Eli's eyes but ends up dropping his gaze down to his feet. He cranes his neck so far to the side Eli hears vertebrae pop in the kid's neck.

"What do you know about her?" he asks, trying to keep his voice gentle despite his wolf going crazy inside of him. Something's making his wolf insane, but he doesn't have time for that right now. Steph is his and he needs to know if these shifters think they can take her from him. He thought they were gathering there for him, but now he's starting to question that assumption.

"We know what she did to Clyde's enforcers," the boy says. His voice starts off strong and he even manages to meet Eli's eyes. But then he shrinks back when Eli doesn't quite manage to muffle his growl.

"I'm not going to hurt you," he tells the boy impatiently. "Explain how you know what she did to the bears."

"Ash talked to Lee," the boy says.

Behind the boy, Ash grimaces and mutters, "Oh shit."

He'll be having a word with her about privacy within the clan later, but for now he needs to focus on the kid in front of him.

"Go on," he demands.

"Word started to spread that Steph is Mother embodied. Things have been so bad for so long that some started to talk. You know, that the Goddess Mother has to do something. Everyone knows the Mother won't stand for this kind of imbalance for too long."

Murmurs of agreement chorus through the crowd at the kid's words. He can hear some of their comments.

"The Mother is giving us Steph to restore the balance."

"Goddess Mother picked her. She's ours."

"Mother embodied for us."

The crowd's words make the kid bolder. He squares his shoulders and meets Eli's gaze bravely "That's why she needs to be clan leader, not you." Many voices of approval sound from the crowd at the teenager's words.

"She's destined to be our clan leader."

"Goddess Mother embodied *her*, not you."

"An obligation is created. The Mother gifted her, so she must serve us."

Staring out in the crowd, Eli frowns darkly. "She's not a shifter," he reminds the crowd. "She can't make clan ties."

"Are you sure?" a woman in the front asks in a soft voice. "My daughter met her in the grocery store parking lot today." She looks over to the young woman next to her. "Go ahead, Jennifer tell him what you told me." Jennifer looks anxiously at her mother then Eli.

"She felt like one of us," she states, using up her courage in that one quick sentence.

"She felt like one of us?" Eli questions. Jennifer's mother hugs the girl close, both shielding her from Eli and giving her courage.

"Her power," Jennifer mumbles into her mother's shoulder. "When she soothed us, I felt the Mother in her touch. Just like back when Clan Leader Jennings was in charge, but Steph is stronger."

This is all news to Eli. He knows she's powerful, but he's never felt the Mother's touch in Steph's magic.

Then he hisses out a breath. He did feel the Mother in her when she used her power against Clyde's bears. Of course, their link means she doesn't need much of her gift to touch him, so maybe she's pulling more from other sources when she's using her gift on anyone but him.

"The Mother has gifted her," Eli agrees slowly, thinking it through as he talks. "But that still doesn't mean she'll be able to create clan ties."

"She will," another shifter announces with confidence. Murmurs of agreement echo through the crowd, and Eli realizes they believe Steph's going to be their savior, not him. As much as he wasn't looking forward to being clan leader, he finds it's a blow to his ego that he's being dismissed.

Next to him, Troy is laughing softly. When Eli glowers at him, Troy's laugh gets louder. "I'm sorry, but the expression on your face is priceless," Troy says between gasps. "I mean, I know you dreaded the idea of being a leader, but it never occurred to you that anyone else might be picked over you if you ever did decide to lead. This is hilarious!"

"It's complicated," he retorts and then looks over to find a distressed Mason running to him.

Fear coils in Eli's gut. "Where is she?"

"I don't know," the polar shifter admits. "I found her car on the far side of the park, but her scent just disappears. I smelled a few shifters near there, but I don't recognize them. Do you think someone took her?"

Looking at the crowd, Eli decides now is not the time to be patient or subtle. If it turns out she just wandered off to get a coffee, she can yell at him later for sending everyone scrambling to find her. Right now, he needs to know she's safe.

"Everyone, go look for Steph," he orders. "She's missing."

"I'll get some of her clothes for those who don't know her scent," Troy calls out and most of the crowd gets up to follow him. The rest all fan out to start searching. Eli desperately wants to shift but knows it's a bad idea. No need to bring animal control or local authorities into the area to deal with a "wild animal" on the loose.

Suddenly he feels her connection to him disappear. He cries out and drops to his knees, clutching his chest. Looking down he's surprised to find no blood or gaping wound. The link between them being severed felt like he got stabbed. His wolf howls from the intense pain as Eli's human eyes water.

"Fuck!" he shouts when he can breathe again.

"Eli?" Chris is there, crouching next to him.

"I can't feel her," he whispers, grabbing the other shifter's hand hard enough to make the man wince. "She might be dead. She can't be dead. I just found her. I can't lose her!"

His panic is making it hard to keep his wolf in check. He feels his teeth growing in his mouth and his jaw starting to reshape. His wolf is pushing out, demanding control of his body. Squeezing his eyes shut he fights off his inner animal. He needs to stay human. He needs to communicate with the others.

"She's not dead," Chris assures him.

Willing to accept even the slightest hope, he forces his wolf back. Snarling, he stumbles back to his feet, clutching at Mason. "How can you know?"

"Because the Mother wouldn't let that happen." The polar bear's confidence is so absolute Eli finds himself believing also. The Mother wouldn't put Steph in his life just to rip her away so quickly.

But she's human, not a shifter. What if she's not Mother embodied? What if she doesn't have that protection? Humans are so fragile. She could easily die from treatment that a shifter would shrug off.

He's never been one for prayers, but Eli finds himself sending words to the Goddess Mother. Begging the deity for Steph's life. *I'll do anything*, he tells the Mother he stopped believing in when he was a child. *I'll give anything. Just keep her safe.*

And just like when his mother died, he gets no answer from Goddess Mother. Faced with silence from his deity, and the roaring of his wolf filling his head, he turns to Mason.

"Fuck the Goddess Mother," he mutters. Mason gapes at his words, but Eli doesn't care. "It's our job to protect Steph, and I'll be damned if I'm going to live without her."

An hour later Steph hasn't been found, but two wolf shifters are dragged in front of Eli, cursing and fighting.

"Do you know who we represent?" one of them spits out as he's pushed to his knees in front of Eli.

"Don't care," Eli snarls. "Why do you smell like Steph?"

The wolf sniffs and then sneers at Eli. "You're the maned wolf everyone's talking about. You don't look so powerful."

"Brave words for a shifter on his knees," Mason growls, punching the man hard enough to send him to the ground. Reaching down, he grabs a handful of hair and brings him back up on his knee. The wolf spits out blood, his sneer still in place.

"I wouldn't do that," the wolf tells Mason. "If I die you won't know how to get the human back."

With a roar of rage, Eli steps forward and rips the man's head off. Warm blood hits him in the face and chest as Mason yelps with surprise and scrambles backward. Turning to the second man, Eli grabs him by the front of his jacket and lifts him up.

"Where is she?"

"Clyde has her," he screams out frantically. "Please don't kill me. It's all Clyde. It's all him. He has her."

"Eli, we need to move this back to the house," Troy says, tugging at his arm. "Chris, Mason, grab the body." Barely containing his wolf, Eli half drags and half carries the captured man to Steph's house. He hears Troy address the crowd as he leaves, telling them to go home and wait. Uninterested in the rest of the clan, Eli storms through the side gate into the backyard and tosses the man down. The dogs all barrel out of the house. As if sensing this man is their enemy, they surround him and start growling. Even Grey, the most mellow of all the dogs, is showing an impressive number of teeth.

Troy, Ash, and Dray all stand behind him.

"Talk!" he orders the sobbing shifter.

"He t-t-took her today. At the park. He was just going to talk to her at first, try and scare her into talking you into backing off. Then Stan told him they should take her, that way you'd have to do what they said."

"What did they do to her?" Eli roars. "Why can't I feel her?"

"Geas," he stammers out. "He hired a witch to put a geas on her. She won't be able to use her magic at all. Not until the geas is burned off."

"Burned off?" Ash whispers, horrified.

"The witch marked it into her skin," the shifter explains, eager to be useful. "She said that's the only way it will work on someone so powerful. She has this weird needle that she kept dipping in red ink. She said another witch can undo it, or someone can burn it off. That's the only way."

Rage washes over Eli. They took his Steph. They hurt her. They throttled her power.

"She didn't feel it, what the witch did. Clyde drugged her. She was out of it the entire time," the man tells him as if that would make it better.

The worst part of all of it is the fact that none of this would have happened to her if he'd never entered her life. He brought this trouble with him. This is all his fault.

Guilt and fury war inside him.

"What does he want her for? What do I need to do to get her back?"

"He wants you to challenge him."

"That doesn't make sense," Ash whispers behind him. "Clyde knows he'll lose. Eli's much more powerful. Even pulling power from the clan ties, Clyde can't win."

"He knows that," Troy states grimly. "Let me guess," he says to Clyde's shifter. "He wants Eli to allow himself to be beaten?" When the man on his knees nods, Troy makes a bitter noise. "He wants to show everyone how strong he is by winning against Eli, so he cheats."

Eli doesn't even need to think about his response. He picks the shaking man up and puts him on his feet before shoving him toward the gate. "I'm letting you go. Tell Clyde I accept his challenge. Deer Glen, at moon rise."

Without a second look, the man turns and runs. They all watch him as he flings the gate open so violently it breaks, sagging backward on a single hinge. With the man gone, they all face each other. Eli sees his fear and desperation reflected in the faces around him.

"He won't let Steph go," Troy points out.

"I know."

"Then what are you going to do?" Ash asks.

"I'm going to talk to my father," Eli explains as he strips out of his clothes and shifts. As he runs for the woods and toward Hunger Valley territory, he sends out his magic to find his father, a bright beacon of power. He plucks at that power until his father responds, sending an image of a section of woods they're both familiar with. When he hits the dirt trail head, he notices Grey is right behind him. Ignoring the pit bull, he flies over the uneven ground with only one goal in mind.

His father might be a self-serving bastard, but hopefully, Eli can convince him to save Steph.

CHAPTER 23

As far as Steph is concerned, waking up disoriented and uncomfortable is getting old fast. At least this time, when she opens her eyes there's nothing over her head to obscure her vision. She's lying on the floor of what looks to be a storage room. The place is dark, illuminated only by one bare lightbulb over the door, but she can see shelves filled with boxes of beer and other alcohol all around her.

Trying to sit up, she winces when she only ends up flopping around a little. Her ankles are bound together and her wrists are tied behind her back. Both bindings are connected by a rope. She's hogtied.

Going still she assesses her body. Nothing feels broken, but she's bruised all to hell, and a dull, burning sensation is emanating from her arm. The sleeve of her shirt has been ripped off, but she can't see anything that would be causing the pain. She notices some dark marks like someone drew on her. The pain from her arm is probably just more bruising, maybe deeper than the others.

Next, she feels for her gift. That's when her fear really starts building. She can sense it's there, but it feels held away from her somehow. After her gift showed up in her teens, she's never been without it. The familiar weight of magic has always been in the back of her mind, pressing there like a warm presence. Half the time it's at work without her even being conscious of it. Now it's almost like a thick plexiglass wall sits between her and her power.

Fighting to reach it makes the burning in her arm get worse until the pain becomes too much, so she stops trying to draw her gift back to her. Panting from the pain, she fights the panic that's threatening to overwhelm her. This isn't the time to get hysterical. She needs to stay calm and controlled. Without her gift to use against her captors, she's going to need to get free the old-fashioned way—by being clever.

Eying a row of whiskey bottles on a bottom shelf, she contemplates the best way to break one and use a shard of glass as a knife. It'll be dangerous, and she could end up cutting herself badly. But then again, remaining tied up isn't all that safe either.

She's just starting to wiggle her body toward the shelf when the door opens. Two men she doesn't recognize walk in. "She's awake," one of them says.

"I can see that," the other one mutters. "Come on. Clyde wants her in the breakroom."

Clyde. In the back of her mind, she'd known he was probably responsible for her current predicament, but she hoped it might be someone else. Anyone else.

"You guys really should let me go," she says as they move to stand on either side of her.

"No, we shouldn't," the first one says as they grab an arm each and haul her up, dangling her between them. The move makes her shoulders hurt and doesn't help the throbbing in her head.

"Let me walk. You're going to dislocate my arms," she protests, hanging helplessly between them. "You're going to kill me!"

Both men freeze. "Is that possible?"

"She's human," the other says. "They're pretty fragile." Thanking the universe for sending two idiots to get her, she lets out a pained moan.

"My shoulder could dislocate and fill my lungs with blood," she whimpers. "I don't want to die that way."

Letting go of her like they've been burned, she thumps back down to the ground and lets out a painful cry as her knees impact with the unforgiving concrete.

"Assholes," she hisses out through tears. They ignore her as they talk to each other.

"Can humans die from just having a limb dislocated?"

"I don't know, but we better not risk it."

"Yeah, Clyde wants her alive for now."

"We might as well untie her feet," one says as he kneels next to her bound legs. "She can't get away. She's only human, and the witch said the geas is strong enough to hold her."

She hears the snick of a knife being opened and suddenly her ankles are free. Taking positions on either side of her again, they grab her a little more gently and haul her to her feet. She's shaky but manages to keep upright.

"What's a geas?"

Neither one answers as they walk her out of the storage area. She walks as slow as she can get away with, but all too soon she's led into a room where Clyde sits on a large worn couch, molesting a scared looking woman in his lap. Several men lounge around the room, beers in their hands and talking in low voices. When she enters, all talking stops, and Clyde pushes the woman off his lap. She whimpers a little when she lands hard on her ass but then scrambles unsteadily to her feet. She staggers a little as she tries to leave the room.

"In the corner, Mari," Clyde barks and she changes course to a far corner of the room. Sinking to her knees on the bare floor, she puts her face in the corner. "I've got her trained right," Clyde tells Steph with a sneer. "Took a little while, but she finally figured it out. Didn't you, Mari?"

"Yes, Clan Leader," the woman says in a soft voice. She's wearing a short tight dress that showcases a painfully thin body. Steph wonders if lack of food is one of the reasons the woman was so unsteady on her feet.

"And now I've got you to train," Clyde says, drawing Steph's attention back to the most dangerous person in the room. It takes a lot of effort, but she drops her gaze to the floor and cants her head to the side, like she's seen so many shifters do. She knows all about men like Clyde. Bullies. Those who like to feel tough by tormenting others. If she pretends to be subservient, she might have a better chance at escape or at least time to figure out what the hell they did to bind her gift.

"I can see you want to be a good little human, already learning your place," Clyde coos, watching her show of submission. "Why don't you come sit on my lap and take Mari's place." Clyde pats his thigh in invitation. "If we can get that power of yours under control, you'll stand a good chance of being my girl." Steph doesn't move, and Clyde's sneering smile turns to a frown. "Don't make me come get you." His tone carries a warning to her.

"If you want my power, we need to bargain," she says in a soft voice. Some bullies understand bargaining, but she isn't so lucky with Clyde. She watches out of the corner of her eyes as his smile disappears. He stands up and strides over to her with a dark expression.

Grabbing a handful of her hair, he drags her to the couch, sits down, and pulls her to her knees in front of him. "I offered you my lap," he growls at her. His breath smells of alcohol and rot, and she can see his yellowing teeth. "Now you get to be on your knees instead."

She prefers her knees to his lap but knows better than to say anything in that vein. The last thing she should do is challenge Clyde in front of his men.

"I'm sorry," she whimpers. "I'm overwhelmed." That seems to mollify him as he lets go of her hair and leans back.

"Overwhelmed, huh?" Reaching his hand out he snaps his fingers. "Mari, beer." The woman scrambles from her kneeling position and hurries to a miniature fridge. She grabs a can out of it and practically runs to put it in Clyde's hand. Then she rushes back to her corner. "Good girl," he calls out, popping it open and taking a long drink.

"You're going to be doing that for me soon," he tells Steph. "But for right now, we're going to talk and get to know each other a little first. Did you let that mutt put his dick in you?"

Completely thrown by the question, Steph blinks up at him. "M-m-mutt?"

"Eli, the freak who can't talk. He's been at your house, but I heard he sleeps in your backyard like a dog. Did you let him get between your legs?"

"Why—"

Blurring with speed, Clyde wraps a large hand around her throat before she can get her question out.

"Don't think of lying to me, human. I'll be able to smell it. I can smell your fear right now. I like it," He leans over and rubs his cheek against hers. "You and I are going to have a lot of fun. Now tell me: Did you let him fuck you?"

Helpless, Steph answers. "Yes."

Letting go of her throat, Clyde leans back again and finishes his beer. He tosses the empty can at Mari, hitting her in the back. She doesn't even flinch as she just picks up the can, deposits it in a nearby trash can, and then puts herself back in the corner.

"That's too bad," Clyde tells her with deceptive gentleness. "I hope I don't have to untrain too many bad habits. Freak like that," Clyde shakes his head in disgust. "He must be pretty weird in bed. He do you in wolf form?"

Wordlessly, she shakes her head. "Well, we might need to try that. Get you used to the fur."

"Are you gonna share her like you do with Mari?" one of the men asks.

"Maybe," Clyde answers and then barks at Mari. "I'm hungry. Get some food from downstairs."

The woman is out the door faster than Steph can track her movements. She can hear the poor thing hit against a wall as she makes her way down the hallway outside. The other men in the room laugh along with Clyde.

A new man arrives, wide eyed and shaking. "Levi where's Mark?"

"He k-k-killed him," Levi stutters out. "Eli ripped his head off while he was in human form. Just ripped it right off." Instead of getting angry, Clyde laughs.

"Dumb motherfucker, he's got no control. He'll be easy to defeat in a challenge circle." For some reason that makes Levi slide his gaze over to Steph.

"I told him what you said," Levi says. "I told him about the human. He agreed to the challenge."

Everything smug and superior, Clyde smirks at Levi. "Of course he did. He's a dumb cunt."

"He said Deer Glen at moonrise tonight."

For the first time, Clyde doesn't look smug or confident. "Goddamn it. That's not long from now. We need to get moving. Spread the word, a challenge for clan leader is happening tonight. Tell everyone to come so they can watch me defend our clan."

Clyde looks down at her as Levi hurries off. "I was hoping to have a little time to play with you, but I guess we'll have all the time in the world later." He rubs a hand on her arm, making the burning sensation worse. It's too much. She cries out and tries to pull away from his touch.

Looking down where his hand rubbed her arm, she sees a strange tattoo on her skin. She doesn't recognize the emblem there, but the way it hurts tells her this new marking is what's keeping her gift at bay. This must be the geas the men were talking about earlier.

"What did you do?" she whispers, horrified. Clyde doesn't answer but just closes a big hand around the tattoo and squeezes. Screaming, Steph tries to jerk away. Laughing cruelly, Clyde stands up and uses his grip around her tattoo to drag her to her feet. His grip loosens slightly once she's standing.

Mari comes rushing into the room, a plate full of hamburgers in her hand. Clyde casually backhands her, sending the food flying. The blow knocks Mari to the ground where she curls up in a defensive ball, probably waiting for more blows.

"Corner," he shouts at her. "Next time learn to be faster. No food for two days as punishment." The woman whimpers quietly and crawls back to her corner. Shoving Steph toward the door he calls out to the other men, "Get the truck and meet me out back. We need to hit the road if we're going to get to Deer Glen in time."

As she's walked across the room, Steph doesn't look where she's going. She keeps her eyes on the woman facing the wall, her shoulders shaking from sobs. A quick glance over her shoulder and Mari's eyes catch Steph's.

Steph mouths, "It'll be okay," as she's shoved toward the door. The woman gives her a wide-eyed, hopeful look and then whips her face back to the wall, but not before Steph can see the swelling already forming around her left eye.

Clyde jerks at her arm, sending pain coursing through her body from the pressure on the geas. He laughs when she yelps, obviously enjoying the way she stumbles from the agony of his touch. "You're going to need to toughen up, human," he tells her as he drags her down a flight of stairs. "Or you're not going to last too long."

Biting her lip to keep from saying anything that will piss Clyde off, she concentrates on wishing Clyde dead. If Eli doesn't do it, she's going to make damn sure she figures out a way to make it happen herself, geas or no geas.

Eli is running so fast he almost crashes into his father. Skidding to a halt, he shifts in one fluid motion. Frantically, he grabs his father by the shoulders and shakes the man. They're in the woods right on the border between Hunger Valley clan territory and Lowell clan.

Without waiting for Richard to ask questions, Eli rushes to talk. "Clyde has Steph. He's challenged me. If I win Steph dies. You need to save Steph. You need to show up to the challenge and save her."

Richard frowns and rips out of Eli's grip. "You know I can't do that. I'm not allowed to be at a challenge, no other clan leader is."

"Fuck the rules. I need you there!" Eli screams, scaring creatures in the woods all around him, except for Grey who stands wide legged and panting at his side. The pit bull just managed to keep up with his long-legged, maned wolf but doesn't look too steady on his feet now. Richard casts a curious glance down at the dog but doesn't bother with questions. Richard is one to focus on main issues and not get distracted by petty details.

"Look, son, just kill Clyde. I'm sorry if you lose the woman. She's mighty powerful, but there'll be others. It's more important that you're the clan leader of Lowell."

"How can you say that?" Eli roars at his father, fists clenched at his sides. "She's my mate!"

That news makes Richard look worried. "Shit, are you both Heartmated? Is it two-sided?" Richard slaps a hand on Eli to feel for a Heartmate tie and smiles with relief when he can't find it. "Fuck, you scared me, son. You know better than to let her Heatmate you back, right? You need to wrap your power around her heart, not let her do the same to you. Otherwise she's an equal in the relationship."

"We haven't officially Heartmated yet. There are no ties," Eli admits. "But she's going to be my equal Heartmate. Her power will be wrapped around my heart and mine around hers. She's the only one for me. For the wolf. She's it. She can't die."

"There's not much you can do except let yourself be killed in the challenge and even then, Clyde will probably kill her anyway. I need you to be logical. No woman's worth letting yourself lose a challenge."

The way Richard says that makes something connect in Eli's head. "Not even Mom?"

"Of course, not your mother," Richard scoffs. "You know that's a rule I created. The challenger's family dies after he loses. The price needs to be high or I'd be up to my neck in challenges. She was a sweet little timber wolf but worthless in a fight. When her brother thought to challenge me, I had to punish the whole family, her too."

It takes a long moment for Eli to understand what Richard's saying. "No," he whispers, taking an involuntary step away from Richard. His memories of his mother are vague and half-formed. She died when he was only eight. "You said she died in an accident."

Nonchalantly, Richard shrugs. "I probably should've told you the truth of it sooner. It would have helped prepare you if it ever became necessary for you to sacrifice a mate to keep your position. But you didn't interact with the clan much and certainly never seemed interested in any females, so I didn't think to say anything. But I guess now you need to know. Your mother's family was treacherous and needed to be made an example to the clan. I'm sorry you're going to lose that Steph woman. She could've been useful, but we'll find you someone else. Just don't let them Heartmate Tie you. You tie them only.

If they get to tie you back then it makes you too vulnerable. No one's worth it."

Eli can't believe what he's hearing. Even his wolf sits inside him, stunned into silence.

How can this be? His father isn't an affectionate man, but how could he so callously murder his wife and Eli's mother? Has Eli been willfully ignorant of his father's evil?

As a clan leader, Richard cares for the vulnerable members of the clan. No one goes without housing, food, or basic comforts. The only thing Richard is absolute about is his authority. No one challenges him or they risk their entire family being executed. There have only been three challenges in Eli's adult life. One man had no family. One was Troy's father, and Eli begged his father to spare Troy's life. The third was Damien, and Eli was supposed to kill his family for Richard. An innocent woman and child. That's why Eli ran from the Hunger Valley clan and ended up in Steph's park. He couldn't face carrying out Richard's orders. Couldn't kill innocents.

For the first time, he finds himself questioning Richard's absolutism. He'd always thought that if no one else in the clan complained, what right did he have to go against Richard's laws.

Everyone in the clan seems content, but then again, could anyone in the clan risk voicing a complaint? The clan always did everything Richard told them to, and now Eli understands why. It's a revelation that Richard isn't the kind, benevolent Clan Leader Eli always thought he was. Instead, standing before him is a father willing to sacrifice his young kind wife to cement his power.

He realizes he's deliberately blinded himself to his father's evil his entire life.

"How could you do this?" Eli whispers.

"That tells me you don't understand." Richard's tone is heavy with disappointment. "To be clan leader you need to be resolute. You can't have outside people Challenging you and you can't have your clan thinking you're weak. There's no place for mercy as a clan leader. You need to learn this so you can be a good leader too."

Our mate is strong.

At first Eli doesn't understand why his wolf would say that, but then realization dawns. Steph is strong but kind. She can be tough, but she tempers it with forgiveness and a fervent desire to do right by the people around her.

His father is completely wrong. Clan leaders don't need to be brutal. They need to be compassionate.

"I'm nothing without her," Eli tells him stonily.

"Don't talk like that," Richard says with a concerned frown. "That sounds like you're going to let Clyde kill you. It won't save the female."

"If she doesn't survive, I don't want to survive either." Eli feels his wolf rage against those words. His wolf doesn't know the meaning of desolation. The wolf will always fight, but he's not the stronger part of Eli. The human part of him understands what his future will be like without Steph, and he doesn't want to live through that future.

"Don't be weak, son" Richard tells him, anger making the older man's eyes blaze. "Don't be like those other simpering fools talking about their Heartmates and love. Your mother was like that. She always pressed me to let her Heartmate tie me. As if I was an idiot. Don't be stupid. Don't let some feeble human make you weak."

Both he and his wolf are done with this conversation. Perhaps, if he survives tonight, he'll seek his father out to give his mother justice. For now, he needs to concentrate on saving the living, not avenging the dead.

"Goodbye, Father."

Without sparing the man another glance, Eli shifts and heads to Deer Glen. He hears his father raging into the night but ignores it. He has more important things to focus on.

CHAPTER 24

At least a hundred people have gathered by the time he reaches Deer Glen, including all the people who showed up at Steph's house earlier that day. When he lopes into the clearing, hopeful expressions cross just about everyone's faces, and it makes his heart feel heavy in his chest. He's not sure he's got anything to offer these people.

He knows Richard is right. There's no way Clyde will let Steph go, even if Eli loses the challenge. He might not kill her, but he'll use her. He'll figure out some way to keep her enslaved. Her life will be nothing but pain, humiliation, and shame because she won't be able to save those around her. His Steph would care about all the clan members being mistreated. She would hurt because she can't help them. Their pain would be her pain. She would be in constant agony.

But winning means Clyde's enforcers will execute her on the spot. It's unlikely he'll get to her in time to save her. As if proving how true that is, Clyde steps forward and wordlessly points. Following his gesture, Eli sees Steph, looking bruised, unsteady, and pissed. The thing that makes his heart freeze is the gun pointed at her head. He's strong and fast, but he can't outrun a finger already poised on a trigger.

"They have orders," Clyde warns him with a triumphant smile.

"Fuck you," Eli growls out as he steps into the challenge circle and waits for Clyde to join him. He tries to keep his eyes off Steph. Otherwise, he's sure he'll lose control. Instead of stepping in with him, Clyde addresses everyone gathered to watch the challenge.

"All of you are here to witness a challenge," Clyde bellows, making a few people around him jerk back. "This mongrel thinks he can be clan leader, but he's mistaken. I've accepted his challenge. I'm going to show you all what a real clan leader can do."

A muffled voice makes Eli look at Steph, who struggles briefly with the man holding her. She must have bitten down on his hand because he pulls it away from her mouth with a muffled curse.

"You're going to show what a coward can do," she calls out. "Only a scared bully would treat his people like this. Only a man insecure in his abilities would hold me hostage. No matter what happens here, you all need to remember, he's only one man. One fearful little man with delusions of grandeur."

She manages to keep her face away from the enforcer she bit, but the second enforcer coldly hits the butt of his gun against the side of her head, stopping her struggles and making her gasp from the pain. Then the hand is back over her mouth and the gun muzzle is against her temple. Eli meets her eyes. He expects to see fear and panic. Instead, all he sees is rage.

Our Heartmate is angry, his wolf crows, dancing a little with glee. *We'll kill Clyde. Then kill the man who hit her. Then kill the man holding her.*

Or we kill Clyde and they shoot her before we can get to her.

That won't happen. She won't let that happen. Look at her eyes. She's our true mate. Much too strong for them.

Even though her eyes are full of fire, without access to her power she's helpless. One or both of them has a very good chance of dying tonight.

"Are you ready to end this, mutt?" Clyde taunts. Eli doesn't bother shifting to talk. Instead, he growls, low and loud. Smirking, the clan leader steps into the circle, and Eli feels the snap of power as the challenge circle closes around them. If either of them tries to leave before the challenge is over, the magic will kill them.

Once a challenge starts, one of them must die or concede defeat before the circle's magic boundary will disappear. Of course, even if a challenger concedes defeat, and the challenge is over, it's up to the winner if the loser dies or is set free. The magic in the challenge circle doesn't care about that part, only that a clear winner is declared.

Eli knows better than to expect any concessions from Clyde. One of them has to die.

Clyde doesn't strip and shift right away. Instead, he stands tall, legs apart and a taunting expression on his face, as if daring Eli to charge him. Not one to bother with posturing, Eli sprints at the man, lips curled back in a snarl. His hope is to put Clyde at his mercy so the clan leader will order his men away from Steph.

Without losing his smirk, Clyde attempts to sidestep the charge. But Eli's not some inexperienced pup to be treated like a bull with a matador. At the last minute he checks his speed, adjusts his trajectory, and hits Clyde even though the man tries to dodge.

Recovering quickly, Clyde crouches low, still refusing to shift. Wondering what his game is, Eli doesn't rush him again. He just paces a little, forcing Clyde to move to keep him in sight. Clyde tosses power at Eli, trying to stun him, but even without clan ties to pull strength from, Eli easily deflects the clan leader's magical blow. But those clan ties make it hard for Eli to fight back with magic. Any power he tosses out to hurt Clyde will be felt by the rest of the clan and he risks hurting the very young or old if he tries to subdue Clyde with magic.

It's just another example of what an asshole Clyde is. A clan leader who cared would shut down those ties temporarily to keep his clan safe. But Clyde is keeping them all wide open so he can draw whatever power he needs from them, and in turn, he potentially places his clan members in grave danger.

Then Eli sees the glint of glass. Clyde has something in his hand and because he's keeping it mostly hidden, it must be some kind of hex, geas, or poison. All of those are illegal during a challenge, but because he wasn't thinking clearly, Eli didn't make Clyde strip and shift before entering the circle. Whatever Clyde has, he's just going to have to deal with it.

Faking a charge, he dodges the hand holding the item, and manages to get his teeth into one of Clyde's legs. His wolf takes over and the man is pushed to the back seat as the taste of blood hits his tongue and battle rage engulfs his beast.

The wolf isn't interested in dodging or fancy tactics. It just wants to rip Clyde apart. Eli screams to his wolf to let go of the leg, to get away from Clyde's right hand, but the wolf just holds on to the limb, trying to sink his teeth into the femoral artery.

Clyde screams as he slams his right hand down on Eli's shoulder. He feels a small, sharp pain and then his shoulder goes numb and his leg goes limp. Letting go of Clyde, he staggers backward, still growling. He can see a small, syringe lying on the ground at Clyde's feet. So not glass, not a hex or a geas, but poison.

"Let's see how you fight now, mongrel," Clyde hisses. "Don't forget. If I die, she dies too." He quickly strips out of his pants and shifts. Clyde's wolf is large but not any bigger than Eli and certainly not more powerful. Without the injection, Eli would have easily defeated Clyde, but now he needs to figure out how to win against this man without killing him. And, of course, try not to die as well.

Can't we just kill him? his wolf complains as they watch Clyde pace forward.

No! Think of Steph. Don't fight me or we all die, Eli tells his wolf. For a brief moment he thinks his wolf has left him. Then an answer comes that he never expected.

He and his wolf have always fought. He can't remember a time when the maned wolf wasn't a presence in his head, trying to control or at least cajole the human side of their body. But at this moment, the wolf doesn't fight. He doesn't even answer. He just gives himself over to Eli.

The wolf just seamlessly melds into him—no separation of thought, senses, or instinct. They aren't two spirits sharing a body. They are one spirit and one body. It's glorious and hopefully not too late to save them.

With one of Eli's legs out of commission, Clyde is able to move faster than Eli. He pushes this advantage by circling and charging over and over again. Eli manages to get a few bites in, but soon he's bleeding from several serious wounds while Clyde only has the one major wound on his leg.

When he starts getting unsteady on his feet, he knows whatever Clyde injected him with is doing more than just making one limb numb. His brain feels like it's moving slower and his body reacts sluggishly. Pulling on his magic he tries to push the poison out of his system, but it does little good now that the poison is taking effect.

He's not going to be able to keep this up much longer. When Clyde tries to get his jaws around a rear leg, Eli goes for broke. He draws up everything left in him. Pouring the last of his magic into physical energy, he jumps and spins, jaws gaping wide and neck fully extended.

The move takes the clan leader by surprise. He manages to get his mouth wrapped around Clyde's throat, clamping down just enough to show the other man that he's been defeated.

Clyde goes limp and whines, signaling his defeat and concession to Eli's dominance.

Magic snaps and the barrier around the circle disappears. Eli holds still, jaws clasped on Clyde's neck, eyes focused on the men holding Steph. They look confused, as if they never expected this kind of outcome, and they look to each other for instruction. Eli lets a low ticking growl come out of his throat, a warning to the enforcers.

No one movies.

"I challenge Clan Leader Eli," a voice shouts out. Eli rolls his eyes to see Richard stepping into the circle, his eyes angry and intense. The challenge circle's magic closes with a snap, trapping the three of them together.

"You're not worthy to lead, my son. I'm sorry I have to do this, but I can't have any child of mine displaying such weakness."

Unclamping his jaw from around Clyde's throat, he lets the defeated clan leader slink away to the far edge of the circle. Richard quickly strips off his clothing, talking as he moves.

"Really, this is for the best. You were always reluctant to assume your duties. This will give me a chance to try again. The woman you picked is human but powerful. She might give me a son who can be a true clan leader—a son who will continue my legacy. I tried with you, Eli, but you've been nothing but a disappointment. Still, I regret having to do this."

Stripped to his skin, Richard shifts and faces Eli with a snarl. The poison, wounds, and exhaustion mean it's all Eli can do to stay on his feet as Richard stalks forward.

I'm sorry, Steph, he thinks. *I'm sorry I waited so long. I'm sorry for everything.*

To his intense surprise, a calm voice sounds in his head. *Hush, I'm going to make it all better.*

CHAPTER 25

If only I had my pepper spray, Steph thinks bitterly as she watches Eli and Clyde fight. Eli's maned wolf is a beautiful sight, all sleek muscles, power, and grace. No way could Clyde defeat him, at least not in a fair fight. That's why he took her. That's why he throttled her magic.

She wants to scream at Eli to fight—not to worry about her and focus on killing Clyde. She'll figure something out, even with the damn enforcers holding her with a gun to her head.

Lying to yourself isn't an effective strategy, she thinks bleakly. It's hard to do anything productive when she has a gun to her head. At least not physically. Repeatedly she tries to push her magic out, feeling for Eli and trying to touch him with her gift. But nothing. Her magic is held captive by what they did to her. Held back by an invisible shield.

There she stands, the hopeless heroine she always yelled at in movies. This is not how anything was supposed to play out! Instead of standing tall next to Eli, she's bound magically and physically with a gun pressing hard against her skull. All she can do is helplessly watch the challenge along with everyone else.

When Eli wins against Clyde she sags with relief. But then Richard steps in and issues a Challenge. No! although he's watching with wide eyes, the Enforcer is still holding a gun to her head. There's nothing she can do. After the fight with Clyde, Eli's wounded. He can't defeat his father like this. Is she about to watch the love of her life die?

What would you do to end this? To save him? To restore the balance? a quiet soft voice asks in her head.

She doesn't even need to consider her answer. *Anything!* she screams back.

Suddenly the world around her stops. The enforcer pressing a gun to her head stops moving, his mouth open mid shout. The other enforcer with his hand over her mouth went stiff when Richard entered the circle and then shouted for him to kill Eli. But no sound is coming out of his mouth now. Rolling her eyes around she sees the same thing in the crowd. People have their hands halfway to their faces, and one woman even has a foot in the air, frozen in time.

What's going on?

Nothing moves, but she feels a presence around her, tightening and constricting her chest.

I didn't create you, the voice tells her as warmth floods her body. *But that doesn't mean I'm not willing to take advantage of you.*

What do you mean? What are you doing?

Answer me honestly, the voice demands. *I can stake my claim on you, but it will hurt. I can free your power, but there will be pain.* The voice hardens. *And in exchange for giving you freedom from the geas, I demand you serve me and my children for the rest of your life.*

Who are you? And who are your children?

They call me Goddess Mother, she explains. *Normally I let them live as they wish. A mother shouldn't interfere with her children. They should be free to live their own lives, make their own mistakes. But I demand balance. I can no longer tolerate how unbalanced my children here have become. I thought at first you would set things right because it's in your nature to care for others. But I see you can't do it, even with the help of a maned wolf.*

I'm talking to a god, Steph thinks. *Or a goddess, whatever. This is not how I saw today going at all.*

You find humor despite your dire situation, the Mother comments with amusement. *That's a good trait. Tell me, human, would you be willing to forsake your creator for me?*

My creator?

We are different, your creator and me. Yet, with your permission, I'll claim you. Don't worry. You don't have a Mother creator. Yours is far less involved. There will be no ill will once you're mine.

Putting those revelations aside, Steph focuses on what's of imminent importance. *If you claim me, will I be able to save Eli?*

Probably, the Mother responds. *The two of you together create balance, so I'm inclined to make sure the two of you survive.*

Then do it! Steph shouts in her head. *Claim me or take me. Anything you need to do!*

This will hurt, the Mother warns her.

I don't care.

Then prepare yourself.

With those words her body starts to feel hot. At first it feels like a fever, but soon it's as if fire is licking along her skin. Her body is frozen just like everyone else's. She can't move anything but her eyes. She can't even open her mouth to scream as the pain becomes more intense.

The smell of burning flesh hits her nose. She rolls her eyes down but only sees herself whole and unblemished. Then she rolls her eyes to take in her arm.

The markings on her arm are smoldering and smoking. The burning sensation through her body recedes and gathers at one focal point, the geas tattoo. The markings flare and flame engulfs that small bit of flesh.

I'm on fire! she screams in her mind.

I warned you there would be pain. This voice is much too calm for Steph's peace of mind.

You didn't tell me you'd set me on fire!

Calm yourself. It's almost done, the Mother assures her, amusement back in her voice.

Steph wants to accuse the voice of lying because the agony seems to go on forever. Or maybe it was only a few more seconds. She can't tell because time doesn't have meaning when your world is nothing but pain.

There now, the Mother coos when the burning finally subsides. *It's done.*

With the pain receding, Steph finds she can move her head. She looks down to see that the marking is gone, leaving behind a gaping, burn wound that's already healing. No sooner do her eyes register the wound than she can feel her gift pouring back into her. With relief she pulls it around her like a comforting blanket.

I have another gift. The Mother's voice holds a quiet excitement, as if presenting Steph with a present for her birthday. *Go to your wolf, my child. Go to your mate. The gift is for both of you.*

A mental push makes her stumble as she pulls away from the frozen enforcers and toward the challenge circle. A frizzle of magic pricks over her skin as she steps over the line that marks the circle's boundary, but that doesn't even make her pause. Suddenly she's consumed by the need to touch Eli.

Yes, touch your mate, the Mother agrees and Steph feels power swell into her. With a few long strides she's at his side. Sinking her fingers deep into his fur, she feels the magic gathered in her flow into Eli. The wolf gives a strangled gasp, no longer frozen. Rearing back, he gives a wolfish scream. The air fills with the sound of bones cracking and popping as Eli howls in pain.

Fisting her hand in his fur, she holds on tightly so the magic can do its job. By the time the Mother's voice tells her it's done, Eli stands panting and massive next to her. No longer slightly larger than his wild counterparts, Eli now stands almost as large as a grizzly bear. His canines look more like tusks, something a prehistoric creature might have. Except for his coloring and the shape of his ears, he no longer resembles a maned wolf. Eli's new shifted form never existed in nature. He's a combination of large cat, wolf, and bear.

He's a beast. A pure predator.

No, Steph realizes as she runs her fingers through his fur as he pants and shudders. *He's a protector.*

Return the balance, the voice orders her with another push of magic into Steph's body.

Suddenly, the world starts moving again. A few people stumble and fall as the Mother releases the crowd. Voices cry out in surprise and shock at the sight of Eli's new form and Steph standing calmly next to him.

Richard shrinks back as he shifts to human form, holding up his hands in supplication. "I concede," he cries out. "I concede to Clan Leader Eli!"

"No," Steph says, turning to face him, her fingers still buried in Eli's fur. "You don't get to live now. Neither of you do." Stroking Eli's fur, she speaks to her deadly mate. "End them, my love."

With that Eli leaps at them with a roar.

"I made a promise," Steph whispers as Clyde and then Richard die screaming under Eli's teeth. "And I always keep my promises."

CHAPTER 26

With both men dead, Eli stands triumphant and energized. Whatever Clyde injected in him is all gone, and his new form courses with power and strength.

We are more, his wolf whispers in awe. *We are Mother blessed.*

Steph made us more, he argues as he turns his massive body back to his future Heartmate. He can't wait any longer. The need to cement their relationship has given him tunnel vision. She stands with a small smile, her face serene and without worry or fear as he pads over to her. His new form is massive, putting his head level with hers even though he's on all fours. He wants to rub his face against her but resists because his muzzle is covered in the blood of their enemies. Instead, he crouches down and then rolls on his back, exposing his belly to her as he gives a little whine.

What are we doing? His wolf doesn't like this vulnerable position at all.

Getting her to touch us.

His wolf's concerns vanish. *Oh, good idea.*

With a dazzling smile, Steph leans over and sinks her fingers into the thick fur of his belly. His eyes almost roll back in his head at the wonderful feel of her touch.

Such a good idea, his wolf huffs out with pleasure.

Tentatively he pushes his magic into her, seeking her heart and gently wrapping around it. When she doesn't object, he pushes a little harder until his magic circles her heart and snaps into place. He can feel her heart beating in time with his own as a sound of pleasure comes from her. Heartmating is often an erotic sensation. He feels her lust stirring but keeps his attention on the task at hand. The Heartmating is only half finished. If he left it like this, she would be at his mercy.

He has no intention of letting their Heartmating be one-sided.

The second part is going to be a bit trickier because Steph isn't a shifter and doesn't know how to properly Heartmate. Carefully, he teases her magic into his own body, drawing her in slowly like fingers tugging at a fragile thread. He feels her confusion and sends reassurance. Her confidence grows. As her fingers tighten in his fur, he feels her push her magic into him with more force. He guides her power around his heart, feeling an intense sensation of love and caring as her power starts to cement. When he feels the snap of a finished Heartmate tie, he gives a little howl and scrambles to his feet, shifting as he does and wrapping her in his arms. She feels even smaller in his arms than she did before.

Not only has his shifted form changed, but his human body is substantially bigger too.

Duh, his wolf mutters.

Shut up, Eli admonishes without heat. His wolf doesn't feel like an adversary any longer. He feels like a partner, and it's wholly new and wonderful.

"What did we just do?' she whispers against him. Her voice isn't accusing or scared, just curious.

"We formed Heartmate ties," he explains. "We're Heartmates. I'm yours and you're mine. Until we join the Mother again." His words make her stiffen, and he worries she'll be upset with him, so he pulls away to better see her face.

"The Mother," she murmurs, looking at him with love and awe. "She made this all happen." Steph looks down at her arm, and he hisses with distress when he sees what she's looking at. A massive burn the size of his fist is in the process of healing at shifter speed. It should be completely healed by tomorrow, but for now it's raw and painful.

Then it hits him. Steph is healing like a shifter.

"Did she put an animal in you?" Eli asks as he focuses on their Heartmate tie, looking for her beast but finding nothing. "Did the Mother make you one of us?"

"No, I don't think so," she answers softly, and her eyes become unfocused for a moment. Then she starts to look distinctly uncomfortable. "But she did give me a few other things. I can feel them inside me, pushing to be released." Her face twists from discomfort to pain and she steps away from him, putting her fingers to her temples.

"I'm sorry," is all she says before he feels the clan ties he formed with Chris, Mason, Ash, and Troy all break with a snap, making him clutch at his chest and frown.

"What—" he starts to protest when he feels her reach out. In the heat of Heartmating Steph and the revelation of her newfound power, he forgot they were surrounded by shifters. Looking up, he notices the crowd of a hundred has swollen to several hundred. Most look hopeful and excited, but a few of them look distinctly uneasy.

Eli eyes the individuals with troubled expressions. Those are Clyde's lackeys, his enforcers and pretend guardians. They carried out his dirty work and terrorized the clan with joyful abandon, confident in their position under Clyde. Memorizing faces, he makes a mental list. He won't let those men live long.

"The Mother couldn't let this go on any longer," Steph shouts out to the crowd.

He stops examining the men and turns his attention back to his Heartmate, not surprised when he finds her glowing with power. She possessed strong magic before she got mixed up with his kind, but now that she's Mother embodied, she swells with power.

"These two men created an imbalance too great to be ignored," she tells the crowd, pointing at the dead bodies of Richard and Clyde. The glow around her intensifies, and she lifts into the air, her feet no longer resting on the ground. Her hair flows around her head, and her clothing moves as if there's a strong wind. There isn't even a breeze.

"The Mother understands there must be death as well as life. There must be the strong and the weak, but cruelty has no place in her world. Balance doesn't require brutality like that. Equilibrium must be restored, and all of you must be part of that restoration."

She points to the enforcers who held her earlier. Everyone steps away from them, making space around the men. The one with the gun points it at Steph, and Eli moves to protect her. But with a sweep of her hand the gun goes flying.

"You dare to bring human weapons among us?" she questions, and Eli almost laughs. Not too long ago she was human. Now she sounds all shifter.

"You're not even one of us!" the man shouts, fear coloring his voice. He looks around him frantically. "Are all of you going to just bow down to her? She's human! She's weak! What are all of you thinking? Are you just going to let some human kill a shifter?"

A low laugh sounds from Steph. "I've been chosen to restore the balance," she intones, her voice vibrating with power. "I don't ask any of them to bow down to me, and I don't plan to kill you." She looks out to the crowd. "I need proof that all of you are willing to restore the balance," she demands. "They helped to create the instability, and all of you must take part in eliminating their foul effects."

Everyone stands frozen, eyes going back and forth between her and the two enforcers.

"I think these guys should be part of this proceeding," Chris announces as he and a dozen other men wrestle several more enforcers into the circle created by the crowd around the two original men. Smiling with approval, Steph nods.

"Very well done," she says, and Eli feels a push of magic as Chris and the men with him drop to their knees. At first, he thinks she's hurt them, but when the men stumble upright, they're all rubbing their chests and smiling.

"Thank you, Clan Leader," one of the men says softly. The other men echo his words and Eli realizes she just set up clan ties with them. Far from being outraged to have a human clan leader, they all look overjoyed.

"Tie me!" someone in the crowd shouts and then sets off a round of requests that Steph silences by simply holding up her hand.

"No," she answers the crowd with resolution. "My ties must be earned."

Confusion reigns for a moment, and then a woman steps forward. Eli doesn't recognize her, but half of her face is covered in bruises. She's barefoot and wearing a skimpy dress that fits her gaunt frame tightly. Her eyes are wide but determined as she strides toward the enforcers, pulling her dress over her head as she walks. Just before she gets to them, she shifts. Her small coyote lips curl into a snarl as she lunges for one of them.

The big man easily bats her away, but she scrambles back to her feet and tries again. "Yes, Mari, take your revenge. Set the balance," Steph murmurs approvingly, and that's when Eli and the rest of the crowd realize what she wants.

Clyde couldn't have held power like he did if the clan had come together against him. One shifter, or even several, couldn't stand against him, but if everyone had risen up, he wouldn't have stood a chance.

The same was true for Richard. Neither men would have been easy to defeat in a one-on-one challenge, but their power could've been subverted by the whole clan coming together. Now Steph is demanding they do just that and destroy the enforcers without her help.

This is a revolution. Steph isn't just taking over as another clan leader might. She's forcing everyone to take part in her overthrow.

Almost as if choreographed, the crowd strips down and shifts, all of them flowing at the enforcers like a wave of fur. The men go down, screaming and trying to shift in order to fight their way out, but faced with such superior numbers they don't stand a chance.

Their bodies are ripped apart by the time everything calms. Blood and bits of flesh decorate the ground along with ripped clothing and a few guns. The men didn't even get a chance to fire a single shot.

"Very good," Steph calls out once the frenzy is over, and everyone starts shifting back to their human form, all looking to Steph for guidance.

"I want it known that Lowell clan stood together to save themselves. I want it recounted and retold so that no clan finds themselves in such a situation again. I'm proud of this clan." With those words she shoves power out, dropping everyone to their knees, gasping. Eli feels the ties forming around him in a web of clan connections that make many cry out. He might not have a clan tie with Steph, but through his Heartmate tie with her, he can feel everything going on. The thing that strikes him the strongest is the overwhelming joy coming from everyone.

"This is no longer a Lowell clan. The Lowell clan and the Hunger Valley clan are dead. In their place is the new clan. No more challenges. No more dictatorial leadership. Those are remnants of a system the Mother never approved of. New traditions will be created. New ways of doing things will be established. This clan will stand as the example of what the Mother wants most of all—balance. If you wish to leave, you may. But if you wish to stay, be prepared to change and fight for others to change as well."

Scanning the crowd, Eli sees nothing but adoration in everyone's expressions. Steph might not have started life out as a shifter, but he has a strong feeling she's about to set the shifter world on its ear. He wonders how the Conclave is going to take the news of this. They could face trouble ahead, but Eli isn't worried. The power radiating off Steph tells him the Conclave doesn't stand a chance against her, even if they are made up of the most dominant and formidable shifters known.

Power slowly retreats back into Steph. The glow recedes, and her toes touch the ground. "All are welcome to join us," she tells everyone as her feet come to rest fully on the forest floor. "And all of us are responsible for caring for each other. Uncaring, disregard, or indifference will no longer be tolerated. Together we will be a strong clan, and no one will be left behind."

With those words her magic fades to normal levels, and Eli hears a collective sigh as the tie pulses lightly with connection instead of throbbing with power. Steph looks over to him, a distressed expression on her face.

"Catch me," is all she says before her eyes roll up in her head and she collapses. Even unprepared for her to fall like that, he's still fast enough to get his arms around her and haul her limp body up to cradle against his chest.

The coyote Steph referred to as Mari rushes to his side. "Clan Leader!" she cries out in distress, reaching for Steph, but Eli snaps out a warning and she backs away. He checks with their tie and finds Steph is unconscious but unhurt. Looking up, he sees anxious faces staring at him.

"She's fine," he tells them with a scowl, and then without another word to the crowd, he looks to Chris. "Get the car. I want to take her home."

Steph's job will be to comfort everyone once she's recovered and awake. Right now, his only concern is keeping her safe and comfortable. The clan can figure out what to do with themselves on their own for now.

At his order, Chris and several others spur into action. Soon a four-wheel-drive vehicle is bumping down the narrow path to the Glen. Faces he doesn't know wrap him and Steph in blankets, but no one tries to take her from him. Then they usher him into the backseat and carefully drive out of the forest.

Those in their animal forms accompany the vehicle. The bright moon makes them easy to spot as they escort their new clan leader away from Deer Glen. Cradling Steph to his chest, Eli listens to their yips, barks, howls, and growls echoing among the trees.

Sounds of happiness, joy, and celebration are sung to Steph.

"I hope you know what you've gotten us into," he mutters to her unconscious form, stroking her hair with one of his big clumsy hands. A pulse of contentment comes through their tie, telling him she knows exactly what she did and wouldn't have it any other way. A single word forms in his mind, clear and strong, and carries a wealth of pleasurable emotions with it.

Family.

That's what Steph just created. This isn't a clan. It's a family. Eli has a strong suspicion this new model is going to catch on quickly.

They'll face blowback too. Many clan leaders aren't going to be happy when their leadership is challenged by those under them. They might even target Steph, hoping to eliminate the example in an attempt to keep the clan structures that give them so much power.

It doesn't matter. He'll keep Steph safe no matter what comes.

CHAPTER 27

This time, when Steph wakes up it's to the smell of flowers. The bed under her is soft and her body doesn't hurt.

"That's more like it," she murmurs as she blinks her eyes open.

"What's more like it?" Eli asks. She moves her head to see his haggard face staring down at her.

"You look horrible," she says, lifting a hand to touch his cheek. "Are you sick?"

He makes a scoffing sound. "Shifters don't get sick, but we do get driven mad with worry when our human Heartmate refuses to wake up."

"Huh?" She looks around and notices she's in her own bed, but her room is so filled with flowers that everything's obscured.

"Is she awake?" an excited voice asks, and Steph looks past Eli to see Ash hovering anxiously by the door.

"Hey, Ash, what did I miss?"

"Oh, damn girl." Ash sighs a relieved breath and strides to her bedside, muscling a space for herself next to Eli. "You rocked the shifter world!"

Wincing at Ash's words, Steph tries to sit up but notices an IV in her arm. Looking up she sees a bag of fluid hanging from the headboard of her bed. "How long have I been out?"

"Almost four days," Ash announces cheerfully. "Eli kept saying you're fine because he could feel you through your Heartmate tie, but we were all still really worried. Eli agreed to let Mari set up an IV. She's a nurse. But he hasn't let anyone else but me and Mari get anywhere near you."

Placing a comforting hand on Eli, Steph makes a soothing sound. "I'm okay, Eli. No one's going to hurt me."

"No, they won't," he agrees gruffly. "I won't let them." Grinning at his familiar attitude, she looks over to Ash.

"How is the clan doing? Have they been stable? Is there anything I need to figure out right away?"

Ash and Eli exchange wide eyed looks. "You remember?" Eli asks gently.

Rolling her eyes, she huffs out a laugh. "I don't think I'm likely to forget a goddess shoving a ton of magic into me," she retorts, making Ash giggle and Eli smile.

"You kept pulsing comfort through the clan ties, even while you were unconscious," Ash tells her. "I don't know if I ever heard of a clan leader that could do that. Clyde certainly couldn't. Anyway, the clan has been scrambling to do what you ordered."

"Ordered?"

"Care for the weak and take care of each other," Ash explains, making Steph smile with real pleasure. "Joe's been pouring over the clan accounts and put together a proposal for you to approve. It would set up accounts to help clan members who are financially struggling. Sandra cleaned out the tavern that Clyde used as home base, getting rid of the drug dealing and prostitution Clyde encouraged. It's only been a couple of days and she's already drawing a good crowd of people. Jennifer and Trever started renovating one of the apartment buildings the clan owns. They said half the apartments are empty and we can use them for homeless clan members. The money from the other renters should make the property break even. There's a lot more, but people want your approval before they do anything."

Laughing with delight, Steph grips Eli's hand tightly. "This is amazing! I never thought it would start happening so quickly."

"Steph, did you forget the part where the Mother picked you for us?" Ash teases her. "When you're ready, I think we should call a meeting so everyone can see you up and moving with their own eyes. They can feel you through the clan tie, but this is so new, and the clan is feeling shaky and anxious. A ton of shifters from the Hunger Valley clan that want to join too."

"Absolutely," Steph agrees. "We just need to find a place to accommodate everyone. I—"

"Don't worry about that," Ash cuts her off. "We've got your new house all ready for you."

Flummoxed, Steph stops trying to sit up. "Wait, what new house?"

This time it's Ash's turn to laugh. "A bunch of us got together to figure out where you should live. You decided to shake up what it means to be a clan leader, so we decided to keep going with that theme. The clan owns that bed and breakfast place. The one out on Marshall Road."

"Rose Cottage?" Steph asks. "The place with the amazing garden?"

"Yup, that one. The one you always wanted to stay at but felt silly because," Ash imitates Steph, "why would I spend good money to stay the night in a bed and breakfast in my own town?" Ash's impression makes Steph grin.

"I did say that. Didn't I?" she chuckles. "Well, it's true."

"Right, I know. But things are different now. No more visiting Rose Cottage and wishing you could spend a night there. Rose Cottage is going to be your new home." Ash holds up a hand. "Before you start objecting, you're going to need lots of space because I can already tell we're going to get a lot of shifters in distress showing up here, running away from other clans. You'll probably want to keep them close at first. The property is large, outside of town, and borders the forest. And it has that big area out back that should fit all the clan when we have gatherings. It couldn't be more perfect. It'll be your home and the clan's gathering house."

"I don't know if I should be taking up clan resources like that," Steph balks.

Now it's Ash's turn to chuckle "Trust me, you're not taking up resources. You're making yourself accessible to all of us. This will make the clan happy. Besides, everyone's tired of getting yelled at by Mrs. Leland when they try to visit here."

Shaking her head ruefully, she smiles indulgently. "Poor old Mrs. Leland. This neighborhood used to be so quiet. Then I moved in, then the dogs, then…" Steph notices a guilty look cross Eli's face. "What did you do?"

Looking away, he clears his throat and mutters something she can't hear. Ash must have heard what he said because she slaps a hand over her mouth, barking out a shocked laugh.

"What?" Steph demands. "What did you do?"

"I might have eaten her cat," he mutters low, refusing to meet her eyes. This time Steph laughs, giving him a sympathetic look.

"We need to get you out of here," she murmurs. "Your wolf isn't meant to live in town. Do you miss your cabin in the woods?"

Meeting her eyes now, he shakes his head. "I don't care where I am. Not as long as I'm with you." She wants to hug him, cuddle him close, and have a heartfelt moment, but urgent demands from her bladder turn her attention elsewhere.

"I need to use the bathroom," she announces as she swings her legs off the bed. She's caught by the IV when she tries to stand.

"Mari!" Eli shouts, startling Steph, who gives him a little glare.

"Inside voice, wolf," she admonishes him. He gives her an unrepentant grin.

Mari appears in the room. Her face is free of bruises, and Steph notices she's walking with confidence as she hurries to the bed. "You're awake! This is great. Let me just check," she starts to say, but Steph cuts her off.

"Get this out of me, please!" she begs pointing to the IV. "Need bathroom now!"

"No problem," Mari assures her, gently disconnecting the IV bag from the part still in her arm. "There, you're free. I'll pull the rest of it out when you're all done in the bathroom."

Getting to her feet, Steph sways a little. Eli grabs her arm to keep her steady but then leads her out of the room and down the hall to her bathroom. Then he tries to come in with her.

"Oh no," she objects and gently pushes him back out. "I can do this on my own."

"But you might fall. I should be in there with you. It's not a big deal. Everyone needs to piss and shit," he growls out.

"True, but I still want to do my business in private. Now out," she demands, smiling as he grudgingly lets her push him out of the door.

With intense relief she empties her bladder. If she's been out for four days, this can't be the first time she's needed to pee. Briefly she wonders what they did while she was out cold recovering but decides not to ask. She doesn't want to know. Sometimes ignorance is bliss.

After flushing the toilet and washing her hands, she opens the door to find a scowling Eli waiting for her. "See, I survived the dangerous bathroom on my own," she teases him. His lips quirk at her words.

"This time," he counters, making her laugh.

"Every time," she retorts and lets him lead her back into the bedroom. On the trip she notices the living room seems to be covered in greenery also. Her entire house is nothing but vases and pots of plants. Most are flowers, but some are exotic-looking plants she doesn't recognize. She raises an eyebrow at Eli.

"Ash mentioned to everyone you loved your garden," Eli explains to her unspoken question. "Now they all want to give you plants."

"That's sweet," Steph murmurs. Eli makes an annoyed sound.

"They stink," he grumbles. Poor Eli with his sensitive shifter nose.

Back in her bedroom, Mari takes out the IV and wraps the tiny wound, chattering the entire time about what Steph should eat and drink for the next few days to make sure her body isn't depleted of any important nutrients. The entire time she talks, she keeps her eyes firmly downcast.

Placing a hand on the woman's shoulder, Steph waits for their eyes to meet. When Mari reluctantly looks up, Steph gives her a warm smile and pulses reassurance through their clan tie.

"It's okay, Mari. You're safe. No one's going to hurt you again."

The woman's eyes fill with tears, and she falls against Steph, sobbing. Eli growls, but Steph silences him with a look as she wraps her arms around the nurse. She doesn't speak, just lets Mari weep while making sure the clan tie between them is strong with comfort. Everyone in this clan is traumatized, but some are worse than others. Those like Mari will need extra care.

"I've got you," she murmurs to the woman as the sobbing calms. "You're safe. All of you are safe."

Pulling away, Mari wipes her eyes with the backs of her hands. "Thank you, Clan Leader." She makes a show of straightening her back and lifting her eyes to meet Steph's. "I'll make you proud. We all will. Balance is already being restored."

"That's all I want," Steph assures her and then makes an exaggerated shooing motion. "Now all of you get out. I need to change, and that doesn't require an audience." She looks over to Ash. "Could you tell everyone to gather tonight at Rose Cottage so they can talk to me? And I can meet with anyone who needs me to approve something."

"I'll get on it right now." Ash hurries out of the room, and Mari reluctantly follows. Unsurprisingly, Eli stays.

Stripping out of her pajamas, something occurs to Steph. "Do I even still have a job?"

Reaching out to draw her naked form against him, Eli nods. "Chris and Mason have been covering for you. And Oscar. I've been told things aren't going smoothly, but at least everything's still mostly getting done." Steph breathes out a sigh of relief.

"That's good then," she says as she wiggles against Eli. Burying her nose into his shirt-covered chest, she breathes in his warm masculine smell. She runs her hands up his muscled back. "You feel so good."

He lowers his head, and she cranes her neck back so they can kiss. She moans from the taste of him. Lust flares in her, and she tugs at his shirt, giving him a one-word command, "Off."

With a smirk, Eli pulls his shirt off over his head. "Anything my clan leader wishes."

Smirking as well now, Steph pulls him toward the bed. "We have hours," she points out. "Hours until the meeting. I think your clan leader needs your personal attention right now."

Following her down on the bed, Eli pushes her legs apart and settles his shoulders between her thighs. "Can I taste you?"

She echoes his earlier words. "Anything my wolf wishes."

CHAPTER 28

It's a good thing Steph has never been shy. In high school, she enjoyed a few drama classes and even had minor parts in a couple of plays. Then she got a job where she needed to tell a bunch of burly men what to do. Within the first month of working at Larson Towing, she learned to be confident in the face of doubt or displeasure. She won everyone at the company over with her professionalism, competence, and friendliness.

Now, standing in front of a crowd of over a hundred shifters, she feels like her entire life was teaching her how to deal with this moment. Twenty minutes earlier an entourage of shifters showed up at her house and urged her and Eli into a large luxurious SUV.

Protesting, she told everyone she and Eli could just drive her car. Troy told her it was just this one time and to let the clan spoil her a little. Steph caved to pressure, but she has a strong suspicion she's going to need to put her foot down in the future.

The small parking lot at Rose Cottage teemed with cars, and many more were parked along the picturesque drive up to the inn. Wyatt, the coyote shifter driving the SUV, pulled up right in front of the inn, blocking anyone from leaving. Steph tried to say something, but he waved off her concern as Ash and Mari hurried up to the vehicle to open her door and greet her, earning a growl from Eli that they both ignored. Eli trailed behind the trio as Ash and Mari took an arm each and guided her around the inn to the large expanse of well-tended lawn in the back. All voices quieted the moment she appeared.

Now, a sea of anxious faces stares back at her as she stands on a small, raised dais. There's no microphone, but with shifter hearing they should be able to catch everything she says as long as she enunciates. With Eli at her side, she smiles at the crowd.

"Hello, clan," she calls out. "I'm so glad you could all make it. After this, I'll meet with individuals and groups about clan business. Even if you don't have a proposal or request, feel free to stay, and I'll find time to talk to you."

Many nod their heads, and everyone looks relieved. She pulses out reassurance through the clan ties, and smiles appear. *That's good*, she thinks. She was mildly worried her magic might not work as strongly on such a large scale. Whatever the Mother did, she made sure Steph has the power to be an effective clan leader.

"At this point I hope everyone here knows what happened to Clyde and Richard. They weren't clan leaders. They were tyrants. The whole point of leadership is to care for those under you. I want all of you to know that the clan will always be my first priority. That means I expect you to make the welfare of your fellow clan members your first priority as well."

Everyone's eyes focus intensely on her, but she feels fervent agreement sing back to her along the clan ties. These people are hungry for compassion and eager to care for each other. It fills her heart with joy. She always wanted a big family; it turns out she got one much bigger than she ever expected.

She wouldn't have it any other way.

It's very late by the time Steph finishes going over proposals, giving permission, and meeting all the clan members. A few too old and infirm to attend sent her handwritten letters. Accepting the letters graciously, she makes a mental note to visit these clan members as soon as she can. It's important that no one feels left out, especially during these early days when so much is changing.

"You're an impressive human," a new voice drawls, and Steph turns to find a man towering over her. Frowning, she feels along the clan ties and finds this man isn't one of her people. Before she can start asking him any questions, Eli is in front of her and growling at the stranger, his teeth shifted into long fangs protruding from his mouth.

Her power flares and she hears several people around them gasp. Looking at her hand, she realizes she's glowing again. Taking several deep breaths, she calms her power and places a soothing hand on Eli.

"It's safe, my wolf." She pushes her gift through their Heartmate tie, comforting his aggravated beast.

"I don't think I've ever seen tusks on a wolf," the stranger comments, unruffled by both her show of power and Eli's partial shift. Stepping to the side so she can have an unobstructed view, she regards the man with interest. She can't tell what he is because she doesn't have a clan tie and whatever magic he possesses is hidden behind strong shields.

"My name's Steph, Miss Garmin, or Clan Leader," she states coolly. "Not human."

Giving her an equally cool look, the man cocks an eyebrow. "Do you find the term insulting?"

"In this setting, yes," she answers honestly. "You're implying I'm lesser than you. I'm not. I'm just different. It's an important distinction."

"There's never been a human clan leader before. That's not just an important distinction. That's an outrageous development," he says with derision.

Eli growls again and she feels his power surge.

"No, Eli. This is my battle and no place for a physical altercation," she tells him. His power stops building, but it doesn't recede. He's standing ready to shift and defend her. At that point she notices several more men gathered behind this rude stranger. They are wary and tense, looking at both Eli and the tense faces of her clan gathering behind her. Many of her clan went home earlier in the evening, but several dozen remain and none of them look happy with this stranger's presence.

Tilting her head to the side, she gives the man a small smile. "Are you afraid your clan will start to filter to mine?"

Her words hit home when the man in front of her visibly stiffens and scowls at her. "You have no idea what you're doing," he growls out, his hands in fists.

Now it's her turn to raise a mocking eyebrow. "Really? Tell me what the Mother expects of her clan leader more than anything?"

"Strength," he says without hesitation. Steph lets her newfound power flood into her. She feels it wash over her skin, letting her skin glow and her hair start to float around her. She almost sighs with the sensation. Using her power like this is intense and pleasurable. She feels the connection with the Goddess Mother who claimed her. Warmth and satisfaction fill her.

The stranger pales and steps back. "Mother," he whispers. The men behind him look shell-shocked as they stare at her with wide, unblinking eyes.

Sending her power out, she caresses it along the man's shields, a request for him to lower them but not forcing the issue. She's so filled with magic right now she could rip through his shields without much effort, and by the look on his face, he knows it too.

When he lowers his shields, she lets her power flow around him in a gentle wave, lapping at his skin and caressing his aura. He shudders, his eyelids falling shut as he absorbs what she's offering him.

"Answer the questions now," she murmurs. "What does the Mother expect of her clan leaders?"

"B-b-balance," he stammers out, his eyes fluttering open. His expression is no longer mocking or hard. His eyes are glazed, and his mouth curves with a soft smile. "Mother," he whispers.

"She likes strength," Steph explains. "But it must be tempered with softness and caring. Many have forgotten that. I may have been human once, but she's made me more and given me a task."

"She's embodied you," one of his men whispers.

Ignoring that, she keeps her focus on the man who challenged her right to lead. "What's your name and clan?"

"Donovan," he murmurs. "Donovan Martin, clan leader of Two Trees clan."

"You care for your clan," Steph says as she feels around in the man's mind. "But you're harsh, especially toward those you view as weak. This isn't what she wants. It's never what she wanted. She promoted the strongest among her creatures to protect the weak, not to neglect them." She focuses her power inside of him, letting him feel the Mother. He makes a strangled gasp and clutches at his chest, going down on one knee. Instead of stepping forward to help him, his men all step back, their faces full of fear.

"Do you understand now?" she asks quietly. He tries to say something, but he's breathing too hard to get the words out. Pulling her power back into herself, she gives him a moment.

When it looks like his breathing has steadied, she leans over and puts a hand under his chin. She urges him to look up and meet her gaze.

"You're safe. You have no need to fear me or her."

"No," he shudders. "I won't fear."

"But you will change," she prods, and he pulls away from her hand so he can nod vigorously.

"Balance," he states as he struggles to stand on shaky legs. "My clan will have balance." He takes several breaths, holding his hand to his chest. "Is it true you killed both Richard and Clyde?" he asks, his voice no longer holding judgment or censure.

Putting a proprietary hand on Eli, she gives the man a gentle smile. "No, Eli killed them." The man shifts his gaze to Eli, and after a moment shakes his head.

"The two of you..." he argues. "She gave you Eli to be your shifter side. Together you two embody balance. His aggression and violence are tempered with your patience and caring. He'll always be quick to strike, to fight and defend. Your first reaction will always be compassion and care."

His words strike a chord in Steph, reminding her of the Mother's words in her head. *The gift is for both of you.*

"Perhaps," she replies, her lips quirking into a small smile. "She does like things to be balanced. Light and dark and all that."

"We've strayed," Donovan murmurs thoughtfully. "When I was little, my grandmother told me stories about the entire clan voting for who would be clan leader. But I thought it was an old woman remembering things wrong. Perhaps it's time to consult the history books. See how things were done before."

"That's an excellent idea," Steph enthuses. "Are there actual books?"

"Scrolls," a man behind Donovan volunteers. "Our clan kept scrolls until about a hundred years ago. After that, it was all oral and not passed down very well. My great-grandfather was a keeper, but he was the last one I know about."

"Keeper?" Steph asks, looking toward Eli.

"Keepers are like historians," he explains. "We had one in my clan, but he died a few years ago without training anyone to take his place. Richard thought it was a waste of resources."

"As did my father," Donovan adds.

"Not anymore," Steph says with determination. "The past is a good place to look, both for instructions and warnings." Looking at Donovan, she holds out her hand. "I'd like our clans to share history. Share knowledge. Figure out ways to do things. Bring the balance back."

Eagerly, he takes her hand in his. "I'd like that too."

CHAPTER 29

One month later

The phone rings, distracting her from the numbers on her computer screen. Oscar ended up running the office for an entire week while she recovered from the challenge, and now, a month later, she's still unraveling all the mistakes.

"I'm a witch, not an accountant," he grumbled when she complained about his office skills. Then he laughed at the expression on her face. Even after a crash course in all the different magical communities from Troy, Steph is still caught out when someone identifies themselves to her as if she's a shifter.

At least work, for the most part, is a pleasant familiar thing to distract herself with. "Larson Towing," Steph says into the phone, her eyes still on her computer screen.

"Steph, it's good to hear your voice," Lonny's deep voice sounds in her ear. Owner of Custom Choppers, he exclusively uses Larson for transporting his bikes anywhere on the West Coast. Considering the motorcycles he creates are basically works of art, it's a vote of confidence that he trusts

Larson Towing so much. At the start Larson Towing specialized in transporting vintage or expensive vehicles. They got out of that business a decade ago, but still grandfather in a few original customers, like Lonny.

"What can I do for you, Lonny?" she asks, taking her eyes off the computer and sitting back in her chair. Looking up makes her notice Eli sitting in a corner of the waiting room, engrossed in a book. She's rarely alone any longer. Eli is never far from her side, and on the rare occasion he can't be with her, he assigns at least two enforcers to guard her. Sometimes up to five. She doesn't raise too much of a fuss because she knows he's doing that out of an overabundance of caution and his over-the-top love for her.

In the end, it's good that he's always with her, not because she's in danger but because he keeps the clan at bay when she needs to concentrate on work. If it wasn't for him, Larson Towing would be constantly inundated with clan members asking for her attention. She's learned to use her wolf to create space when she needs it.

She might adore her clan, but sometimes a girl just wants to concentrate on accounting.

"I've got a bike that needs to be hauled all the way to Arizona in a climate-controlled vehicle," Lonny explains. Steph almost snorts out a laugh. It hits her as ironic that an emblem of toughness and freedom needs to be babied so much.

"Sure, no problem, give me the details and let me have a few hours to make arrangements," Steph picks up a pen and starts writing as Lonny talks.

She hears Eli greet someone coming in but is too busy writing things down to look. Once she's finished, she says goodbye to Lonny and then brings her gaze up to greet the visitor only to find the figure of her boss standing over her.

"John!" she exclaims and scrambles to her feet. "You're back!"

Chuckling, he waves her to sit back down as he drops into a chair. Eli hovers in the doorway, glaring at John but thankfully remaining quiet.

"I got back yesterday," he explains.

"How was St. Martin?" Steph asks, resuming her seat.

"Amazing. It was hard coming home. That's why I'm here. I'm hoping to talk you into buying Larson Towing."

Gaping at him with shock, Steph slumps back in her chair. John chuckles and looks over his shoulder at Eli, who's still scowling. "Can you tell your wolf to back off? I've never attacked a woman and I don't plan to start."

"Wolf?" Steph sputters.

Furrowing his brow, John looks back at her. "Isn't he a wolf? I'm usually pretty good at figuring out their animals, but sometimes I get it wrong. He's just too big to be a coyote." Glancing back at Eli, John tilts his head. "Black Bear?"

"It's not polite to ask, witch," Eli retorts, striding around the room and assuming a position next to Steph. She can feel his hackles are up, and she lays a soothing hand on his arm while sending John a quizzical look.

"Witch?"

"You didn't know?" Now it's John's turn to look surprised. "You always shimmered with power, so I assumed you just knew. I can't imagine anyone with that level of magic not being aware that I'm a witch."

"Judy too?"

"Yes, Steph," John says gently, his face turning soft as he realizes the extent of Steph's ignorance. "Judy and the kids. We both come from a long line of full-blooded witches. That's why I picked this building to move the business to. Remember we used to be on Market Road? When Clyde took over the Lowell clan it was too dangerous for me to operate there. So I move us all into neutral territory."

"You knew," she whispers, blinking rapidly. "You always knew."

"And you didn't," John says softly. "Well, now you do, obviously." He nods toward Eli. "I can feel that you two are Heartmated. Congratulations."

"Thanks," she mumbles and frowns at him. "What the hell, John! A heads up would've been nice."

Laughing, John shrugs. "Hi, I'm a witch. You're a gifted human, and we're surrounded by shifters."

Joining in with his laughter, Steph shakes her head. "Put like that, I guess I understand the lack of communication." She pauses, thinking about when John moved the business and then started giving her more and more responsibilities. "Was it because of Clyde that you started traveling so much?"

"Mostly," he answers. "He was getting worse, and I didn't feel like moving the company again. With you here to run everything, traveling seemed like a viable solution."

"It's different now," Steph assures him. "Clyde's gone. The clan's being run without the use of violence and terror."

"So I've heard," he says with a big smile. "You've caused quite a stir in the community." Glancing up to Eli, John's smile falls a little. "And I guess you probably know that or this one wouldn't constantly be at your side. He gives Oscar the creeps, by the way. You might want to find some kind of job for him to do so the guys don't feel annoyed with him hanging out here all the time."

A growl ticks out of Eli's throat, but John doesn't bat an eye. "Ease back. I've never been a threat to Steph. I'm only stating facts."

"We know some clans out there don't like what we're doing," Eli states gruffly. "They can go fuck themselves."

Barking out a laugh, John waves a hand in the air as if dismissing the naysayers. "I agree with you. I just wanted to make sure you're aware that the Conclave is involved now. I heard they're organizing a Cortege."

"Conclave? Cortege?"

With an unconcerned shrug, Eli glances down at her. "The Conclave is our governing body, but they aren't very involved. A Cortege is a group they send to investigate a clan or individual. Let them come. They can't do anything to you. You're Mother embodied."

John gives a low whistle of appreciation. "Mother embodied? I did miss a lot while I was gone."

Nodding, Steph sounds a small sigh. "It's been a wild ride."

"Then we're going to need to have dinner. Judy's going to want to hear all about this too. We can also discuss you buying this place."

"I can't," Steph says with real regret. "There's no way I could get approval for a loan that large."

Again, John chuckles and looks over to Eli, who huffs a displeased sound. "Tell her."

With a petulant look, Eli crosses his arms over his chest. "I don't want to."

"Eli?" her tone is full of warning, and Eli instantly relents. It's not that he's scared of her. It's that he doesn't like it when she gets upset. When she cried over a dog she found wounded in the road, he rushed the two of them to the nearest emergency vet. Now they have four dogs that visiting shifters spoil rotten.

Despite his bitter complaints about the newest dog, a medium-sized mutt scared of her own shadow, Steph's caught him more than once cuddling the dog and cooing to it when he thinks no one's looking. Her wolf has a soft squishy center that she adores.

"You're clan leader now," he explains grumpily.

"I think I'm aware of that," she states, feeling a little exasperated. Getting information out of Eli is like pulling teeth sometimes. "Spit it out, wolf."

"You can buy the business with clan resources. Make it clan property. Profits will feed back into the clan coffers, but you could be in charge of it."

"Oh," she feels her face light up with excitement. "I'll bring it up at the next clan meeting for approval."

"Don't bother," Eli mutters. "No one would dare say no to you."

That makes Steph frown. "Are people still afraid of me? I thought they were getting over that."

"Not afraid," Eli explains. "Enamored. They want to make you happy because they adore you so much. Buying this business so you can keep a job you like would be a no brainer. They'd approve without asking a single question."

"Then it's all decided," John says, standing up. "I'll talk to Judy, and we'll set a date to have dinner and hash out the details. Who's the clan custodian?"

Steph sputters as Eli and John talk over her.

"Troy Desta," Eli answers. "I'll have him contact you."

"Perfect," John answers. "Steph has all my contact info. I'll see you two soon." With that, he strides out. After a few beats of silence, Eli speaks.

"I don't like you working a full-time job on top of being clan leader, but if this place makes you happy, we'll buy it for you."

Swiveling her chair so she's facing Eli, she wraps her arms around his waist. His big hands come down to rest on her back. "Do they really adore me?" she asks, trying to keep from sniffing.

"Are you crying?"

"No," she lies.

With a sigh of resignation, Eli moves his hands until he can pick her up. She's gotten used to being manhandled by her wolf, so she doesn't protest as he sits down in her chair and cradles her in his lap.

"We all adore you."

"That's good," she breathes out, blinking back the tears she knows will make Eli insane. Even when they're happy tears, he hates it when she cries.

"Can we go home now?"

"No," she gives a watery chuckle. "But give me another hour and we can leave a little early."

"I still don't like it," Eli mutters as he swivels the chair to face the desk. He does this occasionally when one or both of them needs to be touched. He'll have her sit on his lap as she works, the close contact comforting them both.

"Being clan leader does take up a lot of time," she agrees as she looks up the contact numbers for a long-distance hauler that has climate-controlled trucks. "Maybe I can hire an assistant and cut back my hours here."

"That's a good start," Eli agrees, nuzzling his nose into her neck.

"An hour," she reminds him, and he pulls his head away with a discontented growl. She can feel the wolf inside of him whining, and she sends a little pulse of love to both of them.

"We love you too," Eli whispers in her ear.

Epilogue

Six months later

A big black SUV is parked smack dab in the middle of the parking lot of Rose Cottage. She's already late for work, so she huffs in frustration when she notices the large vehicle is blocking her car. It can't be a guest because Rose Cottage isn't an inn any longer. Now it acts as a halfway house, transitional housing, or a place for injured shifters to convalesce.

Right now, three shifters are housed in Rose Cottage, all new to the clan—a black bear so scared she won't come out of her room, a red wolf with aggression issues, and a depressed tiger who refuses to shift. All three of them have been horribly abused by their former clans and will need time and a lot of patience to heal.

That's partially why she's running late. She had to calm the red wolf down after an innocent comment by the tiger at breakfast set her off. Then she got a call from a family who needed her advice about their son. That conversation ate up all the time she usually spends enjoying a last cup of coffee before leaving for work.

Realizing she needed to leave, she looked for Eli but couldn't find him. He said he was just going for a quick run in the woods, but there's no sign of him. Now she's out of time and needs to get going. She's not worried. Someone else will drop Eli off at Larson Towing when he gets back. She almost smiles at what his reaction will be when he realizes he missed driving in with her. Her grumpy wolf hasn't gotten any less protective over the last six months.

Unfortunately, the clan isn't very intimidated by him any longer. When he growls, they don't even blink. They just focus on Steph and what they need to talk to her about. Between Larson Towing and the clan, her every waking moment is full.

Eli isn't a fan.

She doesn't resent her clan for all the time they demand, but sometimes she needs a break, and right now is one of them. Losing herself in the familiar repetition of Larson Towing sounds like a little slice of heaven except someone is parked right in her way, making a quick escape impossible.

Plenty of spots are free, so why the hell didn't this person park in one of them? A rare bout of frustration rises up inside her, and she just barely keeps it from traveling down the clan ties. She learned very quickly that if she isn't careful, the clan feels everything she feels. With positive emotions, that's a good thing. But anything negative takes a toll on her traumatized clan, so she does her absolute best to keep them from suffering any further.

Taking a deep breath, she's about to march back into the house to find the owner of the vehicle when large arms circle around her, picking her up off her feet. Someone inside the SUV opens a door and she's shoved inside. "She's in," a familiar voice calls out. "Go, go, go!"

She's pushed hard against the body holding her as the SUV slips and slides down the gravel drive.

"Dude, don't get us killed!" another familiar voice next to her calls out to the driver.

Wiggling herself into a sitting position, she looks over to Troy and narrows her eyes. "What the hell do you guys think you're doing?"

Next to her, Mason chuckles. He must have been the one who grabbed her. "Kidnapping you," Troy explains with an unrepentant broad grin.

"Thanks for not frying me," Mason says as he reaches for the seat belt to buckle her in. Very aware of her more fragile human body, the entire clan takes every care to keep her safe from potential danger, including car wrecks. Mason might be able to go through the windshield and shrug it off, but even with her better healing, Steph would likely suffer grievous wounds.

Batting his hands away, she growls out. "I can buckle my own goddamn seatbelt."

"Now you're starting to sound like Eli," Donovan says from the driver's seat, and Steph looks up to glare at the Two Trees clan leader.

"What are you doing here? Why am I being kidnapped? Start talking, guys, or I might fry you anyway." Instead of being intimidated, they all laugh. So much for being a scary, Mother embodied clan leader.

"We've decided you need a vacation," Troy explains once their laughter dies down.

"I can't take a vacation right now," Steph argues. "I've got Mellissa, Grace, Ryan, Summer, and Liam at the inn. I'm behind with the quarterly financials at Larson. And there's the meeting with Sandra tonight to go over the renovations at the tavern."

"And that's why you're being kidnapped," Troy says, interrupting her. "None of us wanted to say anything, but then you fainted last week and scared everyone."

"I didn't faint," she protests.

"That's not what I heard," Donovan counters.

"Mari says you're overworked, underfed, and not getting enough rest," Mason grumbles, looking deeply unhappy. "We can't lose you, Steph. You're the best thing to ever happen to the clan."

"To all the clans, really," Donovan pipes in.

"You're not going to lose me," she soothes and sends power pulsing down the clan ties. Both Troy and Mason relax and smile. "I promise I'm fine. Mari talked to me, and I've been making sure to eat regular meals now."

Neither Troy nor Mason argues with her. They're too busy being blissed out from the power she's sending down the clan tie to them. Both of them have closed their eyes and let their heads drop against the headrests.

"And that's why I'm here," Donovan says when he glances over at the quiet backseat.

"Just drop me off at Larson's," Steph orders. "I can get someone else to pick me up later."

"Nope."

Frowning, Steph leans forward until her head is between the front seats. "I can fry you."

"You won't. You like me too much. And I'm not a member of your clan so you can't use clan ties against me." Sliding a glance at Mason, he shakes his head. "That wasn't nice, by the way. The guys are just trying to help you."

"I'm not hurting them," she counters defensively, but a small shaft of guilt hits her. She's used this trick more and more often in the past few months. Whenever a clan member tries to start a conversation about her health or wellbeing, she just sends them into a state of forgetful happiness with the clan tie. That trick doesn't work on Eli, but distracting him with sex does the same job.

Of course, she can't use her clan tie or sex to get her way with Donovan.

"After you fainted the clan held an emergency meeting last week," Donovan explains as he drives, ignoring Steph's glower. "Mari explained that you needed more rest. They're all very aware of your humanity, Steph. When you fainted you scared them badly."

"It's fine," she grumbles, sitting back in her chair and crossing her arms, very much the cranky child. She even kicks the front seat with her foot, making Donovan laugh.

"No, it's not," he counters. "Look, I'm not saying you're weak. I'm saying you're important. You're the clan leader of the biggest clan. Ever. You eclipse the next biggest clan by almost double, and new shifters are showing up every day. That's a lot of clan ties for you to maintain. That's a lot of people for you to care for. If you get sick, who's going to care for them?"

"I'm eating," she protests weakly.

"But not resting," he counters. "That's the reason the clan made an executive decision. For four days at the beginning of every month you're going to stay at Eli's cabin. He's already there, waiting for you."

"He's in on this?" How did he keep that secret from her?

"Don't worry. We tricked him too," Donovan assures her, accurately reading her expression. "He thinks you asked him to get the cabin ready for a shifter who can't be around people. We hinted it might be someone who's like him, with a schism between the human and the animal side. That's probably the only reason he agreed to leave you for Mason and Troy to take to work.

"My wolf's a good man," she murmurs.

"For you he is," Donovan counters with a smile. "Before you, well, I've heard the stories. Anyway, we packed enough food and goodies for both of you. Four days from now someone will pick you guys up."

"Sneaky," she mutters.

"Loving," Donovan counters. She can't argue so she closes her eyes and concentrates on all the clan ties. What started out as a simple web of connections has grown to be complicated and requires a lot of her concentration to maintain and monitor. With care she pulses affection down the ties so that every shifter can feel it. It's a light touch because she doesn't want to startle anyone, but it's strong enough for her clan to know she loves and appreciates them.

Hundreds of clan members pulse right back, telling her in many voices the same thing: *We love you too.*

"Feeling better?" Donovan asks. She opens her eyes to meet his gaze in the rearview mirror. He must have noticed her relax and smile.

"Yeah," she says. "I guess a break isn't a bad idea. Not if my clan wants it."

"That's the right attitude," Donovan says with approval.

Troy and Mason come out of their daze forty minutes later as Donovan pulls the SUV up to the remote, rough cabin. Steph casts a glance at Mason. "This place doesn't look like it's got indoor plumbing."

With a wince, Mason shakes his head. "Uh, maybe we can upgrade?"

"Plumbing," she demands firmly. "I don't ask for much, but outhouses are out of the question."

"Right," Troy says with a firm nod. "It'll be done by next month. Indoor plumbing. Sorry about that, Steph. None of us were thinking about that."

"Men," she mutters.

"Shifters," Donovan counters with a chuckle.

Laughing, Steph starts to say something else, but then Eli is there. He flings open the door. Leaning in, he hauls her out across Mason's lap and into his arms.

"What going on?" he asks, worried. "Why are you here?"

The guys get out of the vehicle and start unloading the trunk, hauling coolers, boxes of food, and bundles of bedding into the cabin.

"The clan's giving us a honeymoon," she tells him. When her words register, a brilliant smile lights up his face.

"Just us?" he asks hopefully.

"Just us," she assures him. Gathering her up in his arms, he sprints into the cabin.

"Out!" he roars at the three men, startling all of them.

"We're going," Troy says with a smile. "Everything's inside anyway. Have a good time, you two." Eli doesn't answer, just growls loudly. Laughing, the guys pile back into the SUV and drive away.

Hugging her to him, he whispers in her ear. "My beautiful Steph."

"My wolf," she breathes. "I think we're both wearing too many clothes."

"I can fix that," he says with an eager grin.

Hours later he carries her outside and sits on the narrow porch. They watch the sunset together, the Heartmate tie thrumming strongly between them. They're both naked, but he's not bothered by the chilly air and she's kept comfortable, surrounded by his warm flesh.

"I never thought my life could be so perfect," she murmurs as golden light floods the world around them.

Perfect, his wolf sighs happily.

"Perfect," Eli agrees.

She's marveling at how everything turned out. She went from having no family to having all the family. Lucky doesn't even begin to cover it. *Thank you,* she whispers to the Mother.

You're very welcome, the Mother whispers to both of them. *I'm pleased.*

"Don't worry," she murmurs out loud with a little laugh at Eli's shocked face. It's the first time the Mother has talked directly to him. "You get used to it."

Dear Reader,

Thank you for reading *Stray Wolf*. Eli and Steph were some of the first vibrant charaters that came to me when I started my writing carreer. They will always have a special place in my heart.

If you want more **New Clan Shifters** the next book in the series is ready for you to read: *Lost Lion*

I hope you enjoyed *Stray Wolf* enough to leave a review! As an indie writer without the support of a publishing company, I need all the help I can get. Your good reviews keep me writing.

If you have any questions, comments, or suggestions feel free to contact me via email: author@rk-munin.com

Want some free novellas? You can find the links for them and much more on my website:

www.rk-munin.com

Cheers,
Rye

Other books by RK Munin

-Science Fiction-

Hissa Warrior Series
Rescuing Halin (Mian and Halin)
Buying Tiran (Mara and Tiran)
Tempting Selon (Lara and Selon)
Defying Kilan (Deena and Kilan)
Healing Mavito (Raleen and Mavito)
Claiming Yopin (Mouse and Yopin)
Teasing Woken (Safena and Woken)
Defending Revin (Kamaril and Revin)
Trusting Warik – Coming soon

Human Pets of Talin Series
Loving Captivity (Sora and Searin)
Escaping Captivity (Lakin and Dalt)
Negotiating Captivity (Nalia and Derani)
Fighting Captivity (Zia and Palforma)
Tender Captivity (Jinna and Holian - This is a novella you can get for free by signing up for my newsletter)
Craving Captivity (Lasha and Tamerin)
The Twelve Nights of Halloheen: A holiday mashup novella (Isla and Tisuran)
Stealing Captivity (Kasi and Ignatias)
Redeeming Captivity – Coming soon

Origins (A Human Pets of Talin Series)
Creating Captivity (Ari and Bazium)
Gossamer Chains (Rain and Hesarium)
Golden Cages – Coming soon
Purring, Presents, and Parties – Coming soon

-Paranormal /Urban Fantasy-

Ours Evermore Series
Two Wolves for Soren (Soren, Kalli, and Quinn)
A Hacker, Vampire, and Chimera Walk into a Bar… (Tobias, Briar, and Memphis)
When Darkness Meets Dawn (Imani, Lex, and Mac)
Tag, You're It (Novella)

Kidnapping Their Third (Cora, Pike, and Kimble)
Pastries on a Plate and Blood in a Mug – Coming soon

Alpha Series
Alpha Mage (Emma and Kade)
His Alpha Mage (Avery and Jason – Novella)
Alpha King (Cathleen and Lazlo)

New Clan Series
Stray Wolf (Steph and Eli)
Lost Lion (Maeve and Cyrus)
Reluctant Cervid (Tavi and Donovan)
Broken Thorn (Sabina and Theodosius)